Praise for Jeffrey Siger

Island of Secrets
(First Published as *The Mykonos Mob*)
The Tenth Chief Inspector Andreas Kaldis Mystery

"A perfect setting and first-rate storytelling."
—Ragnar Jónasson, bestselling author
of the Dark Iceland series

An Aegean April
The Ninth Chief Inspector Andreas Kaldis Mystery

Best Books of 2018 in Crime Fiction by *Library Journal*

"The great man behind Greece's crime mysteries."
—*Greek City Times*

"Vivid local color, agreeable central characters, and exciting action scenes make this a winner."
—*Publishers Weekly*

"The ninth case for Siger's Greek detective, brimming with suspense and a distinct sense of place, continues to deepen the backstory of its band of heroes."
—*Kirkus Reviews*

"Siger's ninth atmospheric mystery vividly depicts the political and economic issues involved in the European refugee crisis. VERDICT: Fans of Adrian McKinty's Sean Duffy books and other police procedurals that handle violence and political issues with black humor will welcome this outstanding crime novel."

—*Library Journal*, Starred Review

"This latest outing also offers a perspective on the Balkan Peninsula and the thorny issue of asylum seekers. A fast-paced international series."

—*Booklist*

Santorini Caesars
The Eighth Chief Inspector Andreas Kaldis Mystery

"[This is a] novel that's both a rock-solid mystery and comments incisively about so many issues besetting Europe and the world today."

—*Huffington Post*

"The eighth case for Siger's police hero has a timely plot and a handful of engaging back stories about its detective team."

—*Kirkus Reviews*

"As always, Siger provides readers with an action-packed plot, well-developed characters with lots of attitude, breathtaking Greek scenery, and a perceptive take on the current political and economic problems affecting Greece. International-crime fans need to be reading this consistently strong series."

—*Booklist*

Devil of Delphi
The Seventh Chief Inspector Andreas Kaldis Mystery

2016 Barry Awards nominee for Best Novel

"Siger brings Chief Inspector Andreas Kaldis some very big challenges in his seventh mystery set in troubled contemporary Greece… The final plot twist proves well worth the wait, but it won't take readers long to get there as they will be turning pages at a ferocious clip."

—*Booklist*, Starred Review

"Though the reader is always several steps ahead of the police here, Siger's sublimely malevolent villains make the book a page-turner."

—*Kirkus Reviews*

"A killer named Kharon (for the mythological ferryman who transports the dead across the River Styx) and bomba, or counterfeit wine, complicate the lives of Chief Inspector Kaldis and his team. The seventh book in Siger's Greek procedural series features a strong sense of place and a devious plot."

—*Library Journal*

Sons of Sparta
The Sixth Chief Inspector Andreas Kaldis Mystery

"Siger paints travelogue-worthy pictures of a breathtakingly beautiful—if politically corrupt—Greece."

—*Publishers Weekly*, Starred Review

"Kaldis's sixth case offers a lively, gritty plot, an abundance of local color, and two righteous heroes."

—*Kirkus Reviews*

"Filled with local color, action, and humor, this story will give readers a taste of modern Greek culture and its ancient roots."

—*Booklist*

Mykonos After Midnight
The Fifth Chief Inspector Andreas Kaldis Mystery

2014 Left Coast Crime Awards nominee for Best Mystery in a Foreign Setting

"Vibrant with the frenzied nightlife of Mykonos and the predators who feed on it. A twisty page-turner."

—Michael Stanley, award-winning author of the Detective Kubu mysteries

"The investigation that follows—highlighted by political interference and the piecing together of a complicated international plot that threatens to disrupt the easygoing, anything-goes life that Mykonos is famous for—keeps the reader engaged, even as it makes obvious that in Greece, it really matters whom you know. The emergence of a shadowy master criminal bodes well for future adventures."

—*Publishers Weekly*

"Gorgeous Mykonos once again becomes a character when conflicting forces battle for the resort island's future in Siger's fifth series entry. Greece's financial vulnerabilities play a key role as Chief Inspector Kaldis digs in."

—*Library Journal*

"From the easy banter of its three cops to its clutch of unpredictable villains, Kaldis's fifth reads more like an Elmore Leonard caper than a whodunit."

—*Kirkus Reviews*

"Acclaimed (particularly by Greek commentators) for their realistic portrayal of Greek life and culture, the Kaldis novels are very well constructed, and this one is no exception: not only is the mystery solid but the larger story, revolving around the political machinations of the shadowy global organization, is clever and intriguing. Fans of the previous Kaldis novels would do well to seek this one out."

—*Booklist*

Target: Tinos
The Fourth Chief Inspector Andreas Kaldis Mystery

"Thrilling, thought-provoking, and impossible to put down."
—Timothy Hallinan, award-winning author
of the Poke Rafferty thrillers

"Nobody writes Greece better than Jeffrey Siger."
—Leighton Gage, author of the Chief
Inspector Mario Silva Investigations

"*Target: Tinos* is another of Jeffrey Siger's thoughtful police procedurals set in picturesque but not untroubled Greek locales."

—*New York Times*

"A likable, compassionate lead; appealing Greek atmosphere; and a well-crafted plot help make this a winner."

—*Publishers Weekly*, Starred Review

"An interesting and highly entertaining police procedural for those who wish to read their way around the globe and especially for those inclined to move away from some of the 'chilly' Scandinavian thrillers and into warmer climes."

—*Library Journal*

"The fourth case for a sleuth who doesn't suffer fools gladly pairs a crisp style with a complex portrait of contemporary Greece to bolster another solid whodunit."

—*Kirkus Reviews*

"Siger's latest Inspector Kaldis Mystery throbs with the pulse of Greek culture… Make sure to suggest this engaging series to fans of Leighton Gage's Mario Silva series, set in Brazil but very similar in terms of mood and feel."

—*Booklist*

Prey on Patmos
The Third Chief Inspector Andreas Kaldis Mystery

"A suspenseful trip through the rarely seen darker strata of complex, contemporary Greece."

—*Publishers Weekly*

"Using the Greek Orthodox Church as the linchpin for his story, Siger proves that Greece is fertile new ground for the mystery genre. Sure to appeal to fans of mysteries with exotic locations."
—*Library Journal*

"The third case for the appealing Andreas will immerse readers in a fascinating culture."
—*Kirkus Reviews*

Assassins of Athens
The Second Chief Inspector Andreas Kaldis Mystery

"Jeffrey Siger's *Assassins of Athens* is a teasingly complex and suspenseful thriller... Siger and his protagonist, Chief Inspector Andreas Kaldis, are getting sharper and surer with each case."
—Thomas Perry, bestselling author

"Siger is a superb writer... Best of all, he creates the atmosphere of modern Greece in vivid, believable detail, from the magnificence of its antiquities to the decadence of its power bearers and the squalor of its slums."
—*Pittsburgh Post-Gazette*

"This is international police procedural writing at its best and should be recommended, in particular, to readers who enjoy Leighton Gage's Brazilian police stories or Hakan Nesser's Swedish inspector Van Veeteren."
—*Booklist*, Starred Review

"With few mysteries set in Greece, the author, a longtime resident of Mykonos, vividly captures this unfamiliar terrain's people and culture. Mystery fans who like their police procedurals in exotic locales will welcome this one."

—*Library Journal*

Murder in Mykonos
The First Chief Inspector Andreas Kaldis Mystery

"Siger's intimate knowledge of Mykonos adds color and interest to his serviceable prose and his simple premise. The result is a surprisingly effective debut novel."

—*Kirkus Reviews*

"Siger's view of Mykonos (where he lives part-time) is nicely nuanced, as is the mystery's ambiguous resolution. Kaldis's feisty personality and complex backstory are appealing as well. Solid foundations for a projected series."

—*Publishers Weekly*

"Siger…captures the rare beauty of the Greek islands in this series debut."

—*Library Journal*

"Siger's Mykonos seems an unrelievedly hedonistic place, especially given the community's religious orthodoxy, but suspense builds nicely as the story alternates between the perspectives of the captive woman, the twisted kidnapper, and the cop on whose shoulders the investigation falls. In the end, Andreas finds more than he bargained for, and readers will be well pleased."

—*Booklist*

Also by Jeffrey Siger

A DEADLY TWIST

A DEADLY TWIST

A CHIEF INSPECTOR ANDREAS KALDIS MYSTERY

JEFFREY SIGER

Published by Poisoned Pen Press, an imprint of Sourcebooks
P.O. Box 4410, Naperville, Illinois 60567-4410
(630) 961-3900
sourcebooks.com

Library of Congress Cataloging-in-Publication Data

Names: Siger, Jeffrey, author.
Title: A deadly twist / Jeffrey Siger.
Description: Naperville, Illinois : Poisoned Pen Press, [2021] | Series: A
   Chief Inspector Andreas Kaldis mystery
Identifiers: LCCN 2020021161 (hardcover) | (trade paperback) | (epub)
Classification: LCC PS3619.I45 D43 2021 (print) | LCC PS3619.I45 (ebook)
   | DDC 813/.6--dc23
LC record available at https://lccn.loc.gov/2020021161
LC ebook record available at https://lccn.loc.gov/2020021162

Printed and bound in the United States of America.
SB 10 9 8 7 6 5 4 3 2 1

To Barbara G. Peters and Robert Rosenwald
I owe it all to you.

"Happy is the man, I thought, who, before dying, has the good fortune to sail the Aegean Sea."
—Nikos Kazantzakis

Naxos Island

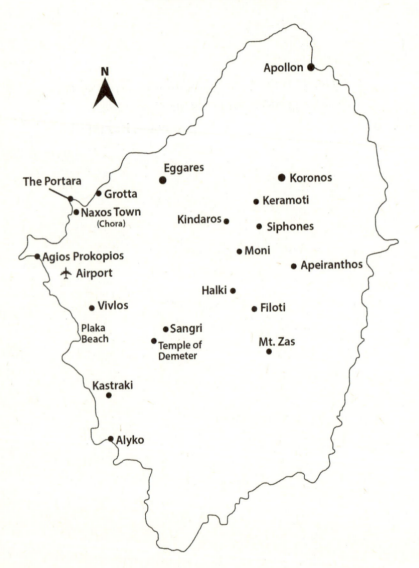

N

Apollon

The Portara

Eggares

Koronos

Grotta

Keramoti

Naxos Town
(Chora)

Kindaros

Siphones

Agios Prokopios

Moni

Airport

Apeiranthos

Halki

Vivlos

Filoti

Plaka
Beach

Sangri

Temple of
Demeter

Mt. Zas

Kastraki

Alyko

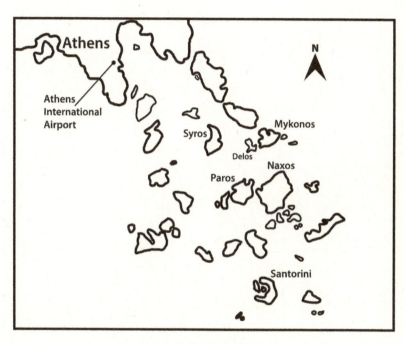

Cycladic Islands

Chapter One

"The key to getting away with what I do is lacking any possible motive. Motive's the first thing cops look for. Which is why I've never taken a job that could tie me to a target, no matter how tenuous the link or big the payday. I'm a conservative businessman, and if my work has taught me anything, it's that fast money comes with excessive risk. It's the gradual accumulation of wealth that makes a person secure in old age, and that's what I'm aiming for."

Chief Inspector Andreas Kaldis sat in his office in Greece's Central Police Headquarters in Athens (better known as GADA) reading and rereading a front-page newspaper article that opened with that paragraph.

A reporter named Nikoletta Elia claimed to have landed an exclusive interview with "the computer underground's most successful hacker" while on holiday on the Greek island of Naxos. Andreas took it to be a made-up story, likely pieced together by a seriously hungover reporter following an all-night booze session with some braggart trying to impress his bar mates with tales of international intrigue.

Strangers admit to weird things late at night in island bars, but this confession made no sense. It was inconceivable to Andreas that a "conservative" computer hacker who wanted to make it to "old age" would be stupid enough to open up about his business to anyone, let alone a reporter, about how he used his elite hacking skills on behalf of clients to ravage businesses, steal state secrets, and mask murders behind accidental equipment malfunctions.

Still, the article was in today's issue of Athens's most respected daily newspaper, and Andreas expected it would kick the city's many conspiracy theorists into overdrive. *What does the hacker's presence in Greece mean? And why are the police doing nothing about it?* As head of Greece's Special Crimes Unit, charged with investigating matters of national concern or potential corruption, Andreas expected his phone would soon light up with calls from members of Parliament looking to show their constituents that they cared about who visited their country.

Andreas looked at his watch. It wasn't yet eight a.m., too early for MPs to be calling. His administrative assistant, Maggie, would be at her desk any minute. He'd tell her to take messages. He didn't have the patience to be diplomatic with politicians this morning. He'd spent most of last night listening to his kindergarten son and toddler daughter coughing. Their colds had kept him awake longer than they had the kids.

I guess that's what it means to be a parent.

A compact, five-foot-three, redheaded ball of energy poked her head in through the doorway. "Morning, Chief."

"Morning, Maggie."

"So, what fresh hells do you have for me today?"

"Just your routine international bad guy on holiday looking for publicity blowback day."

"That should do wonders for Naxos tourism."

"You saw the article?"

"Who didn't? It's a front-page story by a crime reporter with a big following."

"But it makes no sense. Don't people realize it has to be phony?"

"Since when did being phony keep a story off the front page? At least this one's entertaining."

"Good, then keep entertaining yourself by taking messages on any calls for me about it."

"I'll need to requisition a few more message pads."

Andreas and Maggie had been doing their variation on a vaudeville routine since he'd returned to GADA from a brief stint as the chief of police on Mykonos. The luck of the draw had landed him with Maggie, GADA's mother superior and source of all wisdom about its many secret ways.

Ring, ring.

Maggie headed for her desk to answer the phone. "Let the games begin."

Andreas drew in and let out a deep breath. *It's gonna be a long day.* He picked up the newspaper and stared at the byline. "Nikoletta Elia, there must be more to this story than you're telling us."

Another line rang. He looked up. *A very long day.*

———

Despite a lifetime of reporting the news, Nikoletta Elia had never expected to write that story, nor had she anticipated the surge of international attention it received. Her editor had sent her to Naxos for a few days to do a piece on the simmering conflict between the island's traditional agrarian population and its growing cadre of tourism advocates.

She'd been surprised by the assignment and wondered what she'd done to draw the ire of her editor. After all, it wasn't the kind of hard-hitting reporting on which she'd built her byline. Breaking new ground on the crime and corruption beat was her forte, not rehashing the age-old debate about the pros and cons of tourism.

"Give it to a business or features writer," she'd argued to her editor.

"Don't be so negative. After all, it is an island steeped in myth, poised on the cusp of modernity."

"Get a travel writer, then. You know it's not my thing."

"Try it, you might learn something. Besides, you could use a break from chasing cops and robbers."

Nikoletta crossed her arms and scowled. "I couldn't care less that Naxos is where Zeus was raised, Ares took refuge, or Dionysius called home."

He feigned a smile. "Okay, point made; you know your mythology."

"Oh, that's just the start. Theseus, Ariadne, blah blah blah." She raised a hand to stop him from interrupting. "I also know that Cycladic life began on Naxos before Minoan Crete and Mycenaean Greece. Oh, and let's not forget that Naxos flourished as a society through most of antiquity up until the Persians ended its long independent run. Then came the Athenians, the Spartans, and a string of other Greeks, followed by the Romans, Venetians, Turks, and a touch of Russians, though the most lasting influence is clearly Venetian."

The editor chewed at his lip.

She waggled a finger at him. "I don't do historical pieces because I *prefer* running around with cops and robbers."

He held up his hands. "Fine, so write about modern-day conquerors—tourists and real estate developers. Do the piece however you like, but I want you over there and writing it *now*."

Nikoletta shut her eyes and silently counted to ten. She needed this job. Greece was still deep in financial crisis and, besides, she liked what she did. At least most of the time. She opened her eyes, smiled, curtsied dramatically, and headed for the door.

"Send me a story," he yelled after her.

She didn't stop but shot a hand above her head and flashed him the middle finger.

———

Nikoletta's assignment was getting lousier by the minute. The newspaper refused to pay for a plane ticket that would have had her on the island in less than forty minutes. Instead, it paid for a boat that took four hours. That she wasn't forced to take a ferry, which would have made it a six-hour trip at best, did nothing to improve her mood.

Her boat sailed into Naxos harbor past the massive marble Portara, the 2,500-year-old gateway to a never-completed grand temple to Apollo and the modern-day symbol of Naxos. Beyond the harbor the old town spread out and rose along a hillside covered in low whitewashed buildings. Flagstone lanes beneath soaring stone archways led up to a thirteenth-century Venetian castle that still dominated the town. The Castle, or Kastro area, constituted the upper part of the old town, distinguishing it in topography and social standing from the old town's lower Bourgos section.

Nikoletta barely glanced at any of that, choosing instead to maneuver to where she could grab her bag from the luggage storage area and disembark as quickly as possible.

She'd packed lightly, hoping to spend no more than a couple of days, and had arranged to stay in the island's main town of Naxos, also known as Chora, as every island's namesake town is called.

She'd picked Chora because it sat on the island's west coast, virtually equidistant from its northern, southern, and eastern edges. She also assumed that, because it was the island's capital and largest town by far, it would give her the best chance of ferreting out interviews with island officials and tourism advocates. Locating the island's agrarian defenders in the rural parts of the island would prove more logistically challenging, but she'd worry about that later.

She walked along the pier past a phalanx of waiting empty taxis and through a gauntlet of locals hawking places to stay and stopped by a driver holding a small placard with her name written in bold letters. He took her bag and led her to a van bearing the name of the hotel. After five minutes of winding through a maze of one-way streets, they arrived at a bright-white stucco-and-glass hotel just north of the harbor and perched atop a steep bluff overlooking the Portara.

Now free from her four-hour internment on the boat, caressed by gentle winds rolling in off the sea and catching the scent of wildflowers, she thought that a few days away from the madness of Athens might not be so bad after all. She shut her eyes, drew in a deep breath of sea air, and stood quietly for a moment. She opened her eyes, exhaled, and stared out to sea.

Yes, not bad at all.

Nikoletta checked into the hotel, put away her few things, and decided to stroll into town to catch the sunset at a harborside café. Unfamiliar with Chora, she asked the receptionist for the best walking route into town. The receptionist pointed toward the sea, and said the most direct way was to follow a rock-and-dirt path running down along the edge of the bluff through a field of gorse, maquis, stonecrop, and smother weed.

Nikoletta hesitated at first, but the route did offer spectacular views of the Portara set against its islet of Palatia, plus a shimmering orange sun and a deep-blue sea. Besides, it was still daytime, and despite a sign at the top of the path marked BEWARE DANGER, many were walking along the same path. Returning in the dark would be a different story, especially since she was intent on finding a bar in which to drown her sorrows at her lousy assignment.

She easily made it down from the bluff, across a not so busy road, and into a lane opening on to a square in front of the island's eighteenth-century Greek Orthodox cathedral. It was built on the remains of ancient temples and faced the ancient city's agora, or meeting place, but she did not pause, and two minutes later she was at the north end of the harbor.

She strolled by what seemed an endless line of tavernas, bars, and tourist shops, many trying to look more modern and chic than the next but not quite pulling it off. If they were examples of the sort of modern development tourism advocates had in mind for the rest of the island, she could understand why the island's traditionalists were so adamantly opposed.

She paused beside a wide marble harbor-front square and watched as local children rode their bikes and scooters helter-skelter among the passing tourists. It was as if all the world were their playground. She smiled. This was Nikoletta's idea of a Greek island experience.

Her eye caught a flagstone stairway tucked away between a jewelry shop and a *kafenio*, and she headed straight for it. A sign above the stairs read TO THE CASTLE & THE MUSEUM.

She wound her way up the hill along archway-covered lanes lined with stone and stucco buildings, all plainly laid out without any plan other than to confuse marauding pirates. She kept climbing through a residential area randomly trimmed in geraniums and bougainvillea, determined to make it to where signs promised she'd find the Kastro and the seventeenth-century Naxos Archaeological Museum.

As expected, given the hour, the museum was closed.

Nikoletta stood in front of the museum, looking back on to the square, and wondered what to do now. To her right sat a well-tended garden of oleander, geraniums, bougainvillea, and a host of flowers she could not identify; to her left stood the Naxos Cultural Center. She sat on the wall outside the cultural center and watched an amber-colored queen lead her onyx and amber kittens scampering into the garden. This seemed to be the right place to contemplate the direction of her life. After all, she now sat before what once had been the Ursuline School for Girls, representing seventeenth- and eighteenth-century efforts at educating them.

She shut her eyes and listened to children playing nearby. She imagined what life must have been like here so many centuries before and wondered whether the sounds of children at play would have been any different back then.

Amid this unexpected tranquility, Nikoletta decided her editor had been right in asking her to do a piece on tradition versus tourism. She'd made her reputation reporting on the basest of human propensities, stories in which brute force was the currency of choice. It was time to write about humankind's better nature, how those of goodwill could battle over a contentious issue without violence and reach a balanced result acceptable to all sides. Or so she'd like to believe.

She didn't move from her perch until well past sunset, listening all the while to the birds and children. She felt at ease as she backtracked down the hill, but before the harbor a waiter called out to her to please come try his tiny bar. She hadn't noticed the place on the way up, but it had a certain charm reminiscent of the sort of Bohemian café you'd expect to find on a Paris backstreet.

Why not? she thought and made her way to an empty table

by an open window, ordered a glass of red wine, and sat staring out at people passing by.

She didn't notice the tall, fit man until he stood next to her table. He wore the stylized haircut and week-old black beard of men in their late twenties but struck her as considerably older. At first she thought he was another waiter.

"Excuse me, miss, are you Nikoletta Elia?"

She stared at him. "Do I know you?"

"May I sit down?"

"Not until you tell me who you are."

"Someone with a story to tell that I know you'll be interested in hearing."

He'd said the magic words.

She nodded for him to sit. "This better be good."

"I'm a big fan of your work. We must have arrived on the same boat, because I saw a man holding up a sign with your name on it. I waited to see what you looked like but didn't want to bother you. Later, I saw you walking along the harbor front and decided to follow in hopes of getting the chance to speak with you."

"If you've been following me, how come I didn't notice you up in the Kastro? I was virtually alone up there."

He smiled. "Precisely. Which is why when you went into the Kastro, I waited until you came out. I didn't want to spook you."

"How did you know I'd come out the same way I went in?"

He smiled again. "I see you're not familiar with the town. There are only two gates into the Kastro, the Paraporti to the south, and the Trani to the north. You went in through Trani, and I guessed you'd come out the same way."

She stared at him. "Okay, so you guessed right, and now you have your chance to tell me your story. So, tell me."

"If I expect you to believe me, I first better demonstrate my bona fides." He waved to a waiter. "Bring us a bottle of whatever the lady's drinking and a glass for me. Then leave us alone unless I call for you." He turned to Nikoletta. "The wine's on me, and I'm pretty sure that what I have to say will take at least a bottle."

Whatever's on his mind, he has a unique way of getting to the point.

"I'm going to tell you facts about stories you've covered that I could only know if I'm who you'll think I am after you've heard me out."

"Uh, okay?" She picked up her wineglass and leaned back in her chair. "I'm listening."

Over hours of conversation, and just as many bottles of wine, he delved into a half dozen sophisticated ransomware attacks, three embarrassing government document dumps, and two mysterious deaths officially recorded as accidents, all reported on by Nikoletta. He did not object when she pulled a notebook out of her bag and started taking notes but warned her not to record his voice or take his photo.

She pressed him with questions, and he answered with details she already knew, plus many she did not but that were consistent with her long-held suspicions. Details that only someone intimately aware of the ransomware and documents involved, and how the victims' deaths were made to look like accidents, would know.

"It's easier than you can imagine to interfere with a computer that controls a vehicle's antilock brakes, and if you do that on a twisting mountain road, investigators will just chalk it up to another tragic accident."

Nikoletta stared at him. "You do realize how nonchalant you sound in talking about the harm you've done to so many."

He shrugged. "All I want to know is have I told you enough to establish my credibility?"

"I assume you won't tell me your name."

He smiled. "Next question."

"What about your online nickname?"

He smiled again, saying nothing.

"Why are you telling me all this? You're implicating yourself in major crimes, including murder."

"I don't view them that way. I think of myself as employed to make computer systems do what my clients want. It's an intellectual challenge. I'm a black hat hacker, battling the white hats trying to keep me out of their systems."

Her eyes narrowed. "This is not a video game. What you're doing literally destroys lives. You can't seriously believe that's just an *intellectual challenge*."

He leaned in. "My bottom line is that however you wish to characterize my past, I'm giving up that life. I no longer feel the rush I once did on achieving what others had thought impossible. It is time for me to leave the game and, having made that decision, I want to set the record straight."

"Some might say this is all hubris on your part, a desire to see your exploits glorified in the press."

He smiled. "They can say what they like, but that's not in keeping with how I've lived my life." He picked up his nearly empty wine glass. "My reason for this conversation is simple. The world should know that there are people out there like me. Plain, seemingly ordinary folk, paid to do very bad things for calculated purposes without leaving a trace of guilt or motive. We thrive in places where officials are quick to embrace innocent excuses for anything bad that happens on their watch—and where the media are reluctant to question authority."

He slugged down the rest of his wine and leaned forward. "In other words, I mean this conversation as a warning to you and your readers. Beware: we are among you."

He called for the check. "I think you should leave now, Nikoletta. I'll take care of paying. You just take care of yourself."

———

Nikoletta couldn't believe her good fortune at the widespread attention generated by her story. Magazine and TV crews tracked her down on Naxos for interviews, and her editor told her to forget about writing the tourism piece. He wanted her back in Athens, where he'd assigned two reporters to assist her on follow-up stories tied to her mysterious interviewee.

She told him she wanted to write the Naxos article. When he asked why, she said fate had sent her to Naxos for a reason, perhaps an even bigger one than meeting with the hacker. She'd only know for sure once she completed the piece.

Her editor pointed out that it was he, not fate, who'd sent her to Naxos, and now *he* wanted her back in Athens ASAP. They argued back and forth and compromised on her returning in Athens in four days' time.

"But I can't promise you that the police won't be hounding you before then," he told her. "They keep screaming for access to you, and I don't know how much longer I can stall them."

"I'm sure you'll do your best, as you always do."

"Stop with the BS and just make sure you're back here in four days."

"You mean on the fifth day."

"First thing in the morning. Bye."

As soon as they hung up, Nikoletta set off in search of sources for her other story. With her newfound celebrity, she had little trouble getting politicians to talk, but they spoke only in platitudes reflecting the interests of their particular constituencies. Representatives of the tourist industry were also readily available and eagerly expressed their polished, politically correct views on each topic she raised. She completed those interviews in one day, all without leaving Chora.

Her next three days had her trekking across rural Naxos, trudging from one remote location to another, following one introduction to the next, charming and cajoling opinions out of largely taciturn farmers and herders. Most interviews were frustrating, teeth-pulling exercises, but every so often she came across a tiger anxious to devour a perceived adversary with sharp-toothed rhetoric.

It was a grueling four days, but she got what she wanted for her story, and more.

Nikoletta returned to her hotel in Chora exhausted. It was well after dark, but also her last night on the island, and she'd promised a group of locals who'd helped her with her story that she'd celebrate with them at a bar in town.

She made it to the bar by eleven with the intention of putting in a quick appearance and heading back to her hotel. But her friends had brought along homemade food and a bouzouki band. She had to stay—and didn't escape until after two in the morning.

Alone and a bit tipsy, she stumbled in the direction of the hotel. At the base of the path leading up along the bluff, she paused, wondering if she dared risk going that way. As she was about to take the longer, safer route, she noticed fireflies moving along the bluff path.

Fireflies? she thought, shaking her head. It couldn't be fireflies. Then it hit her, and she laughed. They weren't fireflies but folks like her, hiking along the path with light from their mobile phones to guide them. She dismissed her earlier pangs of anxiety, lit up the flashlight on her mobile, and struck out on the path.

The wind had come up, and she could hear the sea crashing on the rocks below. It was a bit trickier a walk than she'd imagined, but somewhere up ahead, others were headed the same way, and from the sounds she heard coming toward her, likely even more intoxicated than she. In a matter of minutes, she'd be safely in her bed. She had nothing to fear.

———

Ring, ring.

The phone rang four more times.

A grasping hand knocked a book off the nightstand before finding the mobile phone.

"Hello."

"Nikoletta, I must see you right away."

She looked at the time. "It's four o'clock in the morning. Who is this?"

"The storyteller who bought you several bottles of wine a few nights ago."

She sat up in bed. "What do you want?"

"Trust me, it's important. *Very* important. Meet me outside the lobby of your hotel in ten minutes. *Don't be late.*"

He hung up before she could say another word.

How did he know I was in this hotel? How did he get my mobile number? Did I tell him? Those were the first questions running through her mind. *But…he was a skilled professional.* She pulled on her jeans, a sweatshirt, and sneakers; grabbed her room key; and hurried down to the lobby.

"The game's afoot" is what Sherlock Holmes would say at a moment like this, she thought.

Ah, the joys of the reporting life…even at four in the morning.

Chapter Two

Conventional wisdom holds early summer in Greece to be a beautiful time of year. The water is warm, the winds are mild, and the tourists are better behaved. But as far as Andreas Kaldis's workload was concerned, he saw little difference from season to season. The nation's criminal underbelly never seemed to go on holiday.

Ring, ring.

Nor do the phones.

He waited for Maggie to answer.

"It's the managing editor of your favorite newspaper," Maggie bellowed in from her desk outside Andreas's open office door. "And he's in his usual foul mood."

"Great, just what I need to make my day." Andreas picked up the phone. "Hi, Gio—"

"Kaldis, it's Pappas here."

Andreas wondered if Giorgos Pappas had purposely patterned his abrupt telephone style after the curmudgeonly stereotypes popularized in film and TV. Though it could be grating, Andreas viewed it as an act—like the cowardly lion in *The Wizard of Oz*—and liked the newspaperman.

"What a pleasant surprise, Giorgos. To what do I owe the honor of this call?"

"I need you to find my reporter."

"I beg your pardon? What reporter?"

"Nikoletta Elia. She should have been in my office hours ago, but isn't."

Andreas wanted to ask Pappas if he'd been drinking but decided to play along for a bit longer. "Do you think something's happened to her?"

"Of course I do. Otherwise why would I be calling you to find one of my reporters?"

"What do you think happened?"

"Damn it, man. If I knew, I wouldn't be calling you."

Andreas counted to three. "Giorgos. If you want my help, *back off.*" He paused for Pappas's response. None came, so he continued. "Why do you think her being a few hours late for work involves something that would interest the police?"

"Five days ago, we published a story she wrote about a mysterious computer pro operating on the Dark Web. It sent cops all over Europe scouring through their closed files, looking for clues to who he might be."

"Yes, I recognized her name. But what makes you think something's happened to her?"

"We agreed that she'd stay on Naxos until today to finish up a story on the push to expand tourism there. When she didn't show up in the office this morning, I tried calling her, but my calls kept going into voicemail." He paused. "So, I called her hotel to see if she'd left yet. I was told she'd not checked out, and when I asked to be put through to her room, again there was no answer. I convinced the manager to check if she was there. He said she wasn't, but her things were."

"Please excuse the indelicacy of this question, but perhaps she spent the night elsewhere?"

"I thought the same thing, but her mobile was next to her bed, and she'd never go anywhere without it."

"I'd like to help you out, but frankly, this still doesn't sound like a police matter."

"I'm not done yet. I haven't told you about the body?"

Andreas sat up in his chair. "What body?"

"The hotel sits on a bluff high above the sea. According to the manager, a body was found early this morning on the rocks just below the hotel. Police have been there all morning looking for evidence."

"I take it the body was not your reporter's."

"Correct. Police haven't identified him yet, but their thinking is he was a tourist unfamiliar with the terrain who lost his footing in the stiff winds that came through there late last night."

"Sounds plausible."

"Yeah, just like Nikoletta's hacker made his handiwork look like accidents."

"Are you suggesting that the body somehow ties into your missing reporter?"

"According to the manager, a hotel security guard saw Nikoletta leave the hotel a little after four in the morning to meet someone over by the edge of the bluff."

"And was that someone the body they found?"

"The security guy never saw who she met, but she never returned."

Andreas picked up a pencil and began drumming its eraser on his desktop. "So, what do you think happened to her?"

"Not a clue. But I'm worried her disappearance is somehow tied into the hacker."

"If you're suggesting he had second thoughts about talking to her, or was worried that she could identify him, I'd think *she'd* be the body they found on the rocks."

"That's why you're the detective, and I'm just the hysterical editor."

"There's another obvious angle," said Andreas, "but it, too, doesn't explain why a tourist ended up dead instead of your reporter. Nikoletta must have alarmed anyone who'd ever hired her hacker. Even though the cat's out of the bag for those exposed in her article, his other clients could be worried about follow-up articles covering other activities pointing back at them."

Andreas heard a deep swallow on the other end of the line.

"Um, we do have an investigative series planned to look into other incidents potentially linked to him."

"Who beyond you knew of those plans?"

"My publisher and the two reporters I assigned to work with Nikoletta." He gave Andreas the names of the two reporters. "But anyone familiar with the newspaper business could guess that's what we'd do. I mean, that's how you sell papers."

Andreas leaned back in his chair. "Okay, you've piqued my interest. I'll send someone over to Naxos to look into this. Just one promise I need from you."

"What is it?"

"Don't publish anything about your concerns for your reporter—or my unit's involvement in this. If she's been abducted and is still alive, the last thing she needs is for her captor to think we're onto what happened and closing in."

Silence.

"Well, do we have a deal?" asked Andreas.

"I had to tell my publisher what happened. He went ballistic at the possibility of someone kidnapping one of his reporters. No telling what he might do."

"Just tell him what I said. Publicity at this time will only endanger her more. And keep your fingers crossed that he listens."

"Following directions is not a customary strong point among publishers."

"I'll take that as a yes, you'll try."

"Let me know as soon as you hear anything."

"That's a two-way street," said Andreas.

"Understood."

"Great. Now let me get back to work."

"Thanks, Andreas."

Andreas stared at his dead phone. That was the first time Giorgos had ever called him by his given name.

He's worried.

———

Detective Yianni Kouros looked forward to spending the coming weekend in Athens with his girlfriend, Toni, something her job playing piano in a Mykonos bar rarely permitted. This weekend, though, the bar was closed for a wedding, giving Toni the opportunity to visit him, and Yianni a break from his weekend ferryboat commute to Mykonos.

He planned on showing his American-born girlfriend the *real* Athens, not the heavily promoted version sold to tourists. But that was still two days away, and at the moment he had a message to see his boss "as soon as you get in."

Yianni had been Andreas's right-hand man since their days together on Mykonos, when Andreas was the island's police chief and Yianni a brash young bull of a rookie cop. He stuck his head through the open doorway to Andreas's office.

Andreas was talking on the phone but waved Yianni toward a chair in front of his desk. "Yes, Minister, I understand the importance of protecting members of our free press from violence." He rolled his eyes. "Yes, we are not Turkey."

Andreas put his hand over the mouthpiece, "It's our Public Order and Citizen Protection Minister grandstanding for a publisher demanding that we find his missing reporter."

"What missing reporter?" whispered Yianni.

Andreas took his hand off the mouthpiece. "Of course I'm listening. I was just telling my best detective to clear his desk to take charge of this matter." Andreas rolled his eyes again. "Absolutely. I'll let you know as soon as we learn anything more." Andreas nodded. "Yes, the best to you and your wife too. Bye." He hung up the phone, sighed, and looked at Yianni.

"Every day I thank the Fates that I gave up that position as Minister of Public Order and returned here to the relative calm of chasing bad guys." Andreas pointed at the phone. "The gyrations he has to go through to satisfy all the interests demanding his attention is enough to drive a person mad. In order to keep the jackals constantly nipping at his heels from getting a clear shot at his throat, he has to keep his constituents thinking only he can be relied upon to make things happen. This time he had to put on an act for a publisher who'd burst into his office venting about us failing to find a reporter I just learned *might* be missing."

Yianni leaned forward. "I get all that political stuff, so let's get to the part about me clearing my desk."

"The reporter who broke that story on the mysterious hacker has gone missing, or so her editor thinks." Andreas told Yianni of his conversation with the editor and his request the paper not run a story about her disappearance until Andreas had a better handle on what happened. "At this point, we don't know if she disappeared willingly or unwillingly. She might just be out somewhere partying." Andreas leaned back in his chair. "Then again, with so much of our world facing lethal attacks on the media, we do have to consider the worst as a possibility."

"I take that to mean the worst is about to happen to *me*."

"Hey, don't complain. It's why you get paid the big money."

Yianni waved off the teasing. "I've got plans with Toni for the weekend."

"You've got a couple of days before then, and besides, Naxos is only an hour from Mykonos."

"But our plans are for Athens."

Andreas nodded. "Well, let's see what you can turn up by Friday, and we'll take it from there."

"I'm not happy."

"Understood. I'll find some way to make it up to you."

"Your bigger challenge will be finding a way to make it up to Toni. After all, she's become best friends with your wife."

Andreas nodded. "Neither of whom is shy about speaking her mind to me. I guess that means you should be on your way ASAP. The sooner you get a handle on things, the better our chance of salvaging your weekend." He paused. "And my domestic bliss."

"Where do you suggest I begin?"

"I spoke to the Naxos police chief and told him to keep Nikoletta's hotel room sealed off until you get there. She apparently left in a hurry, taking nothing with her. I'd say that's the place to start."

"I'll get going." Yianni stood. "Can you get me a list from Nikoletta's editor of everyone she met with on Naxos?"

"I'll get Maggie on it."

"Thanks."

"It's the least I can do for you."

Yianni headed for the door. "You mean the *very* least."

———

Yianni caught a flight from Athens that had him to Naxos in about the same time as it took to fly to its neighboring island of Mykonos, two islands different in practically every way imaginable. Shaped like a broad granite and marble arrowhead pointing north, Naxos was four times the size of Mykonos, and the largest island in the Cyclades. It also boasted the Cyclades's two tallest mountains, Zas and Koronos. Naxos had long ago been deforested but was still green, agriculturally blessed, and since antiquity, famous for its marble and emery mines. Though Mykonos had its barite mines and grain windmills, it was a dry, arid, and rocky place, with modest agriculture that in no way rivaled Naxos's natural riches and virtual self-sufficiency.

But times had changed, and today Mykonos possessed a high-end tourism reputation that was the envy of every Greek island seeking to maximize its own tourist potential. Yianni wondered how long it would be before Naxos embraced the same tourism fervor so many of its island neighbors had.

He stared out the window as the light plane approached Naxos Island National Airport. A relatively modest facility, it stood approximately two and a half miles southwest of Chora, east of a massive salt pond, and surrounded by a patchwork of chocolate, beige, and green open fields. Its short runway kept big international jetliners away, an obvious check on tourism expansion. Yianni wondered if that was intentional and, if so, who wanted it that way.

As Yianni walked across the tarmac toward the tiny terminal building, the final scene from *Casablanca* popped into his mind—Humphrey Bogart and Claude Rains strolling through the fog along a lonely stretch of airstrip on their way to neither knew where.

Naxos's local police chief stood waiting for Yianni at the gate. They knew each other from Yianni's time as a cop on Mykonos. Back then, they'd worked together at catching thieves who'd milk one Cycladic island until things got too hot for them there, then jump to another.

"You haven't changed a bit, Dimitri," said Yianni, hugging the chief and exchanging cheek kisses.

"Too bad I can't say the same for you," smiled Dimitri. "But in your case, you look better than ever."

"Puh, puh, puh. That's all I need, you giving me the evil eye with bullshit compliments." He slapped Dimitri on the back.

"How's your chief doing?"

"Andreas? Great. You know he's married now with two kids."

"I've heard, to the only daughter of one of Greece's wealthiest old-line families."

"Yeah, that's what gets played up in cop gossip, but she's a down-to-earth, no-bullshit lady. In fact, she and my girlfriend created a program to mentor vulnerable young girls."

"Sounds impressive."

"It is, but I want to hear all about your family."

As they made their way to Dimitri's car, he filled Yianni in on the expanding size of his family and listened to Yianni go on about the state of his own love life.

"Your friend sounds like an interesting woman."

"She is, but this case is threatening to wreck our plans for the weekend."

The chief shrugged. "Have her come over. You can stay with us."

"That's kind of you, but I was hoping to show her Athens."

"Well, the offer's open." Dimitri pressed a button on his key fob to unlock the doors to his cruiser. "I assume the first thing you'll want is to see the reporter's hotel room."

"Yes," said Yianni as he slid into the passenger seat, "then the people she talked to."

"I'll arrange to have one of my local Naxos cops drive you around the island. Trust me when I say that'll be a hell of a lot easier than turning you loose with a GPS, a map, and a car. The island's too big, and the places and people you'll want to see way too difficult for you to find on your own."

"Thanks, but how do you know who exactly I'll want to see?"

"I don't." Dimitri pulled out of the airport onto the main road leading back to the heart of Chora. "But from what I've heard, your reporter was all over the island, speaking to some of its most *interesting* characters."

"What's that supposed to mean?"

"This island is filled with strong opinions, rooted in a deep pride in Naxos's historically independent ways. Some show it in words, some in dress, some in actions. I expect every one of them will have an opinion on what happened to her."

"Are you saying word's out that she's missing?"

"We're trying to keep it quiet and officially have said nothing, but there's no way this sort of thing stays out of the local gossip mill for long. After all, the story she wrote about meeting up with that cyber guy attracted international attention in a way that gave the island a bit of celebrity. People know who she is. When word gets out that she disappeared the same night that tourist died"— Dimitri waved his right hand in a small circle—"I can only imagine the theories that will be circulating. Each one undoubtedly aimed at implicating someone the teller of the tale despises."

"Why would locals want to spread that sort of bullshit? It seems sort of self-destructive for the island."

"The answer to that question, my friend, has been a mystery haunting Greeks for centuries. For example, our illustrious mayor made it clear to me this morning that he's prepared to turn this into a political issue aimed directly at me. To quote him, 'Unanswered questions surrounding a dead tourist and missing journalist cannot be allowed to hang over our island.'"

"I take it you two don't get along."

"That's putting it mildly. We have serious disagreements over what he and I see as legally permissible behavior on the part of his political cronies."

"Hmm." Yianni changed subjects. "Any evidence of the tourist's cause of death?"

"Yes, a header off the top of a cliff onto the rocks below."

"What else do you know about him?"

"No ID yet, but we know his physical description." Dimitri described him.

"That's it?"

"No signs of foul play, no drugs or alcohol in his system."

"Then what the hell was he doing out there in the middle of the night?"

"That's what half the island wants to know, and the other half doesn't care because it's already convinced he was murdered."

"I can see you're feeling the pressure. Any leads?"

"That would be too much to expect. A lot of accusations are being lobbed back and forth between rival interest groups, and of course, a rash of conspiracy theories abound. All, at least so far, unsupported by evidence."

"In other words, business as usual."

"Yes, but I've compiled a list of everyone preaching me theories." Dimitri handed Yianni an envelope. "Take it for what it's worth. It just might give you a place to start."

"And give your harassers the sense that you took their opinions seriously enough to pass them on to me." Yianni smiled.

Dimitri grinned. "One must keep one's public happy."

They fell back to talking about old times and how much the world had changed in so few years.

Yianni paid little attention to the neighborhoods they passed through on the two-lane road into Chora. To him, the modern areas that developed around the outskirts of virtually every town of sizable population, be it an island or mainland town, looked the same. The perennial favorite choice of construction remained two- and three-story buildings thrown up for the rents they generated, from street-level commercial space to residential apartments above. Gas stations, hardware stores, and electronics shops mixed in among supermarkets, pharmacies, bakeries, butchers, and banks. Doctors, lawyers, and accountants worked in offices next to fast-food shops, nail salons, hairdressers, and lotto sellers, plus the ubiquitous *kafenia* and tavernas.

Dimitri wove though Chora's maze of one-way streets to a tiny parking area wedged between the edge of a cliff and the hotel.

"Here we are. I've taken the liberty of arranging for the security guy to be here for you to interview. He's our only witness to whatever happened. I figured you'd like to speak to him first."

Yianni followed Dimitri into a reception area decorated in pale grays and whites. Walls of glass enclosed two sides of the adjoining bar and restaurant area, affording sweeping views of the Aegean, Portara, and Chora.

Dimitri introduced Yianni to the hotel's owner, a tall, slim man with the practiced, welcoming smile of a hotelier. He showed the two cops into his office. A squat, swarthy man wearing blue jeans, a Grateful Dead T-shirt, and a scruffy, Jerry Garcia–style gray beard, slouched in one of two taverna chairs in front of a simple wooden desk.

"Anargyros, these are the policemen who want to speak with you," said the owner. He pointed to the upholstered office chair behind the desk. "Please, Detective, feel free to take my chair."

"Thank you, but Dimitri can sit there. I'll take this one." Yianni sat in the chair next to Anargyros and turned his head to face the hotel owner. "You've been most kind. We'll let you know as soon as we're finished with the interview."

The hotel owner looked disappointed at being subtly told to leave but nodded and left the office, shutting the door behind him.

Yianni smiled at Anargyros. "First of all, thank you for seeing us at a time when I assume you're normally asleep. My name is

Detective Yianni Kouros, and I have some questions that you may have already been asked by others."

Anargyros shrugged.

"I'd like you to tell us everything that happened last night conceivably having anything to do with Nikoletta Elia."

Anargyros shut his eyes and rocked his head from side to side. "Do you mind if I smoke?"

"No."

Anargyros reached into his jeans, pulled out a small sack of tobacco and rolling papers, and began making himself a cigarette.

Yianni shot a where-the-hell-is-this-headed look at Dimitri.

"Anargyros," said Dimitri, "this isn't one of your group therapy, addiction support sessions. We need answers *now*."

Anargyros stared at Dimitri and kept quietly rolling his cigarette.

"Do you want to keep this job or not? Just answer the detective's questions and you can be on your way. Otherwise…"

Yianni jumped in as the good cop. "We really don't want to take up any more of your time than necessary, but we do need your cooperation."

"Or else I'll drag your ass down to the station and keep you there until you answer his questions," added Dimitri.

Anargyros finished rolling his cigarette, pulled a plastic lighter from another pocket, lit the cigarette, and drew in a puff. "She came into reception at about three a.m." He exhaled. "Pretty close to shitfaced when she did."

"Did she say anything to you?" asked Yianni.

"Just took her room key and said good night." He took another draw on the cigarette. "About an hour later she burst into reception, wearing blue jeans and a gray sweatshirt and asking if someone was looking for her. I said no, and she went running off into the breakfast room and bar area."

"What did you do?" said Yianni.

Exhaling a cloud of pungent smoke, he said, "I got up from behind the reception desk to see what she was doing. Considering how drunk she'd been an hour before, I didn't want her grabbing anything from behind the bar. My job would be on the line if I'd let her."

"What was she doing in there?"

"I never got to see—she came out before I had the chance. She seemed panicked. Then she asked if anyone had been in reception since she'd come back to the hotel at three. I said no. I also suggested she calm down and go back to bed."

"What did she say to that?"

"She never answered, just pointed to one of the windows looking out toward the bluff and yelled, 'There he is.'"

"Did you see who she was pointing at?"

"It was so dark I couldn't see if a tall, short, thin, or fat he, she, or it was out there. Whoever it was stood beyond the hotel's lights."

"Then how do you know someone was out there?"

He took another drag. "Because when I turned to see what she was looking at, I saw a blinking light coming at us from the dark."

"How do you know it was aimed at you?"

"Aimed at her." He exhaled. "When I turned to her, she was running for the front door. I looked back at the light and it stopped blinking right after I heard the wind slam the front door shut."

"And she never came back?"

"Correct." He let the smoke drift out of his nose.

"Didn't that seem odd to you?"

Anargyros stared at Yianni. "Are you serious? This is a holiday island. A woman staggers back to the hotel at three in the morning after too much to drink, and an hour later comes down from her room looking to hook up with some guy who'd just called her, and you expect me to wonder why she didn't come back before my shift was over at seven?"

Yianni nodded, "Good point. But how do you know someone had just called her?"

"I don't. I just assumed it."

"Could the call have come through the switchboard?"

He shrugged. "I'd have had to put it through, and none came in for her."

"Are you sure?"

"Calls at four in the morning are rare. And if one came in, the caller would have had to convince me to put it through. There were no calls."

Over the next hour, Yianni and Dimitri plumbed Anargyros's memory for every detail of Nikoletta's appearance, words, and behavior that night, but his story and recollections remained the same.

"Well, what do you think?" said Yianni to Dimitri after they'd sent Anargyros on his way.

"I think he's telling the truth. He's a bright guy seduced by a bad meth habit, but he's done a pretty good job of kicking it. I don't see an angle in this for him."

"Well, let's take a look at her room," said Yianni. "There's got to be a clue somewhere."

"You always were an optimist."

——

Nikoletta's room reflected the new minimalist trend in beach accommodations. Tastefully done in pale-gray and white, with marble floors and light-oak wooden shelving and furniture, it perfectly stated what it was: a modern place for a holiday stay.

Yianni stood in the doorway, studying the room before stepping inside. "Have your guys gone through this?"

"Every millimeter, but they left things right where they found them."

"What did they turn up?"

"Fingerprints, likely from housekeepers, workmen, and past guests."

"Anything else relevant to us?"

Dimitri pointed to a pile of notebooks on the nightstand. "Four of them contain the reporter's notes on interviews for her tourism story. The fifth covers her interview with the mysterious cybercriminal."

"What about the mobile phone?"

"It's locked. We assume it's hers."

"Did you try opening it?"

"I thought about asking my five-year-old son to take a crack at it. He always seems to know how to get into my phone, but I decided to leave that challenge to your tech wizzes back in Athens."

"Good decision," said Yianni. "Let's get it couriered to Athens right away."

He carefully made his way over to the nightstand. "I assume the notebooks have been examined for fingerprints?"

"Yes. Only hers turned up."

Yianni sat on the edge of the bed, picked up the top notebook, and opened it. On the first page was a notation handwritten in Greek and English.

IF FOUND, PLEASE RETURN TO NIKOLETTA ELIA, followed by a Greek mobile telephone number and the word REWARD underlined and circled.

On the next page was a neatly printed name, location, date, and beginning and ending time, followed by pages of notes and long bodies of text, presumably recording the words of the subject of her interview. Sections were arranged similarly for each person she'd interviewed.

Yianni looked up at Dimitri standing by the bed. "Have you read these?"

"Not carefully. I glanced at them, but as you can see there's a lot to read."

Yianni held the notebook open to the page he'd been looking at. "Who's the person named here?"

Dimitri leaned in to read the name. "That would be our mayor. I understand he was the first person she interviewed for her story."

"I'll need your help in identifying who she met with. The list my office received from her editor isn't complete."

"No problem."

"She had five notebooks?"

"That's all we found."

"That's a lot to read."

Dimitri nodded. "And steps to retrace."

Yianni shut his eyes and sighed. "No way I'll be able to complete all of this by the weekend."

"Like I said, the offer of a place for you and Toni to stay remains open."

"Thanks." Yianni slapped his free hand on his thigh and stood up. "Well, let's get started. First thing I need is a place to read these notebooks cover-to-cover, undisturbed. I want to finish reading them by tonight so that I can begin retracing her steps first thing in the morning."

"I know the perfect place for you."

"Not the police station. I'll be inundated with gossipers who won't take no for an answer."

"Don't worry, no one will disturb you where I have in mind."

"Good."

"There's only one hitch."

"Being?"

"Do you believe in ghosts?"

Chapter Three

Yianni called Andreas to report on what he'd found, or rather not found, and said he'd call again after he'd read through the reporter's notebooks. He pondered whether to call Toni, but she might be sleeping. Her job as a piano player in one of Mykonos's iconic clubs kept her up until four in the morning. She rarely stirred before noon, and then it was off to her day job playing finder of stolen goods for tourists and locals preyed upon by opportunistic thieves. Her late afternoon nap was sacrosanct, but he decided to risk leaving a message on her mobile.

He leaned against a wall as he patiently waited for the sixth ring to send him into voicemail. "Hi, my love. I'm just calling to let you know I'm on Naxos and will be incommunicado for the rest of the day and likely much of the night, reading documents. I didn't want you wondering why you hadn't heard from me, and—"

Ring, ring.

Yianni looked at his phone. It was Toni. He switched over to take her call. "You're awake?"

"Phones ringing six times have a habit of doing that to me."

"I didn't expect you to leave it on."

"When I sleep alone, I leave it on vibrate. And don't bother to ask why unless you're prepared to handle the answer."

Yianni laughed. "I miss you."

"I miss you too. Can't wait until the weekend."

Yianni swallowed. "Me too. I was just leaving you a message that I'll be tied up into the night reading documents."

"What sort of a case has you cloistered away reading documents? I thought all you big-time cops did was break heads and beat confessions out of bad guys."

Yianni grinned. "That's the fun part, but we can't beat on them until we find them. Which is what has me standing outside a monster medieval mansion atop old town Naxos."

"Sounds wonderful."

"It is. The local police chief arranged for me to have a key to the place so that I could do my reading undisturbed. But now I'm all alone, about to be surrounded by antiquities dating back to the fifth millennium B.C.E., and who knows what ancient spirits, so I decided to call you for company."

"Is it someone's home?"

"No, it used to be the School of Commerce for Boys, but now it's the Naxos Archaeological Museum."

"I think I'm supposed to respond, 'How sweet of you to think of me,' though my instinct is to say, 'You sound horny.'"

"So much for the moment."

Toni chuckled. "I've never been to Naxos. I hear it's wonderful. Maybe we could go there together someday."

Yianni bit at his lip. "Yeah, why not?"

"Well, try not to have too much fun among the artifacts while I labor on among the sinners."

"One man's sin is another's wished-for prayer."

"You sound more like a philosopher than a cop."

Yianni laughed. "On that note, I'll say goodbye, get to work on my reading, and let you get back to sleep."

"Little chance of that now, my love, but bye-bye." She signed off with a kiss.

Yianni lingered for a moment, holding the phone to his ear. Toni was unlike any woman he'd ever known. She could read a bar audience with wildly different musical tastes and come up with the perfect tune to please them all.

He wondered if that same intuitive gift had her somehow sensing that their weekend plans were in jeopardy. By suggesting they "someday" visit Naxos, did she want him to know that she was okay with that? Yianni shook his head and smiled, put his phone away, and stepped inside the museum.

He put the notebooks down on a small table just inside the entrance, picked up a brochure from the same table, and wandered for ten minutes through the museum's warren of rooms, halls, terraces, and staircases. According to the brochure, one of Yianni's favorite authors, Nikos Kazantzakis of *Zorba the Greek* fame, had attended the school that once inhabited this building. Yianni also read that an upper floor of the school had once housed a library full of artifacts and other valuable treasures, but occupying German and Italian forces destroyed them in World War II.

Yianni could easily spend a day in here wandering among antiquities. He decided the best place for him to do his reading would be as far away as possible from those distractions. So, he planted himself and Nikoletta's notebooks at the desk where visitors stood in line to buy their tickets.

Yianni drew in and let out a deep breath, picked up the notebook containing the reporter's earliest entries, and muttered to himself, "In the beginning..."

———

Toni turned onto her left side and stared at a blank wall next to the lone window in her bedroom. There was nothing there for her to see, but she wasn't looking, she was concentrating her thoughts. Since their last weekend together, all Yianni had talked about were his plans for them in Athens. What they'd see, what they'd do, who they'd meet. Now, not a peep.

Something's happened. I hope it's only work.

She rolled onto her back, stretching and yawning as she did. She lived in a hotel close by the sea. It was more of a big house with bedrooms, but its owner called it a hotel and the Tourist Board allowed him to do so, thereby entitling him to charge higher rates for his rooms. Toni had no complaint about the price because as a year-round resident she had a special deal. More importantly, the owner and his wife treated her like family. That meant a lot to Toni, because her mother had died a few years back, and her father's subsequent depression led him to give up his overseas position with the U.S. State Department and move back to New York City, the place of their marriage and Toni's birth.

She'd grown up as a diplomat's child, bouncing from one foreign American school to another. Music was her only constant during those early expat years. Straight out of high school, she skipped college and took off on her own, bumming around Europe, dreaming of setting the world on fire with her music. Ultimately, she landed on Mykonos.

She swung her legs out of bed, faced the bathroom doorway, and shifted her eyes to the mirror to its right. "Good evening, Toni, how nice to see you looking so fine and chipper. Another late night in store for you, I presume? Now don't start complaining, Dearie. After all, you're the one who wanted to be a piano player. In other words, get your ass out of bed."

Toni shut her eyes and shook her head. "I must be crazy talking to a mirror."

She looked back at the mirror. "No, Dearie, you just miss your boyfriend."

———

The more of the reporter's notebooks Yianni read, the more certain he was that his weekend plans were toast. As unhappy as that made him, he saw no alternative. From what Nikoletta had written, there could be any number of reasons why she'd disappeared, several of them fatal.

Her notes of her conversation with the hacker went into details not revealed in the newspaper article. Details pointing fingers at mobsters, private citizens, and government officials he claimed had retained him to target competitors, enemies, colleagues, and spouses. If true, every one of his clients had a reason to want Nikoletta silenced.

But her other notebooks suggested a different sort of suspect, one unrelated to him or his kills, yet with a definite motive for keeping her from publishing her second story. The players ranged from big-money developers to activists to uncompromising fanatics. Nikoletta's plans for laying bare the bad intentions and hidden agendas she saw as stoking a looming, pitched battle over the island's future would not endear her to many.

But enough to kill her?

Yianni leaned back in his chair and stretched. With all the crazies in this world, he wasn't about to play psychiatrist and eliminate any potential suspect. He'd simply assume the worst and say a prayer that it wasn't too late for Nikoletta.

On that thought, he looked at his watch. It was nearly one in the morning. He hadn't eaten a thing since a quick bite with Dimitri on their way up to the museum. He thought to call Andreas and report on what he'd read since they'd spoken shortly before midnight, but it was late and he'd didn't have much more to say than he'd already told him. Too many suspects, too many divergent motives. He'd call first thing in the morning. Tomorrow would be a busy day. Make that, *today* will be a busy day. He should get to bed, but before retracing Nikoletta's every step, he needed something to eat.

———

The path from the museum down to the harbor was a mix of stone steps and inclines, but all well lighted. There was life on the old town's winding streets, not surprising what with it being tourist season. Yianni had no trouble finding the bar where Nikoletta had held her interview, and though its kitchen was closed, a man Yianni took to be the owner offered to microwave a frozen pizza.

Yianni sat sipping a beer when the owner returned with the pizza in one hand and a fresh-made Greek salad in the other. "I thought, what kind of a host would I be if I didn't at least offer you a salad?"

Yianni smiled. "You're too kind. I never expected this."

"You don't like salad?"

"No, I meant this is very generous of you. Thank you."

"I always try remembering that hospitality shows respect not just for my customers but for what I do every day of my life to earn my living. That was a lesson passed on to me by my father." He crossed himself.

Yianni studied the man, who looked fit, in his late forties, taller than Yianni, but wiry, with a broad round face, a three-day beard, uncombed more than tousled hair, and the sort of close-set, dark eyes that suggested feral intensity.

Yianni extended his right hand. "My name is Yianni."

The man shook it. "Stelios. Welcome to this little bit of heaven."

"It's a lovely setting. You must get a lot of business."

The man nodded. "Yes, business has been very good. *Puh, puh, puh.*"

Yianni picked up a piece of pizza and took a bite.

Stelios started to turn away. "I'll leave you to eat in peace."

"No, please. Join me." Yianni pointed to the chair across from him. "No reason for me to eat alone, assuming you don't need to be doing something else."

Stelios sat. "No, the bartender has everything under control. The few customers remaining are just sipping drinks and basking in the notoriety of the place."

Yianni saw his opening. "Notoriety?"

"You didn't know?"

"Know what?" Yianni feigned ignorance.

"That reporter, the one who wrote a story about a mysterious computer guy she met in a bar, she met him here."

"Really?"

"Yes, they were sitting at that table behind you, in the window."

Yianni turned and looked at the table, then turned back to face Stelios. "How long were they here?"

"Two, three hours."

Yianni turned around to look at the table again. "What were they like?"

"He talked; she took notes. And before you ask, I never heard a word they said."

"Why do you think I would ask?"

"Because everyone asks me that."

"I guess that's only natural, but I'd also think it only natural for you not to admit you'd overheard anything, even if you had."

Stelios smiled. "Considering what the newspaper said they talked about, I think you're right."

Yianni nodded. "So, what did he look like?"

"I'm not good at remembering faces."

"Another wise trait. Though probably not a good one for a bar owner."

Stelios smiled again. "Don't worry, I'll remember yours. So, what has you over here on Naxos? Are you on holiday?"

Yianni reached into the front of his shirt and pulled out his ID on a lanyard around his neck. "Nope, I'm a detective with Greece's Special Crimes Unit." He took another bite of the pizza.

Stelios's face blanched. "I guess I've already said too much."

Yianni gave a quick upward jerk of his head. "Not at all." He took a taste of the Greek salad. "This is terrific. I particularly like the touch of oregano."

Stelios's face constricted, and he bit at his lip.

Yianni took another bite. "Tasty."

Stelios started to stand. "I've really got some work I should be doing."

Yianni nodded "no" again. "Stay. I like your company."

Stelios slunk into the chair. "Honest, I heard not a word."

"So, what did he look like?"

"I told you, I—"

"Would you like a piece of pizza?"

"No, I—"

"How about at least a bit of feta?"

"No, I—"

"Then how about a bit of truth serum?" Yianni slid his beer across the table to Stelios.

"He was a tall man, slim, with dark hair, but it could have been a wig. His eyes were intense. My guess is he's from one of those Scandinavian countries, maybe Iceland, but from the little I heard him say, he spoke perfect Greek without any trace of an accent."

"Anything else?"

"A big smile, I mean a really big smile."

"You said he was tall. How tall?"

"A little taller than I."

"When did he come into the bar?"

"Right after the woman sat down at the table."

"Did they know each other?"

"He knew her, but she didn't know him. I watched to make sure he wasn't going to harass her. I protect my customers from that sort of thing."

Yianni nodded. "I'm sure. So, what did you hear?"

"Basically, the things she wrote in the article. I heard him say he had some interesting things to tell her. Once she told him to sit, I lost interest in their conversation. I had no idea who he or she was and didn't have to hear another seduction routine. I think I've heard them all at one time or another. Besides, we were busy, and I had other customers to sit with."

"Did they leave together?"

"I don't remember. And I've never seen either of them again."

"I assume that's another question you get asked."

Stelios nodded.

Yianni extended his hand. "Thanks, for everything."

Stelios quickly stood and shook Yianni's hand. "May I go now?"

"Sure."

Stelios turned to walk away but paused and looked back at Yianni. "You're not so bad for a cop. Your dinner's on me."

"No, I insist on respecting your business by paying for it."

Stelios touched his chest with his hand. "Thank you. But only for the pizza. The beer and salad are on me."

Yianni returned the gesture. "Deal."

Yianni devoured the pizza and salad and ordered a second beer for which he insisted on paying. As he was about to leave,

Stelios came over with a plate of fresh fruit. He placed the fruit on the table and sat down across from Yianni.

"Something else occurred to me. I'm not sure it's important, but just in case it is, I wanted you to know."

"I'm listening."

"Someone else came into the bar at about the same time as the man and the woman. I can't be certain when he arrived, but he sat at the bar sipping beers with his eyes glued to the mirror behind the bar."

"Could he see their table in the mirror."

Stelios nodded.

"Did he speak to either of them?"

"No."

"When did he leave?"

"Right after the woman left."

"Why didn't you tell anyone this before?"

"I didn't even think about it until you asked me whether she and the hacker guy left together. That's when I remembered the fellow at the bar. He could have been her driver waiting for her to leave, but I don't recall her saying a word to him, even when she left."

"Have you ever seen him before?"

"No, or after."

"What did he look like?"

"Your height, a bit stocky, ruddy complexion, dark, normal-length hair, dark eyes, in his thirties."

"His ethnicity?"

"No idea, I never heard him speak. He could have been Eastern European, American, or even Greek. I've no way of telling."

That fits the description of the guy who did a header onto the rocks below Nikoletta's hotel.

"What about the bartender who waited on him. Where can I find him?"

"You mean her. I wish I knew. The staff in this place turns over before I can even learn their names. They move on as soon as they find a better job, whether here or on another island. I'm just happy if they give me notice."

"Do you have a name for that bartender?"

"Uh, that's a bit complicated."

"No working papers? So no legitimate name." Yianni shook his head.

"Hey, I was trying to help you out. Now you're going to burn me?"

"Don't worry, I'm not going to turn you in. Just promise not to do it again."

"Sure. Promise."

Good chance of that one being kept.

"Thanks," said Stelios, hurrying off as if afraid to test his luck with further conversation.

As Yianni walked back to the hotel, he put his conversation with the bar owner out of his mind to focus on his next challenge: telling Toni that their weekend plans were canceled.

———

"Hello."

"Sorry to bother you at work, but I know you take a break fifteen minutes before every hour."

Toni looked at her phone. "It's a quarter to three, and there's no one on the phone except you and me, so what's the story you have to tell?"

"One that I hope won't dampen your sense of humor."

"Try me."

"The case that has me on Naxos is going to keep me here through the weekend."

"Whew, I thought it might be something serious, what with this being so far past your bedtime. We'll do Athens another time. After all, it's not going anywhere."

"I'm sorry."

"Well, I can't say I'm not disappointed. I was looking forward to seeing you."

"Me too." Yianni paused. "You could come over here. I'll still have to work, but at least we could be together part of the time."

"Does Naxos have beaches, bars, and restaurants?"

"Great ones."

"Fine, then count me in. I'll find some way to keep myself occupied while you're busy elsewhere."

"I'm not sure I like that proposal."

Toni laughed. "It's no different than the sort of life I live over here on Mykonos without you. Need I remind you that I'm the experienced partier in this relationship? So, what is it, big boy, Naxos or *nyet*?"

"If Greece had you negotiating its bailout with the European Union, we wouldn't be in the mess we're in today."

"That's not an answer. I'll give you until tomorrow to make up your mind."

"You mean today."

"Whatever day is Friday. I can catch the first boat to Naxos Saturday morning."

"Excellent. Just let me know the boat's name so I can arrange for you to be picked up by the hotel if I can't be there."

"Works for me. Time for you to get to bed, and me to get back to work."

"Miss you."

"Miss you too. Kisses."

The EU wouldn't have stood a chance against her.

Chapter Four

Andreas couldn't remember the last time he'd slept past dawn. With two young children, one of them always found a way to serve as his wake-up call. Lila and he had live-in help who could tend to the children, but Andreas looked upon these early-morning moments as his only guaranteed time with his children, because his evenings far too often belonged to the vagaries of what awaited him each day in his office.

Lila never interfered with her husband's first thirty minutes of daybreak playtime, but then she'd show up and impose order on the chaos her husband seemed ingenious at creating. After all, Tassaki had to get ready for kindergarten, and Sofia needed some semblance of a schedule. All of which meant that by eight each morning, Andreas was out the door and on his way to GADA.

This morning he arrived in his office to find three voicemails from Nikoletta's editor, each a bit more frantic than the one before.

There was also a message from Yianni describing what he'd learned from the bar owner and promising to call in at nine. Andreas dialed the number left by the editor.

The phone had barely rung once when Andreas heard, "It's about time you called back."

"Morning, Giorgos. You should be honored. I'm actually calling before my first cup of coffee. So, what has you so riled up?"

"MY REPORTER IS STILL MISSING!"

"I know that. It's why I have my best detective working around the clock on Naxos to find her."

"Well, get more people over there."

Andreas drew in and let out a quick breath. "There must be another reason why you left three messages for me in less than an hour, other than to bust my balls over how I assign my overworked, underpaid staff."

"He left me a message."

"Who did?"

"The hacker, or at least someone acting as if he's the hacker."

Andreas's voice tightened. "When did you receive it, how did you get it, and what did it say?"

"I found it on my voicemail when I got up this morning. The voice sounded like it had been through a scrambler, and he told me not to worry, Nikoletta was safe, and he was protecting her from those who might wish to do her harm. He said he knew the police were looking for her on Naxos, but they would never find her unless she wanted them to."

"*Unless she wanted them to?* Did he actually use those words?"

"Those precise words."

"Sounds like someone is trying to slow down the search by suggesting all's fine. But it's a rather bizarre way to do it, since it suggests a Stockholm-syndrome situation in the making."

"My feelings exactly."

"Then again, the call could've been a phony," said Andreas.

"Could be. There are a lot of crank callers out there. I'll send over a copy of the voicemail to your office for analysis."

"Better yet, bring us your phone. Our lab might be able to pick up more from it than off a copy of the message."

Giorgos's voice tensed. "I've got a lot of other things on that phone. Confidential things."

"I'm sure. It's why I suggested *you* bring it over. Watching what the lab guys do to your phone might give you peace of mind."

"I'm expecting nothing of the sort until Nikoletta's found, safe and sound."

Andreas paused. "On that point, I've reconsidered your request to assign more people to look for her."

"How many more?"

"Just one. For now."

"One? You think that's going to make a difference?"

"My wife thinks the world of him."

"Your wife? What—" Giorgos chuckled. "Okay, wiseass, when do you leave for Naxos?"

"ASAP."

"I really appreciate that."

"Understood."

"Have you found anything helpful in her notebooks?"

"Just a lot of possibilities to follow up on."

"Any chance of an ID on the hacker from her sketchbook?"

Andreas sat up straight in his chair. "What sketchbook?"

"She always carries a sketchbook with her to draw images of the people she met and places she visited. Interviewees don't always care for cameras, so she sketches them later from memory. We don't put them in her articles, but she saves them in case a source later denies giving her the interview."

"Where did she keep her sketchbook?"

"Usually in the back pocket of her jeans. It's about the size of a thin paperback with a simple brown leather cover. She never goes anywhere without it."

"What are the chances it contains a drawing of whoever called you?"

"If she interviewed him, I'd say it's a given."

"My detective didn't find it in her room. That's too bad. It'd be helpful to know what our kidnapper looks like."

"You think she was kidnapped?"

"She disappeared, no one's heard from her, and you receive a call from a stranger telling you not to worry, she's safe, because he's protecting her. If not a crank call, it sure sounds like a kidnapping to me. Which makes it all the more important that you—and your publisher—don't let the story get out to your media colleagues."

"But the caller didn't ask for ransom."

"All that means is money isn't why he took her."

"Shit."

"And that he's likely a psycho." Andreas's other phone line rang. "Gotta run, it's my detective calling from Naxos. Let me know the moment you hear anything more from Nikoletta's *protector*."

Andreas hung up on Giorgos and answered the other line with a grunted "Yes?"

"That's a cheery greeting to hear first thing in the morning."

"It's not the first thing in the morning, and I'm not in a cheery mood. I made the mistake of answering my phone before having my first cup of coffee and haven't been able to get one yet."

"At least you had the chance to wake up. I may need to glue my eyelids open. I haven't slept. I tried, but my mind kept running through all the things Nikoletta wrote about the people she interviewed. The interviews are blending one into another, and I've got to talk to the mayor in an hour."

"I'm sure you'll handle it fine, but just in case you'd like to slow down, take a nap, or maybe even spend some time at the beach, don't worry, everything's under control."

"Uh-oh. What bad news are you about to drop on me?"

"Nikoletta's editor just received a voicemail from her potential kidnapper telling us not to worry, he's protecting her."

"*What?*"

Andreas filled him in on his conversation.

"I never saw a sketchbook," said Yianni, "and I searched her room thoroughly."

"I know, but when you have the chance, take another look at it from the perspective of someone looking for a hiding place."

"I'll do it as soon as I get off the phone."

"Don't run off just yet. Have you told Dimitri that the bar owner's description of a stranger hanging out in his place the night Nikoletta met the hacker matches the dead tourist?"

"Not yet. I plan on telling him when he picks me up this morning. That should spice up his morning almost as much as you've done mine."

"I have some good news for you too. I'm coming to Naxos tomorrow to help with the investigation."

"Terrific. I can definitely use the help running down suspects."

"Maybe you'll get lucky in your meeting with the mayor."

"Who knows, but it should be interesting. I hear he plans on turning it into a PR event to announce the disappearance of the reporter and claim the local police chief isn't competent to handle the investigation—as evidenced by the fact that Athens sent me here."

"I was afraid of something like that. Why avoid taking a swipe for political gain, even if it risks a woman's life? Does the mayor know you're friends with the chief?"

"Dimitri's the one who told me, so I doubt it."

"Sounds like you're in for a hell of a morning."

"The good thing is, it'll at least wake me up."

"Some folk like to get their morning jolt from a cup of strong coffee, others opt for bare-knuckles conflict. I guess you fall into the latter category."

"Frankly, I prefer sex, but since that's currently unavailable, I think I'll have to settle for doing my best at screwing the mayor."

"On that, I think I'll say goodbye and leave you to your good times."

———

Dimitri had left a note for Yianni with the hotel receptionist apologizing for not arranging to pick him up for his meeting with the mayor, but since the mayor hadn't invited Dimitri to attend, it seemed best that Yianni not show up with a police escort. Instead, he left Yianni the keys to an unmarked motorbike parked outside the hotel.

Greeks and their intrigues. They never end.

Yianni's drive to Naxos's town hall took considerably longer than he anticipated. From a map, he'd estimated five minutes, but a gnarled web of one-way streets filled with tavernas, shops, hotels, and tourists anxious to get to the beach made it seem as though he'd never get there. After twice finding himself caught in a loop taking him away from town hall, he decided to make up a route of his own. He made a U-turn and headed due south along the harbor front aimed directly for town hall, ignoring a host of ONE WAY and DO NOT ENTER signs along the way—not to mention a flurry of honking horns and salty gestures from oncoming drivers.

Town hall overlooked the southern end of the harbor and served the Naxos and Small Cyclades Municipality governing Naxos and its neighboring smaller islands of Iraklia, Schinoussa, Koufonissia, and Donoussa, among others. Of Naxos's 18,400 residents, 13,000 lived in Chora and its environs, which meant approximately seventy percent of the population lived within roughly thirty percent of the island's territory. The balance lived in the sparsely populated but much larger rural territory north, east, and south of Chora. Police divided coverage responsibilities between headquarters in

Chora and an auxiliary office at the center of the island in Naxos's second largest village, Filoti.

Yianni parked directly in front of the town hall in a spot overlooking a smaller replica of the massive marble *Sphinx of Naxos* donated nearly 2,600 years ago by the people of Naxos to the Temple of Apollo at Delphi. Town hall's modern-day version of that ancient guardian stared straight out to sea, ever vigilant for any sign of danger headed its island's way.

The relatively new, two-decade-old town hall bore no resemblance to any ancient architectural style associated with the sphinx, and little to the old town's distinctly thirteenth-century Venetian influence. Still, its neoclassical design, ecru stucco front, and parallel rows of turquoise windows framed in white marble sublimely complemented the Kastro's three-hundred-year-old former School for Girls—perched high atop the old town in the ideal spot for looking down upon her much younger brother.

The town hall's main entrance stood between a pair of Doric columns supporting a second-story marble balustrade and terrace fronting a set of French doors. From his experience with other town halls, Yianni assumed the French doors and Il Duce–style balcony opened into the mayor's office.

Yianni stepped into the vestibule leading to the main entrance and reached for the door handle, but there was none. He tried pushing against the door, but it wouldn't budge. He could see people inside, but no one stepped forward to open the door. As obvious a grand entrance as it was, this wasn't the way in.

He turned around, looked left, looked right, went left, and made another left at the end of the building. There he found an open door leading into a short hallway lined with offices.

He smiled. His superstitious aunt would say he'd just received a message from the gods: *Be wary of the obvious.*

Chapter Five

As soon as Yianni stepped inside, a man asked if he was there for the press conference.

"No, I'm here to meet with the mayor."

"About what?"

Yianni smiled. "I don't mean to sound rude, sir, but my business doesn't concern you. The mayor's expecting me, so why don't you just tell him Detective Kouros is here to see him?"

"Oh, so you *are* here for the press conference. The mayor left instructions for you to go directly inside." He pointed toward an atrium at the center of the building, where a lone olive tree grew beneath a pyramid-shaped skylight. A second-floor balcony, trimmed with scenes from classical Naxos, encircled the atrium floor.

At one end of the atrium, reporters milled about a podium, waiting for a press conference to begin. Yianni shouldn't have been surprised. It wasn't often that a mayor from a traditionally non-newsworthy island had the opportunity to draw national coverage. Announcing the now-famous reporter's disappearance would make headline news for sure.

Yianni recognized some of the reporters from Athens and stood back from them, not wishing to draw their attention.

"Detective Kouros, how nice of you to show up."

Yianni swung around to see a short, well-tanned man with a bouncing belly, badly dyed brown hair, and a well-rehearsed smile.

"I'm sorry, sir. I don't believe we've met."

"I'm the mayor." He extended his right hand. "The reception-ist told me you're here, and I came right down." He pointed to a staircase behind him. "After all, we don't want to keep the press waiting."

"Excuse me, sir, but I'm not here for a news conference. I'm here to ask you about your meeting with Nikoletta Elia."

"All in good time." He patted Yianni on the shoulder. "But first we must alert the press and my fellow Naxians to what has befallen her and assure them that we, their public servants, are doing all that we can to find her."

"We are. But having a news conference to announce her dis-appearance and my unit's involvement could endanger her life."

"I don't see how you can say that. It will mobilize the com-munity to look for her."

"If there's actually been a kidnapping, and the kidnapper learns he's the subject of a nationwide manhunt, the attention might spook him into doing away with her. Your local police are already doing all the right things. I'm only here to provide them with additional manpower."

The mayor's perpetual smile turned sharklike. "That's bull-shit and you know it. The local cops are inept and couldn't find a souvlaki at a soccer match. You're here because the reporter's newspaper and your minister insisted that your unit step in and take over the investigation. I will not be party to a cover-up of this poor woman's kidnapping."

Yianni leaned into the mayor. "I don't know who put those ideas in your head, but I suggest you reconsider whatever you plan on saying to the press."

Any semblance of a smile disappeared. "Is that a threat?"

"No, just some professional advice from one public servant to another."

"I was hoping you'd participate in the press conference, but it's far from necessary. You're here, and that's all the backup I need for what I have to say on the subject."

"Feel free to say whatever you think serves the interests of your island, but there's something I should tell you."

"What's that, another threat?"

"No, another fact. My chief arrives tomorrow, because he's also concerned with the safety of Nikoletta. You've now been warned about the risks to her life presented by proceeding with your press conference. If Chief Inspector Kaldis thinks that what you say to the media in any way jeopardizes her life, he'll tear you apart in the press, not to mention what he'll do to you in the eyes of all your perceived political friends back in Athens."

"I'm not afraid of him."

"Well, you should be. Perhaps you forget that our unit's mandate extends to investigating suspected official corruption wherever we find it. Why you're so hell-bent on undermining your local police chief, no matter the risk it presents to the reporter's life, will undoubtedly pique my chief's interest." Yianni put his hand on the mayor's shoulder. "Are you up for risking your political career for a few passing headlines and the chance to take a cheap shot at your police chief?"

He let his hand fall from the mayor's shoulder. "I'll be waiting here when you're done. We still have to talk about your conversation with Nikoletta."

The mayor turned and walked briskly toward the journalists, but with a noticeable slump to his shoulders. Reporters began shouting questions at him, but he paid them no attention until he was behind the podium and cameras were rolling.

He stared straight at Yianni as he spoke. "I'm here to answer any and all of your questions, but first let me say why I've called you here. I want you and the nation to know how proud I am of our island's professional hardworking police force, which has spared no effort to identify the poor tourist who tragically perished here."

"Is that why you called this press conference?" yelled a reporter. "Just to say thank you to the police?"

He stared at the reporter. "I wouldn't think any of you'd have a problem with that. On Naxos we value our police and everything they do to keep all of us, tourists and locals alike, safe and secure. Don't you agree it's about time they got the recognition they deserve?"

Yianni smiled. *Nicely played, Mister Mayor.*

———

Yianni had to give the mayor credit. He'd handled the sharp questioning with patience, offering little in terms of substance, yet tossing out a teaser to keep them coming back. "We expect very soon to identify the tourist who perished in that tragic fall onto the rocks below Grotta."

That prompted a shouted round of additional questions.

"It's part of an ongoing investigation," the mayor deflected, "and we'll provide you with more details as soon as we've confirmed them and notified the next of kin."

When the press conference ended, the mayor hurried out of the atrium, made his way up three flights of marble steps to the second floor, and headed straight for a doorway centered on a glass-enclosed office suite marked MAYOR—with Yianni right behind him.

Inside, the mayor stopped momentarily to speak with a woman

sitting at a desk in front of a set of French doors and across from the open door to a corner office. He glanced back at Yianni and grunted, "Follow me."

The office was furnished in what Yianni considered *politician traditional*. An imposing, highly polished wooden desk, a luxurious high-back leather swivel chair, a pair of far simpler guest chairs, an oval conference table with matching chairs, and a comfortable sofa set off to one side of the room. The sofa undoubtedly was meant for those occasions when, by sitting next to his visitor, the mayor could convey that his guest was among his most valued and trusted confidants.

The office also displayed the obligatory photographs of celebrities and powerful officials who'd passed through the mayor's life. Angled on his desk for all to see stood a photo of his wife, children, one dog, and one cat.

Without waiting to be invited, Yianni sat in a chair directly across from the mayor.

"Okay, Detective, I did what you wanted. What else do you need to know so that I can get you out of my hair?"

"I'd appreciate your telling me everything you recall about your meetings with Nikoletta Elia."

"It was *one* meeting, and I found her to be a charming and intelligent woman interested in fairly portraying Naxos to her readers."

"You're done with the press conference, and though I sincerely admire the way you handled the press, don't waste your charms on me. I've read her notebooks, and we both know that at one point she told you to stop bullshitting her with 'Chamber of Commerce' answers."

The mayor rolled his eyes. "Well, if you already know what we said to each other, why are you wasting my time asking me to repeat myself?"

"I have a couple of reasons. One, to see what she may have left out of her notes, and two, to decide whether I can trust you're telling me everything. So let's get back to what she asked and what you answered."

They sparred back and forth for the next twenty minutes, but the answers the mayor grudgingly gave were consistent with what Nikoletta had recorded in her notebook.

"So, my final question—at least for now—is who else did you suggest she interview for her article?"

"Let's be frank, Detective. As I see it, Nikoletta was into this story for the glory. It's why she wrote the piece about a computer criminal. Next, she wanted to write an article about what she thought was a war brewing between our tourism industry and agricultural interests. Contractors versus conservationists. Yes, she asked me for the names of the biggest, most important players on all sides of what she saw as a potential controversy. I wasn't about to give her the names of firebrands who'd stoke her into doing a hatchet job on the island, so I gave her the names of people who I knew would only say good things about the island. If she wanted revolutionaries and naysayers, she could find them on her own."

"Did she find them?"

"I don't know. My job is to protect the island, and that means its reputation. Encouraging bad press falls outside my job description."

"Okay, let's try a different approach. Who are the island's firebrands, revolutionaries, and naysayers?"

The mayor's face turned crimson. "All they'll try to do is wind you up with crazy conspiracies and theories. How's that going to help find the missing woman?"

"I won't know until I speak to them. But let me put your mind at ease. She never believed what you told her. Here's what she had to say."

Yianni read from his notes. "'The mayor must think I'm an idiot. He gave me a list of political cronies who'll give me only politically correct answers. He must be hiding something. I'll have to get leads elsewhere.'"

Yianni looked up. "Sounds like your recommendations didn't cut it with her. So…names, please. It'll speed up the investigation, and perhaps even save her life."

The mayor spit out a list of names, accompanied by various creative epithets.

As it turned out, every name mentioned by the mayor had found its way into Nikoletta's notebooks, which also contained a few that weren't on his list. She'd obviously been thorough in her research. Perhaps too thorough for islanders like the mayor, who don't like the threat of bad press.

Yianni thanked the mayor for his time and cooperation, but the mayor said nothing in reply, only pointed Yianni toward the door, not rising to shake his hand or show him out.

I guess that means I did my job.

———

After calling Andreas to brief him on how he'd indelibly ingratiated himself to the island's mayor and texting Dimitri the description of the man he'd been told was watching Nikoletta and the hacker the night they met, Yianni moved on to the next name on Nikoletta's list, Marco Sanudos, head of the Naxos Hoteliers' Association. They'd arranged to meet at Marco's hotel. A map showed it to be approximately five kilometers from Naxos town hall, close by a popular beach. Since it didn't seem that far, Yianni decided to use the motorbike rather than accept Dimitri's offer of a car and driver.

It was a sunny, warm morning, with very little wind, a perfect day for a bike ride along the miles of open beach that Naxos took such pride in offering to the world. Less than a kilometer into his planned route, Yianni realized the maps were not as precise in describing the state of the roads as he'd hoped, so much so that he should have taken Dimitri up on his offer of a driver.

The paved road running from the town hall south along the sea soon turned away from the beach and into a maze of back streets that had Yianni turning first one way and then another in an effort to keep moving parallel to the sea. When he came upon a broadly paved road running next to the beach, he thought he'd found his way, but it soon turned into a dirt road before joining up with a main road that took him away from the sea in the direction of the airport.

At a sign for Agios Prokopios Beach, he decided to put his faith in the saint whose namesake beach he was looking for and took a right, heading west. It took him past the salt pond he'd seen when his plane landed and along a narrow paved road winding between borders of bamboo windbreaks and ancient stone walls. He drove alongside fields and pastures of varying shades of greens and browns, some no doubt growing seed potatoes for Naxos's most famous crop. It was not the by-the-seashore sort of ride he was looking for, but still scenic. Missing, though, were road signs with even a hint at how to find Marco's hotel.

After a slew of wrong turns and dead ends, Yianni pulled over, took out his phone, and in an act some might see as a repudiation of divine guidance, switched his faith to GPS.

By the time he spotted the first sign for the hotel, he was already there. It sat atop a slight rise overlooking the beach. The resort complex, equipped with two huge swimming pools, a spa, shops, bar and dining facilities, tennis courts, and a private beach, had virtually everything required to keep the clientele happily on property, free to spend their time and money there and nowhere else.

He parked the bike by a freshly painted white building trimmed in cerulean blue and dominated by a soaring all-glass entranceway framed in white marble. Yianni followed a sign marked RECEPTION pointing toward the building. A short, fit man a few years older than Yianni waited for him inside the door.

"Detective Kouros, I presume. I'm Marco Sanudos."

"How did you know it was me?"

They shook hands and the man smiled. "Very few of our guests arrive on motorbikes, and even fewer without luggage. Frankly, I was a bit concerned when you didn't show up at our appointed time, especially after the mayor called to tell me you'd been to see him and left."

"How nice of him to call."

"I think he was more interested in warning me to be careful of what I say to you."

"Does he have a habit of doing that, or is it a special honor reserved just for me?"

"He means well," Marco smiled, "as long as you're not interfering with his priorities."

"What's that mean?"

"May I suggest we continue this conversation in my office?"

He told a young woman sitting behind the concierge desk to send water, coffee, and pastries and led Yianni into a room behind reception. The room's only masonry wall was a long one shared with reception, the rest glass, arranged in a perfect semicircle looking on to the pool area.

"Wow, how do you get any work done in here? I'd either be mesmerized by the view or worried who might be watching me."

"The view you get used to, and the glass is one-way." He pointed to a stylish chrome and leather chair in front of a teak and chrome desk. "Please, make yourself comfortable."

Yianni sat down as a waiter arrived with a coffee tray. After the waiter left, Marco said, "What I didn't want to get into out there in front of my staff was that I'm much closer to your friend Dimitri than I am to the mayor. Dimitri told me you'd scuttled the mayor's plans for sticking it to him, and that really pissed him off."

"How do you know about my friendship with Dimitri?"

"He called me not long after the mayor did. He said you were a friend who could be trusted and that you'd likely get lost on the way here." Marco looked at his watch. "He asked that I let him know if you hadn't made it by now."

"I'm flattered everyone's so worried about me."

Marco smiled. "We've lost a tourist and may have lost a reporter. I guess no one wants us to lose a cop, too."

"So you know about Nikoletta?"

"The mayor told me. He also said not to share her potential disappearance with anyone."

Yianni nodded. "I can understand your concern about losing more folks. From my limited experience in getting from town to here, I'd say Ariadne and her Labyrinth crowd must have played a big role in laying out Naxos's street plan."

Marco laughed. "You're not the first to suggest that. But better roads come at a price, and I don't mean just their construction costs. They change the nature and character of a place. Easier accessibility means greater numbers of visitors to an area, and that brings other changes."

Yianni stared at Marco. "Whose side are you on? I'd expect you to be all in for tourism?"

"I am all in for tourism, just not to the point that I want to see our island trampled to death. I was born and raised here. My grandfather started this hotel, my father expanded it, and now it's my turn to shepherd it forward. I'm committed to sensible planning, sensible preservation, sensible progress."

"Nicely put. Does the mayor know you're after his job?"

"Not interested. This is my passion, not politics."

"Did you have this kind of conversation with the reporter?"

"Yes. I sensed she didn't believe I was sincere."

So far he's consistent with what's in Nikoletta's notebook. "What made her think that?"

"She asked whether I had plans to expand the hotel, and I said yes. Why not? This is a hotel area. We wouldn't expand onto the beach but onto property adjacent to the beach. There are plenty of other virtually undeveloped beaches that can and should be preserved as they are."

"My guess is your fellow islanders who own property on those undeveloped beaches wouldn't agree with you."

"They don't, but that's not unique to Naxos; it's a national problem. We only want *others* to bear the burdens of preserving our country's natural resources."

"Perhaps I was wrong in suggesting you're running for mayor. Sounds more like prime minister to me."

He shrugged. "Right now I'm confining myself to simpler issues, such as limiting the number of cruise boats allowed to dock on any given day."

"How big a problem is that?"

"It chokes the old town for the few hours they're in port, but otherwise they have a limited effect on the island. The bigger issue is expanding the airport."

"Is there a plan to do that?"

"There's a lot of wishful thinking in some quarters, and anxiety in others, because extending the runway to accommodate big jets would significantly impact the island."

"What do you think will happen?"

"Frankly, I don't think Naxos will have much say in it, one way or the other."

"Why's that?"

"Because the airlines, cruise lines, and airport authorities don't want Naxos to have an international airport."

"Why not?"

"The most expensive per-mile air route in Europe is between Athens and Mykonos. Mykonos has expanded its airport and operates twenty-four hours a day, seven days a week. It's a transportation hub for this part of the Cyclades. Big jets land there, and tourists head to its ports, where boats transport them to other Cycladic islands. It's a simpler and more profitable arrangement for big-time transportation interests than having another international airport so close to Mykonos. Santorini serves the same role in its part of the Aegean."

"Did you tell that to the reporter?"

"It didn't come up, but she might have heard it from someone else. It's not a secret."

"What *did* you tell her?"

Marco gave a thoughtful recitation of everything he could recall of their conversation, which matched what Nikoletta had entered in her notebooks. She'd also describe him as "cute," but Yianni decided not to share that bit with him.

"So, what do you think happened to her?" asked Yianni after Marco had finished describing his conversation with Nikoletta.

"I have no idea. Yes, there are strong passions on this island over its future direction, but enough to kidnap a reporter over a story about any of that?" He shook his head. "I don't see it."

"But what if she uncovered something someone didn't want exposed?"

"You mean corruption?"

"That's one possibility."

"I think it's safe to say that everyone on this island already knows who's corrupt, and a reporter threatening to expose what's already known wouldn't likely lead the bad guys to harm her. That would be a surefire way of generating far more serious trouble for them than anything she planned on exposing."

"So what's *not* known that could have endangered her?"

Marco again shook his head. "I don't know. There are crazies everywhere in this world, doing the unimaginable in the most unlikely locales. Who knows what could have happened here, who she met, what she said or did, even innocently, that triggered a response otherwise incomprehensible to rational, sane people?"

"That's not the answer I was hoping for."

"I truly wish I had a different one."

"Do you know anyone who might?"

"Sure, speak to the activist folks."

"Where would I find them?"

"Some of the island's most vigorous activists call Halki home, or at least consider it friendly territory. Besides, it's a cool village to visit."

"I can see why you represent so many disparate interests. You only have nice things to say about everyone."

He gestured no. "No, not everyone. But my disputes with them are unrelated to any of this, and even with my worst enemy, neither of us would go so far as to physically harm the other. It's just not our way." He smiled. "At least not when sober."

"On that note, thank you, I'll be on my way."

"Not yet, please. Dimitri sent a pickup truck to take you and your motorbike to your next appointment."

"Did he say why?"

Marco smiled again. "No, but my guess is that after your experience getting here, he doesn't think it's a good idea for you to be wandering about the island alone looking for whatever village it is you want to see."

"It's marked on a map. How difficult could it be to find?"

"What's the village's name?"

"Siphones."

Marco lost his smile. "Oh."

"What's that mean?"

"That village has been abandoned since the 1950s."

"It can't be the only abandoned village on the island."

"It's not."

"So, then what's with the *oh*?"

Marco hesitated. "Locals claim it's haunted."

"Oh."

Chapter Six

Yianni stood alone outside the hotel entrance, speaking on his mobile with Andreas.

"So, how did your Naxos friendship tour work out with the head of the hotelier association? Better than with the mayor, I hope."

"A lot better." Yianni described his conversation with Marco in detail, leaving out only the parts about his trouble finding the hotel.

"What did you think of him?"

"Came across as a nice guy. He sounds like a politician, always trying to find middle ground."

"Always *seemingly* trying to find middle ground, but as you pointed out, his middle ground allows his hotel business to expand while cutting out potential competition from other beaches."

"But it does make sense, Chief. It might just be a matter of working out satisfactory compensation for those restricted from building on their property."

"I don't even want to contemplate what that process would be like, how long it would take, or the sorts of shenanigans it would bring into play. If Marco thinks getting an international airport on Naxos would be politically difficult to achieve in the face of opposition from other Cycladic islands, imagine what his *middle ground* proposal would involve. I assure you getting individual islanders to give up their property rights so that their neighbors can profit from land they're allowed to use will require nothing short of a political miracle."

"Okay, I get your point. But nothing Nikoletta could've written struck Marco as a reason for a local to kill her."

"So he says. He prefers the *random crazy attacker* scenario or, if not that, perhaps a cabal of vigorous village *activists*."

"What do you think he's hiding?"

"I've no idea if he's hiding anything. But I do think he's trying to take the heat off like-minded Naxians by suggesting we concentrate on crazies and activists. To me the bottom line is simple. He may not like the mayor, and certainly the two men have very different styles, but they share a core principle: Above all else, protect the reputation of the island."

"In other words, I should continue doing what I'm doing. Question everyone, believe no one, and be ready for your arrival tomorrow."

"I'll let you know what flight. By the way, what are you driving?"

"Funny you should ask. I think I see my new ride headed this way."

"Come again?"

"I've been using a motorbike, but it's not good for the terrain I have to cover next, so Dimitri is sending me new wheels and a driver who knows the island."

"What kind of wheels?"

"Give me a minute; it's almost here." Yianni paused. "My oh my, you're not going to believe this."

"I'm all ears."

"Then I guess I should start humming the tune to that Eagles song about a girl in a flatbed Ford, because that's precisely what's headed my way."

Andreas groaned. "Call me later."

———

Officer Popi Sferes was twenty-three, two years out of the police academy and freshly married to a local. She wore her dark-brown hair in a tight bun, no makeup, a light-blue police blouse, dark police trousers, and black leather high heels. Yianni never understood why so many female cops wore heels, but in this case he did. Without them, Popi would've been barely tall enough to meet the police force's minimum height requirement.

She introduced herself as his driver and official guide to the island. "My chief thought that since my husband is local, my presence might help convince other locals to talk with you."

"Sounds reasonable."

"Reason doesn't necessarily work here."

"Meaning?"

"Let's get the bike into the bed of the pickup, and I'll explain later."

Yianni nodded and rolled the bike to the truck as Popi dropped the tailgate. Yianni braced himself to bear the brunt of the weight on the lift, and together they counted, "One, two, three, *lift.*"

Yianni nearly lost his balance and dropped his side of the bike while Popi lifted her half with the strength of a man twice her size.

She smiled. "Surprised you, didn't I?" She reached for a set of tie-downs in the bed of the pickup, tossed one to Yianni, and together they lashed the bike in place.

"Sure did. Could you let me in on whatever brand of vitamins you use?"

"No vitamins, just the hard life of a farmer's daughter in the rock-infested Peloponnese, plus years of weightlifting competitions to make up for what has me wearing high heels whenever I'm asked to meet a visiting dignitary."

"I'm hardly a dignitary."

"Maybe not, but you didn't try mansplaining me into why I shouldn't be lifting the bike, so I'd say you qualify as a pretty good guy."

"My girlfriend gets the credit for training me well."

"Good for her." Popi walked toward the driver's door. "Are you ready?"

"Sure." Yianni opened the passenger's door and noticed a pair of women's flat shoes on his seat. He held them up. "What do I do with these?"

She slid onto the driver seat, kicking off her heels as she did. "I hate wearing heels." She took the flats from Yianni and put them on.

"So, what is it you promised to explain *later*?"

"It's a pitch I have for visitors to explain the nature of the people here. It saves them asking me a lot of questions." She turned on the engine and edged back out onto the road, headed in the general direction of the airport. "I can give you the Chamber of Commerce-approved version, or my cop-to-cop one."

"I think you know which one I want to hear."

"Just stop me if I bore you." Popi swallowed. "Naxos spent so many centuries occupied by foreign powers that some Naxians seem bred to be naturally suspicious of everyone and jealous of their neighbors. For example, the Venetian aristocracy that once lived within Chora's Kastro walls literally and figuratively looked down on whoever lived outside their privileged castle. That same sort of snobbery exists in many respects today among their descendants."

She reached for one of two bottles of water in a cup holder between the seats. "The other bottle's for you."

"Thanks."

"Then you have the farmers and herders who live outside of town. They're not only considered ignorant peasants by many who live in town, but they're also often consumed by rivalries with neighboring villages." She took a slug from the bottle. "On top of all that local bullshit, you've got the resentment Naxos as an island bears toward its neighbors, Paros and Syros, and vice versa."

"What gripes does Naxos have with them?"

"Basic islander jealousy pretty well covers it. But with Syros it runs a bit deeper. In antiquity, Naxos was rich and important far beyond any of its Cycladic neighbors, other than the holy island of Delos. But all that changed once Naxos was conquered. Centuries later, after Greek independence, Syros emerged for a time as the cultural and economic center of the Cyclades, and the airs adopted by Syriots riled Naxian pride to an extent they've never forgiven."

"You make them sound like rival football fans."

"Not a bad analogy," said Popi. "Which means I may not be of much help if whoever we're meeting with sees you as rooting for the other team."

"And the rival team for where we're headed would be…?"

"Greeks have a penchant for paranoid conspiracy theories. No telling how what you have in mind fits into their frame of reference."

Yianni shook his head. "So, what can you tell me about Siphones?"

"It's in a lovely location that's been abandoned for nearly seven decades for reasons no one seems clear about. Some suggest it was a lack of water, others say floods, a few claim villagers moved away after the emery mines closed and they lost their jobs or because it lacked a school for the children."

Yianni looked at her. "What do you think's the reason?"

"Hard to say, but other villages have persevered and continue to this day with far less in natural beauty and resources than Siphones. In fact, farmers still work the land there during the day but leave before dark rather than turning any of the abandoned homes into their own."

"Like I said, what do *you* think's the reason everyone moved on?"

"Honestly, I've no idea. There are rumors it was leprosy, but that seems somewhat dramatic…another quality we Greeks are known for." She paused. "Then again, there's the marble cross and plaque someone mysteriously erected at the village some twenty years ago. The plaque contains an engraved prayer dedicated to a saint revered for his magic and makes mention of healing the wounds from demons and their works of magic."

"And thus arises the haunted angle Marco mentioned."

"Some would even say cursed. At one point the plaque was smashed to pieces, and though it's been pieced back together on the ground, there's been no explanation for why someone went to the trouble of destroying something bearing a prayer asking for a saint to heal wounds."

Yianni shut his eyes and shook his head. "At the moment, I've got more than enough open mysteries on my plate. This new one I respectfully leave for you to solve."

"I just thought you might like to know the background of the people and place you're about to visit."

Yianni opened his eyes. "I know. I'm just complaining for the sake of complaining. Thank you for listening."

Popi smiled. "That's an admission I rarely hear from a man. Your girlfriend really did raise you right."

"It's been a challenge. For us both." He smiled at Popi. "But it's worth it."

She smiled back. "I know."

———

At a juncture with a main road just north of the airport, Popi turned left, then headed north.

"Are we heading back to town?" asked Yianni.

"Who's doing the driving?"

"Okay, I'll take that as a 'please shut up.'"

"No need to say please."

Yianni stared at her. "Why do I feel your husband and I have a lot in common?"

She turned right off the highway onto a narrow dirt road passing between broad swatches of farmland mixed in among fields of tall grass and newly baled hay. Tall bamboo, planted to protect the crops against strong Cycladic winds, lined both sides of the road, and of the handful of structures Yianni saw along the way, half looked to be businesses catering to tourists.

"Is this what most of Naxos is like?"

"Around here, yes. Away from here, no. We're on the edge of a fertile plain that spreads out south and east into major growing areas. Once we hit the highway, we'll be heading into the mountains and you'll get a bigger picture of where we are now."

"I think what you're trying to tell me is that down here, I can't see the forest for the trees."

"Yes, but more like you can't see the farmland for the bamboo. Naxos no longer has forests. Thanks to the practices of those who lived here before us."

Yianni stared out the window, wondering how this area might look a few years from now.

"Are you into goat herding?"

Yianni looked at Popi. "That's a strange question to come out of nowhere."

"You said you thought my husband and you had a lot in common."

Yianni paused for an instant. "Are you saying your husband's a shepherd?"

"That's for sheep. He's a goat herder and one of the best." Popi glanced at Yianni. "You seem surprised."

"I am. It's just so different from what we do."

"Not really. He spends much of his time like us, trying to keep critters in line who'd otherwise go astray at the first opportunity."

"Interesting perspective, but you must admit it's not the sort of career you hear much about these days."

"You do if you live in a rural community on Naxos. You may think being a cop is glamorous, but at least herding has profound biblical significance."

"We have more TV shows."

She smiled. "Good point."

Popi turned left onto a paved road, then right onto a two-lane highway lined with a hodgepodge of buildings and unkempt grounds typical of the sorts of businesses necessary for supporting a community.

She kept left each time the highway split. "Here's the road we want." She nodded toward a sign pointing left and marked KOUROS, KINIDAROS.

"Ah, at last, a chance to find myself," smiled Yianni.

"Huh?"

"That sign, it has my last name on it."

"Oh, I see, that was a joke. Next time warn me."

"I assume Kouros is where Naxos's famous six-meter long, unfinished marble statue of a young boy has lain on its back since the seventh century B.C.E."

"How'd you know that?"

"Trust me, if your last name also happens to be the term used to describe nude statues of young boys, you learn all about them, whether you want to or not."

Popi laughed. "Now *that's* funny."

"And I didn't even have to warn you." Yianni stretched. "So, how much longer until we get to Siphones?"

"We should make it in about a half hour, depending on traffic."

"What sort of traffic?"

"Slow buses, slow trucks, slow tourists, and of course, the ever-present possibility of goats on a road."

"You must know all the tricks for driving through a herd of goats."

"Yes, sit back, relax, and wait, because if you want to see a pastoral herder turn wildly insane, try driving through his herd and scattering his goats in every conceivable direction."

"Oh."

"Enjoy the ride."

They left the developed part of the island behind them, passed through rich bottomland plains, and began their climb up into the mountains. Each time the road narrowed down to run through a village, Yianni'd catch glimpses of the weathered faces of old men sitting on the front porch of their local *kafenio*. He wondered what thoughts passed through their minds as they sipped their coffees, watching so many vehicles stream by on their way to who knew where. Perhaps they thought of their children and grandchildren out working the farms and tending the flocks in the same age-old ways as they once had.

More likely how naive we city types are. Why would their kids, let alone their grandkids, be willing to put in the sort of fifteen-hour days of hard labor their lives once demanded?

As the pickup slowly passed close by a tiny, bougainvillea-draped stone house surrounded by daisies, poppies, and anemones, Yianni rolled down his window for a whiff of the scents. With that, he caught the rhythmic beat of cicadas nesting in a roadside patch of fig trees.

"Can it get any better than this?"

Popi smiled. "Just wait."

Once up in the mountains, the road turned to twists, switch-backs, and panoramic views of long, fertile valleys and stone-edged mountaintops. At times he'd see a slice of the distant deep-blue sea, or a mountain face shaved white for its marble. Down in the valleys, rows of olive trees swept up against fields of copper, emerald, and sage, while stone walls streaked with age held planted terraces snugly in place against sharply slanted hillsides.

In the bright early afternoon sunlight, every color showed true. Dots, dashes, spires, and blotches of green popped out against a richly earth-toned land deep into its seventh millennium of cultivation.

Roadsides boasted colorful flowers mixed with grasses, herbs, maquis, and gorse in among eucalyptus, fig, olive, oak, and other such hardy trees the ever-present rock and winds permitted.

Even the occasional concrete plant or marble quarry could not diminish the awe-inspiring majesty of the mountains' natural beauty or the timeless charm of old stone villages nestled against their slopes.

"This is truly beautiful," said Yianni, not taking his eyes off the view.

"I'm glad you like it," smiled Popi.

"It's hard not to. Do you live out this way?"

"I live south of here, by the Temple of Demeter."

"What's it like down there?"

"The temple sits on a hill with a view that every time I go by gives me more respect for the ancients' uncanny ability at picking the perfect sites for their holiest of places. Many consider it the most significant archaeological site on Naxos."

"Sounds like somewhere to take my girlfriend if she manages to get here this weekend."

"What's the lucky lady's name? My husband's is Mamas."

"Toni. She lives on Mykonos. Plays piano in a bar. Not exactly Mamas's biblical career, but it's a living."

"Speaking of intriguing, do you mind if I ask why we're going to Siphones?"

"I assume Dimitri told you about the missing reporter. She met some farmers in Siphones who were pretty outspoken about big money trying to ruin the island."

"They're not alone in that feeling. Especially among Naxians living outside of Chora."

"But aren't they used to that? After all, between the emery mines and marble quarries, this island's been getting sliced up for eons. And for much of the time, by foreigners."

"True, but what locals fear this time is a new type of foreign conquest. One fueled by big-money investors making changes in a few brief few years that outstrip the sum of all that the island has experienced in the past *six thousand* years."

"Sounds like the sort of fevered rhetoric that gets passions running high."

"You better believe it."

"Enough to kill someone?"

"I'm a cop; how could I ever rule that out?"

"What's your instinct, based upon living here?"

"There's a lot of tough, hard-thinking people on this island, and if they thought their way of life was under siege, I've no doubt they'd do what they felt they had to do to protect it."

"So much for the pastoral life."

She shook her head. "No, it's consistent. It is, after all, the responsibility of the herder to protect his flock from wolves."

Yianni stared at the side of Popi's face. "Are you suggesting it's reached the point where herders are going after the wolves?"

"No, I'm just answering your request for my instinctive opinion on what I believe could happen if those concerns aren't addressed."

Yianni looked straight ahead. *What the hell have I walked into?*

———

Just before the village of Moni, Popi turned left at a sign marked KERAMOTI-APOLLON. "We're ten minutes away from Siphones."

"I appreciated this brief chance at being a tourist. Thanks for driving."

"No problem. As often as I've been up here, I'm still blown away every time I see the mountains. I miss the ones back home in the Peloponnese."

She pulled off onto the side of the road just past a sign reading SIPHONES.

"Where's the village?"

"On the other side of the road. It steps down the hillside in terraces still farmed to grow crops like potatoes, cabbages, onions, tomatoes, and eggplants."

"How many old houses are here?"

"Hard to say, with so many in ruin, but I'd guess around thirty-five."

"That many?"

"This used to be a vibrant community, with lots of kids, lots of grapes, and lots of wine."

They walked across the road and stood at the edge of the hillside looking at the mountains to the south and west.

"They must get a hell of a sunset here."

"This view always makes me wonder why everyone left and, more significantly, why no one has returned."

Yianni nodded in the direction of a marble cross. "I assume that's where I'll find the plaque with the mysterious message."

"Yes."

He walked up the road to the cross and stared down at the remains of a broken plaque. Yianni knelt down to read the inscription. "It says precisely what you described." He took out his notebook and began to write.

"It's getting to you, isn't it?"

"That's the downside of being a detective. We can't resist a good mystery. But this time it's only curiosity, not professional interest." He stood up.

Popi pointed at a group of men gathered on one of the cultivated terraces. "Are those the ones you're here to see?"

"I won't know until I meet them. How do we get down there?"

"We walk under a bridge from the other side of the road. It's a bit overgrown, but that's the only way I know to get there." She started out across the road.

Yianni followed. "What's the snake situation on Naxos?"

"Ah, you're a city boy."

"As a matter of fact, my family is from your part of Greece, the Peloponnese."

"Then don't embarrass our roots by being afraid of snakes."

"I'm not afraid, just asking."

"Make a racket and watch where you step. They don't like you any more than you like them."

"I didn't say I didn't like them."

Popi managed to maneuver through a patch of tall thistle, and down nine stone steps to the edge of an overgrown four-meter stretch that ended at the mouth of a dark culvert running under the bridge. An algae sludge grew where a trickle of water seeped into the culvert from the hillside behind her.

Yianni stopped at the top and stared at the culvert. "You've got to be kidding."

"Don't worry; it's an old sluiceway for water running off the mountain. It's the water that still makes this place so attractive to farmers."

She picked up some stones and tossed a few into the weeds in front of her and the rest into the culvert. "That's to scare away whatever might be in there. But don't worry; I'll lead."

Yianni followed the path she'd made through the thistle and down the steps to where she'd stopped to throw her stones. "I take back what I said before about my having a lot in common with your husband."

"Why's that?" she asked from inside the culvert.

"Because the poor soul obviously has a lot more to contend with than I do."

As Popi continued though the culvert, Yianni heard, "Snakes, snakes, come meet the nice detective."

Chapter Seven

"Minister, I don't know who's pounding down your front door over this, but it's been only a little more than a day since we learned the reporter *might* be missing." Andreas switched the phone from his right hand to his left, picked up a pencil with his free hand, and began tapping the eraser end on his desktop.

"Detective Kouros is on Naxos conducting an investigation alongside the local police, and I'll be joining him tomorrow. If we do what you say you're being pushed to do and announce to the world that we believe she's been abducted, it will most certainly draw a lot of media attention, but as I've said before—and it deserves repeating—*that sort of attention could cause her abductor to panic and kill her.* Let's not forget there's been no ransom demand, so if there's been a kidnapping, her captor's motive is something other than ransom. If we can determine what that motive might be, it could be the lead we need to find her."

Andreas listened to the minister.

"Minister, I'm not questioning your motives or the sincerity of your concern for the reporter's safety. If I'm questioning anything, it's the agenda of whoever is pounding on you to do something that we both know is premature at best and fatal for the victim at worst."

He listened more.

"Of course there comes a time that alerting the media could be beneficial to a search, but we're not there yet."

And listened still more.

"By Sunday evening? That's virtually impossible."

Andreas and the minister argued back and forth on the date, but the most the minister would agree to was Monday at noon.

The minister hadn't revealed who was pressuring him to go public, but Andreas felt certain it was Nikoletta's publisher. What bothered Andreas was why her publisher was pushing so hard. Genuine concern for his reporter's fate? A sincere belief in the power of the media to help police generate leads? Or to sell newspapers and promote his paper's follow-up series on Nikoletta's reporting.

Whatever the reason, Andreas had until Monday to find Nikoletta. After that, the story of her disappearance would be all over the media, along with a slew of finger pointing at his unit for not finding her.

The sooner I get to Naxos the better. Andreas sighed—and snapped the pencil in half.

———

Yianni made it through the culvert, cursing all the way.

"That's certainly a novel way of clearing away critters," said Popi.

"It's the last time I'm doing something like that."

"Sorry to tell you, but that's the only way I know back to the truck."

"You can't be serious." He waved his hand in the direction of three men on a terrace below them. "Just get me over there."

They followed the sluiceway's flagstone bed beneath a canopy of fig trees and climbed up onto a path running by a group of tumbledown homes.

"What's that?" said Yianni, pointing at a dark pit.

"My guess is that's where they once stomped grapes to make wine. They still grow grapes here," she pointed at some vines, "but it doesn't look like there's much stomping going on anymore."

As they approached, the three men stopped their work, stood up tall, and watched the visitors approach. All three appeared lean and fit, dressed in similar jeans, work boots, and long-sleeved cotton shirts. Their difference lay in their choice of hats. One wore a broad-brimmed straw, another a Greek fisherman's hat, and the third an American-style ball cap bearing the symbol of an Asian tractor company.

Yianni waved as he stepped onto the terrace and approached the men. "*Yiasas.*"

The men did not return his wave or hello.

Yianni kept coming, smiling all the way. As he drew closer he noticed significant age differences in the men, accentuated by the varying years spent earning farmer tans on their faces, necks, and sinewy forearms.

He stopped in front of the man in the fisherman's hat, clearly the oldest of the three. "Good afternoon, sir. My name is Yianni Kouros. I'm a detective, and this is my colleague Officer—"

"We know Popi," said the man in the ball cap. "And don't waste your time talking to my father; he's not quite all there. Let him get back to his fieldwork before he gets upset and we have a hell of a time getting him home. He doesn't take well to changes in his routine."

Yianni looked at the one in the straw hat and nodded toward the old man. "Is he your grandfather?"

Straw hat looked at ball cap.

Ball cap nodded. "Answer the man, son."

"Yeah, we're all family."

The old man wandered away, and no one tried to stop him.

"He'll be okay," said ball cap. "He's like an old burro. Knows every inch of his land blindfolded."

"I don't mean to interrupt your work," said Yianni, "but if you could spare us a few minutes of your time, I'd appreciate it."

"The police chief said you wanted to know about that reporter who was nosing about here a few days ago."

"That's right."

"Why do you want to know about her?"

"She wrote a newspaper article about a man she met in Chora, and we're following up on that."

"You mean the computer guy?" said the son.

Yianni nodded. "We're looking for leads on who he might be."

That was the best cover story he could think of to hold off speculation over why cops were running all around the island asking questions about the reporter.

"Why don't you ask her?" said the son.

Yianni liked it better when the son was quiet. "Reporters like to protect their sources, so we have to go at it differently. I'm sure you aren't interested in protecting a criminal."

"What do you want to know?" said the father.

"What you talked about with her."

"How's that going help you find your man?" the son asked.

The kid was getting on Yianni's nerves.

Popi put her arm around the son. "Come, let's go find your grandfather and let your father and the detective talk."

He seemed reluctant to leave, but his father nodded, and he went with Popi.

"The reporter came here looking for dirt on how we felt about the growth of tourism on the island."

"What sort of dirt?"

"Who's corrupt, who are the big players behind development efforts, and what sorts of things they're doing to get their way. She also wanted to know about anyone I knew who was against development and what they were willing to do to stop it."

"What did you tell her?"

"The truth. There's corruption all across Greece. This place is better than most. Same thing with development. Places change; people move on. Just look around you." He waved his hand. "Grandfather was born here, but everyone's moved away. This place died, a new place somewhere else was born. It's part of the cycle of life."

Yianni stared at the man. "What's your name?"

"People call me Junior."

"Mine's Yianni. The thing is, Junior, I've heard you're not too happy with what's happening on your island. That foreign investors are coming to ruin Naxos, and you're all in for doing whatever it takes to see that doesn't happen."

Junior shrugged. "I don't know who'd have told you that, but I'm just a simple farmer. What do I know about foreign investors?"

"You live on an island where for millennia its people have lived under the domination and control of foreigners. Everywhere you look are reminders of that history. So, please don't bullshit me by saying you have no opinion on foreign investors threatening to occupy your island."

Junior glared and clenched his fists. "Are you calling me a liar?"

Yianni looked him straight in the eyes. "No, I'm calling you a bullshitter."

For an instant neither man moved or blinked.

Junior smiled. "Okay, that name I can accept."

Yianni returned the smile. "So, what did you tell her?"

"What I thought would impress her."

"I don't follow."

"Look, let's be realistic. I'm a bit old to be running around with those revolutionary types on the mainland tossing Molotov cocktails at what they see as symbols of their enemies. But I could tell she was looking for just that sort of angle for some story she was writing about farmers versus developers. So I made myself seem like a revolutionary."

"But why would you do that?"

"I may be too old to run around with revolutionaries but not too old to want to get into their pants."

Yianni felt certain his jaw had dropped. "Are you saying you slept with the reporter?"

Junior gestured no. "I tried my best routine—even tossed in a line about how the European Union with its memoranda has been occupying our country for a decade. But none of that worked. She took my story and took off. Didn't even accept my offer of sharing a bottle of homemade wine."

Nikoletta had left that bit about her afternoon out of her notebook. Perhaps because as a Greek woman she was used to that sort of approach from the men she met.

"But I heard that a group of you told her you'd burn down the foreigners' projects if necessary."

Junior smiled. "You heard right. More Molotov cocktail talk. The group you heard about was me, my son, and my father. I'll let you decide whether Grandpa could have agreed on anything. As for my son, he's bright for sure, but as you've seen, he goes along with what his father says."

Yianni burst out laughing. "What is it about Greek men that leads them to think they have a chance with every woman?"

"I don't know, but why do you think my son wandered off with Popi when he was having such a good time tormenting you?"

Yianni turned to look for Popi. She was nowhere to be seen.

"Don't worry. She's in no danger. Aside from her having a gun and a husband who could lift a bull, my son's a gentleman. It's just the thought of the possibility that makes men vulnerable to a woman's charms."

Yianni yelled out her name.

"Besides, Popi was raised on a farm among four brothers and learned how to handle men by watching them grow up making fools of themselves. Something we all seem to do from time to time."

Yianni saw Popi walking toward them with son and Grandpa in tow.

"See, I told you there was nothing to worry about."

Yianni hesitated. "Perhaps you could answer another question for me?"

"I'll try."

"Is there a way to get back up onto the road other than going through the culvert?"

"Yeah, head up the hillside below the monument and over the wire fencing. That will get you back on the road."

"Thanks."

"No problem. Just one thing."

"What's that?"

"Be careful of the snakes in the brush if you go that way."

———

Yianni grudgingly admitted to Popi that a few seconds' scoot through the culvert beat three minutes of not knowing what lay ahead of you in the underbrush.

Safely back in the pickup, he checked his phone for messages and saw one from Andreas telling him they only had until Monday noon before the whole world knew Nikoletta was missing. He called back, and when put into voicemail, left a brief message describing his interview with the Siphones boys.

"Everything okay?" Popi asked.

"Just routine stuff." He put his phone back in his pocket. "Before I forget, thanks for steering the son away from his father so I could speak to him alone. You did well, Officer."

"Thank you. I know the son. In fact, I know the whole family. The father sometimes hunts with my husband."

"That explains how he knew so much about your background."

"Hunting gives hunters a lot of time to talk among themselves. Sometimes too much time."

"He only told me good things, such as how your growing up among four brothers taught you to deal with Greek men."

"I wouldn't say that I'm fully up to speed on the intricacies of what makes them tick, but being the only sister had its advantages, even if I didn't appreciate them at the time."

"Meaning?"

"I was the baby of the family, so my brothers called me *Runt*, as in runt of the litter."

"Ouch. That must have hurt."

"But woe be unto anyone else who dared call me that or messed with me. My brothers were very protective. Too protective at times. They still tease me. Now, though, their favorite line is that I married Mamas because he's the only guy I ever dated big and strong enough to handle them."

"The father mentioned something about your husband being able to lift a bull."

"More like a calf, a big calf." Popi paused. "Do you mind if I ask the context in which that subject came up?"

Yianni wondered how much he should tell her, but if she hadn't drawn the son away he'd likely never have learned a thing from the father. "No, I don't mind. Just keep it among ourselves. This isn't gossip to share with anyone, including our cop colleagues over coffee."

"Understood."

"He claimed that everything he told the reporter was made up to impress her. That none of it was true."

"Did he say why he made it all up?"

"To use his words, he wanted to get into Nikoletta's pants by convincing her he was a Molotov cocktail–tossing activist."

She nodded. "That makes sense. It's priority number one for men in their dealings with women. At least most men, and not just Greek men."

"I'm not sure I'd go that far, but then again, I'm not in your shoes." He smiled. "Either heels or flats."

Popi laughed. "A deft change of subject."

"In this case, though, I believe the father," said Yianni.

Popi nodded. "From what I know of him and his family, I'd agree they're not the Molotov cocktail–tossing sort." She started the engine. "So, where do you want to go now?"

"I'm famished. Haven't eaten since breakfast, aside from a couple of cookies at Marco's hotel."

"There's a terrific taverna up the road in Koronos, and the drive there offers some of the most spectacular views on the island. Every time I'm up this way I eat there. It's a winding mountain road with plunging views into emerald valleys running out to the sea. Are you up for that?"

"How could I not be?"

She edged back onto the road around an old pickup that had parked off to the side of the road just beyond them.

"I've got a whole list of people to chase down, but not an address or telephone number for one of them. All I have are their names and their villages. Nikoletta apparently found them by going to the villages, striking up conversations with locals, and getting them to tell her where she could find their village's main *activist*." Yianni turned to look out the side window. "She must have a real gift for getting people to talk. I find most villagers to be closemouthed when it comes to speaking to strangers."

"That's because you're a cop, and activists are wary of cops. In my experience, once you get them talking, the hard part is getting them to stop."

"But how do I find them?"

"I should be able to help you with that. This is a fiercely independent island, with tough people, but it's still a small community and if you're known and trusted, you can get that sort of information."

"Here are the names." Yianni pulled out his notepad and read off a half dozen names and villages.

"Oh, boy."

"Dare I ask what that means?"

"Remember what I said before about getting activists to stop talking? Well, you've got the equivalent there of a Eurovision competition among the biggest talkers on the island. I suggest you plan on spending the better part of a day with each one on your list. That is if you want a shot at getting any of your questions answered. They'll spend most of the time preaching to you about why they're right, the rest of the world is wrong, and you should join them in their cause."

Yianni thought of the new deadline Andreas had delivered. "I don't have that kind of time."

"I wish I could tell you something different, but they'll bend your ear for sure."

Yianni leaned his head back, shut his eyes, breathed in deeply, exhaled, and opened his eyes. "What's the chance of our getting all of them together in one place to meet with me as a group?"

"You mean turn it into an activist convention? They'll be

competing like cats for attention to show who's the most important."

Yianni smiled. "That's the point. They'll each have heard the other's pitch so many times they'll be shouting one another down to stop with the canned speeches. We might actually be lucky enough to get them competing with each other over who's giving better answers to my questions."

"Optimism is an admirable trait, Detective." Popi bit her lower lip. "I must admit, it's an interesting idea, and if we promise them food, wine, and liquor, it just might work. We can bill it as Athens reaching out to Naxos's leading thinkers in an effort to learn what's truly on the people's minds."

"That's laying it on a bit thick, wouldn't you say?"

"We're talking about self-styled politicians, and regardless of where they fit on the political spectrum, they all share one common trait: they love an audience."

Yianni smiled. "Are we back to your view on men?"

"In this case it's a gender-neutral phenomenon."

Yianni sat quietly for a moment. "Do you really think you can pull it off?"

"I can try. Once they learn who else is being invited, they'll all likely want to be in on it, if only not to lose out to a rival if something good comes out of the meeting. I suggest we hold our little get-together in a place activists consider friendly territory."

"Okay, go for it. Try to set it up for tomorrow afternoon. He'll be here by then, and I'm sure he wouldn't want to miss it."

"Is he a masochist?"

"No, more of a cat wrangler."

———

Andreas was doing his best to clear his desk of a mess of burning bureaucratic emergencies, but his usual approach—handing them off to Maggie—wasn't available. She had her own fires to put out, so he decided to take a different tack: Ignore everything, leave the office early, and spend the rest of the day with his children.

Andreas made it as far as his car before his mobile rang. It was a Naxos caller, but he didn't recognize the number.

"Hello, Kaldis here."

"Chief Inspector?"

"Yes, who's calling."

"It's Dimitri from Naxos."

"Oh, sorry, Chief. I didn't recognize your voice. You sound so serious."

"There's been an accident."

Andreas's heart skipped two beats. "Involving Yianni?"

"Yes."

Andreas swallowed. "How is he?"

"Banged up but hanging tough."

"How banged up?"

"As far as his doctors can determine, it's two broken ribs, but otherwise only sprains, bruises, and cuts. He was knocked around quite badly but doesn't appear to have sustained a concussion or internal organ damage. Still, they're keeping him heavily medicated and want him to rest undisturbed for now. Which means no questions from us."

"Thank God he's okay. Where is he?"

"In our Naxos General Hospital. That's where the ambulance brought them."

"Them?"

"My officer was driving. She wasn't as lucky as Yianni."

Andreas's heart dropped. "How is she?"

"Don't know yet. She was in a coma when they airlifted her to Athens. I'm waiting for word."

"What happened?"

"Their pickup went off the road just outside of Koronos, a mountain village up north. No idea yet if it was mechanical failure, or she swerved to avoid hitting an animal on the road, or something else."

"Something else like what?"

"At this point we're ruling out nothing."

Andreas drew in and let out a deep breath. "I'll be there tomorrow morning. When do you think you'll have a better fix on what happened?"

"We sent a mechanic and accident investigation team to the site. As soon as I hear anything from them, I'll let you know."

"What do you know so far?"

"The pickup went off a narrow two-lane mountain road at a sharp curve to the driver's left, over a cliff edge to the right, rolling before getting hung up on a massive boulder. It was a miracle they hit the boulder, because if they hadn't, the pickup would have rolled all the way down into the valley and they'd have had no chance of surviving."

Andreas crossed himself.

"Who found them?"

"A tour guide driving tourists back from Koronos saw the pickup on its back up against the boulder and called it in."

"Did the guide see what happened?"

"No."

"Bad luck."

"As a matter of fact, very good luck. It turned out that one of the tour guide's clients was a doctor, and she was able to stabilize them until the ambulance arrived."

Andreas crossed himself again.

"What are your instincts on the cause?"

"Let's just say Popi was familiar with the road and used to goats darting out from nowhere. She knew you don't swerve if you can't brake in time, especially in the mountains. Better a dead animal than you."

"So, we're left with something mechanical or your *something else*."

"That's how I see it."

. Andreas fluttered his lips. "Please keep me in the loop on how they're doing, and let me know when I can speak with Yianni."

"Will do."

"Thanks."

They said goodbye, and Andreas put down the phone. He shut his eyes and said a brief prayer. He opened his eyes and wondered whether this was just a tragic coincidence or *something else*.

He knew what he had to do next. He just wasn't sure how best to go about it. He hoped the words would come. He looked at his phone, found the number he wanted, and called Toni.

Chapter Eight

Toni had heard so many good things about Naxos that she couldn't wait for tomorrow to come to join Yianni there. But that was before she spoke to Andreas. By the time they'd hung up, everything he'd told her was a blur, and she could only recall him saying there'd been an accident, Yianni was fine, but the doctors wouldn't allow him any visitors or callers.

To Toni, that did not sound like *fine*.

Her immediate reaction was to call the hospital and ask to speak to Yianni, but all that would do is kick her anxiety level into even higher gear once the hospital inevitably told her what Andreas had said. *No callers.*

She knew what she had to do next. She called her boss and told him she couldn't work tonight because her boyfriend had been in a serious accident on Naxos, and she had to get over there right away. Her boss said that if she didn't come to work tonight, she was fired.

She said that since the bar would be closed for the weekend anyway, what was the big deal?

He said it was nonnegotiable.

She said, fine, if he wanted to play a hard-ass, she'd tell his wife about his girlfriend. He said he didn't care.

Then she told him she'd tell his *girlfriend* about his *boyfriend*.

He paused for a moment before wishing her safe travels and asking that she please make it back to the bar as soon as Yianni was better.

Now she sat in the new port of Mykonos, waiting for the next boat to Naxos. The trip would take less than an hour, but she had absolutely no idea what she'd do once she got there. All she knew for certain was that she had to get to Naxos. Somehow she'd figure out what to do next.

After all, improvisation is how I make my living.

————

Lila hadn't been off the phone since Andreas called to tell her of the accident. She insisted on coming with him to Naxos, if only to comfort her friend Toni.

Her first call was to her mother, who agreed to watch the children and suggested Lila immediately call a close family friend to see if she could stay at her summerhouse on Naxos. The friend told her she was away, but Lila should use the home as if it were her own for as long as she needed.

That led Lila to call Maggie. Lila knew Maggie and her boyfriend, Tassos, would be headed to Naxos to be at Yianni's bedside. Tassos was Andreas's and Yianni's longtime police mentor and chief homicide investigator for the Cyclades. Lila invited Maggie and Tassos to stay with her and Andreas at her friend's house and said she'd pick Maggie up tomorrow in time to catch the first plane to Naxos. Maggie confirmed that Tassos would join them there by boat from Syros, and Lila said to tell him they'd meet him at the port.

With arrangements made, her next call was to Toni.

No answer.

She kept trying.

———

By the time the ferry docked in Naxos, Toni had a plan. The worst it could do was get her arrested, but since her boyfriend was a cop, she figured he'd be able to make things right...once *he* was right.

Stop thinking like that, she thought, and whispered to herself, "He's fine, just like the doctors said."

She knew she had to calm down if she wanted to pull this off, so she decided to walk to the hospital rather than take a taxi. The hike would bring her around. She pulled on her small backpack, disembarked, and headed for town. Her immediate problem was that she had no idea where to find the hospital. She stopped at a car rental agency by the entrance to the pier and picked up a map.

The hospital was about a kilometer away, depending on the route she took. She picked one crossing the harbor front that turned left at the main road into the port. The road ran by storefronts filled with goods aimed at enticing passersby, but Toni noticed none of it in her haste to reach the hospital.

The neat, one-story, white stucco and blue-trimmed medical center sat on the left, just beyond a rotary. She headed straight for the door marked ACCIDENTS AND EMERGENCY and joined three others sitting along a wall in the reception area, while a half dozen more waited in line for the receptionist.

The receptionist paid her no mind, and Toni sat as if patiently waiting for someone to arrive. The opportunity Toni'd been hoping for came in the form of an animated and rapidly accelerating conversation between the receptionist and an elderly local woman complaining loudly over how long she'd been waiting to see a doctor.

Toni stood and matter-of-factly strolled past the two combatants as if looking for a toilet. In the midst of her battle with the woman, the receptionist barely glanced at Toni. With a quick peek back to be certain the receptionist's eyes were not on her, Toni went left and darted through a door reading PATIENTS AND HOSPITAL PERSONNEL ONLY. It led into the emergency treatment room, which, as with most public hospitals these days, was staffed by overworked, underpaid professionals possessing neither the time nor inclination to care about who passed through their unit.

She aimed for a door at the far end, walking as if she knew precisely where she was headed. Once through the door, she circled back toward the reception area but entered the corridor beyond where she could be seen by the receptionist. Toni had no idea where Yianni could be in the building, and though Greek hospitals might not be finicky about who walked through their halls, if she started opening doors to patient rooms, she'd likely be escorted out in short order.

She heard a door open around a corner ahead of her. A serious-looking man in a white coat turned the corner headed straight for her. She gave him her most innocent smile. He said nothing until he'd passed her.

"If you're looking for a patient, Miss, their rooms are down this corridor in the halls to the left and right."

She turned to thank him but he'd already disappeared into the treatment room.

Thanking Lady Luck instead, Toni hurried down the corridor toward the rooms. At the intersection of the corridor with the hallways, she paused to listen for voices.

She peeked around the corner to her left. A nurse sat on a chair with her back to Toni, facing a monitor and chatting on her mobile. The nurses' hallway and the hallway to Toni's right each had four doors, a pair on each wall.

Toni's only chance at getting to Yianni without being seen by the nurse was if he was in one of the rooms to Toni's right.

Lady Luck, I need you again.

She crept along the wall leading to those rooms, paused at the first door, and listened. She heard a young woman singing a Greek lullaby.

She moved on to the next door but heard nothing. She'd reached for the door handle for a quick peek when she heard people in the room directly across saying goodbye. She yanked at the handle and jumped inside, just as a couple walked out of the other room loudly repeating their goodbyes. No way Yianni would be in there.

If Yianni wasn't in this room, or in the fourth room in this hallway, Lady Luck had let her down. Toni turned and looked at an empty bed. She shut her eyes and willed herself to believe Yianni was behind that fourth door.

She drew in a deep breath and reached for the door handle. That's when she heard an alarm.

How could they have found me?

She heard voices shouting and people running down the hall in her direction.

Oh well, I almost made it.

She opened the door, prepared to tell the truth, in time to see the nurse from the monitor race into the fourth room followed by the helpful man in white.

Yianni must be in there.

She ran to the fourth room's doorway and saw the two frantically working on a man hooked up to wires and tubes. An old man.

This was her chance. She raced across the corridor to the other four rooms and opened the first door. No Yianni. She opened the second. No Yianni. She opened the third. Her heart jumped at the sight. IVs, tubes, and monitors all connected to a sleeping, bandaged Yianni. She closed the door behind her, crept around the bed to a chair up by his head, sat, and smiled. "I'm here," she whispered.

She mouthed a thank you to Lady Luck, then thought of the old man whose crisis had generated the distraction. She hadn't seriously prayed in years, and long ago had lost all interest in organized religion, but if ever there were a time for appealing to an everlasting being on behalf of Yianni and the old man, this was it.

Toni sat quietly, drifting between joyful memories and abject fears for the future. She was deep in thought when a nurse bolted into the room, each startling the other.

"What are you doing in here?" the nurse demanded.

"He's my boyfriend. I'm just sitting here, not touching him, not saying anything. Just being here for him."

The nurse raised her voice. "I don't care who you are. You're not allowed in here. I don't know how you got in here, but if you don't leave at once, I'll call the police."

Toni gestured with her hand for the nurse to lower her voice.

"Don't tell me what to do; just get out of here." She pointed toward the door. "And I mean *now*."

Toni smiled and spoke softly. "Let's look at the situation. I've been in here for a good hour. Perhaps you can explain to the police how you allowed a complete stranger to gain access to a critically injured one of their own and remain undetected long enough to have done only God knows what sort of harm to him." Toni shook her head. "Come to think of it, I guess the police aren't your main concern. After all, how are you going to explain to your superiors what happened? This just might rise to the sort of thing that justifies terminating your job. Is that the kind of risk you want to take in this horrible economy? And for what?"

"You don't—"

Toni held up her hand. "Let me finish, please. I'm trying to help you out here. Why get into a fight that you can only lose? After all, the worst that happens to me is my boyfriend's buddies escort me outside, thank me for caring so much for him, and tell me to come back to see him tomorrow."

Toni raised and dropped her shoulders. "So, what's it going to be? A confrontation you can only lose or an act of compassion allowing all of us to win?" She pointed to Yianni. "Especially him."

The nurse closed her eyes and stood perfectly still—as if counting to ten—then abruptly turned and walked out of the room.

"I don't think I won a friend in that exchange," she whispered in Yianni's direction. "But I don't care, as long as I won the battle."

Toni went back to sitting quietly by Yianni's bedside, watching him sleep, and taking care to do nothing to disturb him. She noticed that his hand closest to her had begun to twitch ever so slightly. She reached over so that his twitching hand touched the top of hers. She felt him weakly grip her hand and lightly squeeze.

She struggled to fight back tears.

This battle she lost.

———

Andreas heard his cellphone ring. "Honey, would you grab my phone please? It's on the kitchen counter. I'm in the middle of changing the baby's diaper."

He tickled Sofia's belly. "Promise you'll never tell any of your tough guy daddy's buddies what you just heard him say." He tickled her again. She giggled. "I'll take that as a yes." Andreas finished securing her diaper, kissed her belly, and snapped up the bottoms to her onesies jumpsuit. "They wouldn't believe you anyway."

I can hardly believe it myself. He smiled. *And I owe all of this to the nanny's night off.*

"It's someone from Naxos named Dimitri," said Lila.

"Coming." Andreas carried Sofia from the nursery across the

apartment to the kitchen. He handed Sofia off to Lila in exchange for his mobile.

"Hi, Dimitri. How are our cops?"

"No change, which I'm told is a good thing."

Andreas clenched his jaw. "Let's hope so."

"I have news from my guys at the accident scene. That boulder was a lucky break for them for more than one reason. If the pickup hadn't hung up on it, they wouldn't have had such an easy time determining the cause."

"Easy time?"

"Like a neon sign announcing, 'Look here,' is how they described it. The driver side of the truck was caved in from the front wheel to beyond the door. Something hit it and sent it on its way off the road."

"What kind of something?"

"Likely another truck, or at least something big enough to inflict that much damage without its driver also losing control on impact. The place where it happened and timing were ideal for knocking them off the road. It was in the middle of a sharp left-hand curve, meaning momentum already had the pickup moving toward the edge when the collision occurred."

Andreas rubbed at his eyes with the thumb and forefinger of his free hand. "How can they be sure the damage wasn't caused by the pickup rolling over before hitting the boulder?"

"Indentations along the side of the pickup indicated impact with a bumper, and though the paint color on the impacting vehicle was close to the color of the pickup, it wasn't quite the same."

Andreas dropped his free hand down to his side. "How could Popi have missed a truck swerving into her lane?"

"That's one of many questions I hope each of them will soon be able to answer."

Andreas paused. "So, what's your gut telling you on this one? Another coincidental accident?"

"I'd sure like to think so. Otherwise, someone's out there targeting cops just for asking questions about the reporter."

"Can you think of any other reason why Popi might be a target?"

"Nope."

Andreas nodded. "Same with Yianni. At least not a target for anyone who'd bother to go to the trouble of making it look like an accident."

"That sort of thinking is what has me worried."

"Me too, and why I'm on tomorrow's morning flight to Naxos."

"By then we hope to have an ID on the dead tourist whose description matches the one Yianni obtained of the guy in the bar watching the reporter and her interview. It's not easy identifying foreigners like him unless they're in an accessible database or have been reported missing."

"Let me know as soon as you hear anything."

They exchanged goodbyes.

"How's Yianni?" asked Lila, still holding Sofia.

"No change."

"What about Toni?"

Andreas shook his head. "I don't know. I sensed she was in shock after I told her what happened, and I haven't heard from her since. Have you spoken to her?"

"No. I keep trying her on her mobile, but there's no answer."

Andreas bit at his lip. "I sure hope she's okay."

"She's a tough cookie. Lord knows what she's up to."

"I'm sure we'll find out soon enough." He walked to the refrigerator, opened it, and took out a beer. "Want one?"

"Since when have you switched to beer?"

"I read it's healthier than wine."

"And more fattening."

"Are you suggesting I'm fat?"

"No, but ask me again after you're on this beer kick for a month or so."

"Mommy, Daddy, come see what I did," shouted Tassaki from the living room.

"Dare we imagine?" said Lila, leading the way.

Tassaki sat on an Oriental rug covering part of the room's white marble floor. Spread out on the marble in front of him was a completed jigsaw puzzle depicting the Acropolis.

"Wow," said Andreas. "You did all that by yourself?"

"Yes, and it looks just like the real one." Tassaki smiled as he pointed out the window at the apartment's unobstructed view of the Acropolis.

"We're so proud of you," said Lila.

Sofia gurgled.

"Sofia is too," smiled Andreas.

"Now run off and get ready for bed. Then daddy will come read you a story."

"Yay!" Tassaki jumped up and ran off to his room.

"How many pieces are in that puzzle?" asked Andreas.

"Two hundred fifty."

"I couldn't do it."

"I wouldn't have the patience."

"Maybe you should bring one of his puzzles to Naxos," smiled Andreas.

"What are you trying to tell me?"

"Just that I'm going to be very busy there."

"We've been married long enough for me to have already figured that out."

"Just saying."

She stared at him. "I certainly hope you don't think I plan on getting in your way. I'm going to see Yianni and be there for Toni. Maggie and I—and if she's up to it, Toni—are more than capable of hanging out together and taking care of ourselves."

Andreas cleared his throat. "To pick up on your point, we've been married long enough for me to know your capabilities. I just don't want you doing something that attracts the wrong kind of attention."

"And just what's that supposed to mean?" Lila's hands now rested in fists upon her hips.

"Like drifting over into my line of work."

"That's just your cop brain talking." She waved him toward Tassaki's bedroom. "Go read your son a story. You won't be seeing him for a few days."

"I wish it were only my cop brain."

"What makes you think it isn't?"

"A journalist is missing and two cops are in a hospital, the apparent common connection being questions asked that someone didn't want asked. I don't want your healthy curiosity turning unhealthy."

Lila sighed. "Go read your son a bedtime story." She paused. "You both could use one."

Chapter Nine

The morning flight out of Athens had Andreas, Lila, and Maggie in Naxos by eight. After picking up their rental car, they made it to the hospital by nine. Dimitri was waiting for them outside Yianni's room, unsmiling.

"What's wrong?" asked Andreas.

"Is Yianni all right?" said Lila.

He faced Lila, but his expression did not change. "I'm Dimitri."

"Excuse me, Chief, I should have introduced my wife," Andreas nodded at Lila, "and our police colleague, Maggie Sikestis."

"Better known as his administrative assistant," said Maggie, extending her hand.

Dimitri shook their hands. "It's a pleasure to meet you both. I just wish it were under better circumstances. Yianni is fine. It is my officer who's not. She's still in a coma, but an infection has set in, and they may have to remove her spleen."

"Oh, my God," said Lila.

Andreas's head sagged and he exhaled deeply. "I can't wait to catch the bastard who did this." He looked up at Dimitri. "Have you spoken to Yianni?"

"No, I was waiting for you to get here. But he's awake and talking."

"Talking to whom?"

"His girlfriend."

"Toni?" said Lila. "What's she doing here?"

"That's a story no one seems willing to tell, but she's here. Been with him since late yesterday afternoon and hasn't moved from his bedside."

Lila smiled. "That sounds like our Toni. Can we see him?"

Dimitri shrugged. "You'll have to ask Toni. It seems the hospital has ceded all decisions to her."

Andreas opened the door to Yianni's room and motioned for Lila, Maggie, and Dimitri to step in ahead of him.

Toni jumped up from her chair and hurried around the bed to embrace Lila, tears welling up in her eyes. "I'm so glad to see you."

Lila hugged her tightly. "I've been trying to reach you since I heard what happened."

"I know." Toni released her grip and stepped back from Lila. She took Andreas's hands and kissed him on both cheeks. "I turned off my phone. I didn't want to speak to anyone. I just wanted to focus on Yianni." She hugged Maggie.

"Any chance of me getting included in this party?"

Andreas looked down at Yianni. "Would you please not disturb us while we're commiserating over how worried you had us?"

"Yeah, at least let us get to the really tearful parts we rehearsed on the plane," said Maggie.

Lila walked to his bedside and touched Yianni's hand. "Your buddies over there are all macho now, but you should have seen them on the plane. Never saw them so worried."

"It was a tiny plane and a lot of wind," said Maggie.

Andreas moved in next to Lila. "Good to see you back to your lousy sense of humor self."

"Glad to be seen. When we went off that road, I never thought we'd be seen again, except at the funeral."

"You don't have to talk about any of that now," said Andreas. "How's Popi?"

Andreas glanced at Dimitri.

"She's fine," said Dimitri.

"Where is she?"

Dimitri paused. "Athens."

Yianni's face tightened. "Then she's not fine. Stop bullshitting me."

Andreas stared at him. "She's still in a coma, but stable."

Yianni shut his eyes. "That poor kid. I can't wait to get my hands on the bastard who did this."

Toni went back to her seat by Yianni's bedside and took his hand.

"There seems to be a consensus on that point," said Maggie.

Yianni's eyes remained closed. "We left Siphones and were driving to Koronos for lunch. Everything was going smoothly, until we went into that curve." He drew in and let out a deep breath, and opened his eyes. "This red Fiat came whipping round the curve on its side of the road—"

Dimitri cut in. "A red Fiat knocked you off the road?"

"No. Right behind it, almost up against the Fiat's bumper, was a white straight-job. I thought it was preparing to pass the Fiat once it got around the curve. Instead, as we were opposite the Fiat the truck swerved into our lane, and…" Yianni shut his eyes again and shook his head.

"What's a straight-job?" asked Lila.

"A truck about the size of a small bus," said Dimitri.

Yianni opened his eyes. "How bad off is Popi, really?"

Andreas answered. "They may have to remove her spleen."

Yianni winced. "How's her husband holding up?"

"He went with her on the airlift to Athens," said Dimitri. "That's all I know."

Yianni squeezed Toni's hand. "Good. I'm glad he's there."

Andreas bit at his lip. "Do you think it was an accident?"

Yianni stared at him. "Not a chance. The bastard was looking straight at us when he swerved into us."

"Can you describe the driver?"

"Dark eyes are all I remember."

"How do you think the attacker knew you'd be on that road to Koronos?"

Dimitri interrupted, "From Siphones, there are only two ways to go. Perhaps he just guessed right."

"Or he was virtually certain where we'd be headed," said Yianni.

"How would he know that?" asked Andreas.

"Popi told me that every time she's in the area she eats at a particular taverna in Koronos."

"That means your attacker knew Popi's routine," said Maggie.

"I know."

"Or, assuming a hit team, they were prepared to catch up with you from behind if you'd turned the other way," said Andreas.

"Why do you say team?" asked Dimitri.

"We've heard nothing from the Fiat driver, for one thing. Also, a big truck roaring along a curvy two-lane mountain road likely raises a caution flag in most drivers' minds, but seeing one hugging the bumper of another vehicle makes you more concerned for the other driver than yourself. It slows you down just enough to make you an easier target."

"In other words, we're dealing with an orchestrated hit," said Dimitri.

"Seems like it to me," said Andreas.

"Then we were damn lucky to have survived. According to what I read in Nikoletta's notebooks, that hacker doesn't miss a target."

"Which kind of makes you wonder," said Andreas.

"About what?" asked Toni.

"Our man's trademark has him making deaths look like accidents. What happened here checks that box, but he always works alone and doesn't take risks that might come back to haunt him. In this case, at least two people were likely involved, a truck driver and a car driver, and the paint on Popi's pickup and the straight-job don't quite match. Yes, it might have been overlooked by investigators if the pickup had rolled all the way down the mountain, but the clear paint differences would be just the sort of mistake our man takes pride in avoiding."

"So who else could it be?" said Maggie.

"Anyone." Andreas looked at Dimitri. "Any luck yet on identifying that dead tourist?"

Dimitri gestured no. "Like I said before, identifying tourists is difficult."

"Have you tried our Greek databases?"

"For a foreigner?"

"Maybe he wasn't a foreign tourist?"

Dimitri exhaled. "Will do."

Andreas turned to Yianni. "What were you planning on doing next?"

"Having a big meeting with all the activist leaders Nikoletta interviewed. Popi was going to set it up using her local connections."

"So much for that, I guess," said Dimitri, quickly adding, "at least for now."

"Not necessarily," said Andreas. "Tassos Stamatos's boat arrives in less than an hour. He has local connections everywhere and might just be able to set up that meeting."

"If anyone can, it's Tassos," said Maggie. "Everyone in the Cyclades seems to owe him favors."

"Or worries about what he has on them," said Yianni.

Andreas looked at Dimitri and nodded toward Yianni. "He's Yianni's hero."

"Can't help it; he's my Greek version of John Wayne."

"A shorter, stockier Rooster Cogburn version, no doubt," said Andreas with a smile.

"Easy there, that's my guy you're talking about," growled Maggie.

"Enough already," said Yianni. "Just set up the meeting for tomorrow so that I can make it."

"But you're all bandaged up," said Lila.

"It'll generate sympathy. And make me look like a tough guy."

"Not as tough as the guy who put you here," joked Andreas.

"You're staying right here until the doctors say you can leave," said Toni.

"Then I want to talk to the doctors."

"Fine," she said.

"Alone."

"Why?"

"You intimidate them."

"That's not a good reason."

"Okay then, because you intimidate me."

Toni patted Yianni's hand. "Get used to it."

———

Andreas and Maggie were waiting for Tassos when the massive Blue Star ferry docked at the port. Andreas had used his badge to park next to the Harbor Police post by the end of the pier, saving Tassos a three-hundred-meter walk lugging baggage.

Tassos hugged and kissed Maggie. "Great to see you, my love."

He looked at Andreas. "Good to see you, too, fella." They embraced and slapped each other on the back.

"You look terrific. Slimmer than I can ever remember."

"I owe it all to my prison warden here. Maggie keeps everything I'd like to eat under lock and key, leaving me to battle rabbits for food."

"That visual works for me. You out in your garden on all fours, hopping around after lettuce and carrots."

"Don't knock it 'til you've tried it." Tassos looked inside the three-row SUV. "Hey, where's Lila?"

Andreas picked up Tassos's bag and put it in the far back seat. "She's at the hospital keeping Yianni company while Toni takes a break to shower and catch a bit of a nap in Yianni's hotel room."

"How's the kid doing?"

"He's almost as tough as you." Andreas smiled. "I'm not worried about him. Come on, jump in the car, and we'll go see him."

Maggie opened the passenger side rear door and stepped inside. "Sit up front," she said to Tassos. "I'm sure you two have a lot to talk about."

"Don't we always," said Andreas.

He carefully maneuvered the SUV through the crowd of pedestrians headed toward the taxis, hotel buses, and car rental offices far ahead. "This place is packed."

"Always is when a boat lands. A real bottleneck for the whole town," said Tassos.

"I can't imagine what it must be like when one of those behemoth cruise ships lands," said Maggie.

"Naxians can. It's what motivated some of them to wage a humongous battle against the town's plan to expand the port by seventeen acres."

"When was that?" asked Andreas.

"Back in 2007. Town hall wanted to expand the port to accommodate five cruise ships. Thirty-three citizens filed a lawsuit against their plan and won it in 2008 when the Greek Supreme

Court found the study on which the expansion was based to be insufficient."

Andreas shook his head. "That sort of activism must have really pissed off town hall."

"That's an understatement. Participants in the Case of the 33, as it came to be called, and their supporters were vilified for opposing the plan. Threats of physical harm were reportedly made, CURSE THE 33 appeared emblazoned on signs at rallies and in graffiti, and boycotts were called against businesses tied to the thirty-three. The more overtly threatening tactics largely subsided once the media in Athens got word of what was happening and turned the situation into an embarrassment for the island. But even today, pockets of resentment remain and some still boycott the original thirty-three."

"What happened to the thirty-three?"

"Actually, there were more than thirty-three actively in opposition, but since the law required those acting as plaintiffs to be directly affected by the plan, some of its strongest opponents weren't officially named as part of the thirty-three. After their court victory, the group disbanded, though some members later ran for office, and their party is now the third-largest vote-getter on the island."

"So they gave up good works to became politicians," said Maggie.

"Not all of them, my love. Some of the thirty-three organized an environmental group that's very active on a lot of fronts."

"Such as?" said Andreas.

Tassos looked at Andreas. "Why do I get the impression you're interested in what I'm saying for more than its historical significance?"

"Just keep talking, Professor, and I'll tell you after you're done."

"He's never *done* talking. Here take this." Maggie held out a bottle of water.

"Ignoring those slights, I shall continue." Tassos paused to take the bottle and twist off the cap. "So, back to today's hot environmental issues on Naxos…" Tassos took a long sip of water and stuck out the thumb of his free hand. "Number one is windmills."

"Windmills?" said Andreas, "I'd think environmentalists would be all for them."

"They claim they're not as efficient as other methods and that those behind them are actually seeking to create an industrial park for purposes of selling energy off-island, not to conserve and protect the island."

"Interesting."

"The other hot button issues are much the same as those confronting most islands." He popped out a finger. "Private businesses using public spaces like beaches for their umbrella, kitesurfing, and taverna businesses. Three," another finger shot up, "protection of wildlife, like sea turtles. Fourth," another finger, "where do you place stops on tourist development? And that issue raises more additional and complicated issues than I have fingers to count on."

"And please do spare us your toes."

Tassos waved Andreas off. "Bottom line, there's a lot of activism here, and it's not just a right versus left political thing. Naxians are proud of their independent lifestyle, and many have genuine concerns over what constitutes sustainable development and what threatens to destroy the way of life they treasure. These are not new concerns. Back in the 1990s, there was talk of expanding the airport to accommodate bigger planes, and twenty-three communities came out publicly against it."

"God sent you to me today for a purpose," said Andreas.

"Glad you finally figured that out."

"Stop this blasphemy," said Maggie, crossing herself.

"I need you to reach out to your contacts here to arrange a meeting."

"What sort of meeting?"

"With the activists interviewed by Nikoletta Elia." Andreas brought Tassos up to speed on the case.

"Don't we need Yianni at the meeting?" said Tassos. "He's the only one who's read the reporter's notebooks."

Andreas nodded. "I know. But there's no choice. We only have until Monday before the minister goes public about the reporter's disappearance."

"That could get her killed," said Tassos.

"Tell me about it."

"I guess that means the three of us have some serious reading to do before tomorrow," said Maggie.

"We can divide it up among us," said Tassos.

"If you set up the meeting, we'll do whatever has to be done to make it work."

Tassos pulled out his mobile, found a name, and pressed it. "Now, please be quiet while I try to be charming."

Andreas glanced back at Maggie. "My, Maggie, it sounds as if you and I are in for a novel experience."

She rolled her eyes. "To quote you, oh wise one, 'Tell me about it.'"

———

By the time they reached the hospital, Toni was back in her chair next to Yianni.

"I thought you were taking a nap," said Andreas.

"Couldn't sleep. Too wired," said Toni.

"You should take one of the pills they're giving me. It will put you right out," said Yianni.

"Or take a ride with this guy, listening to him attempting to be charming." Andreas nodded at Tassos walking into the room behind Maggie.

"Tassos, you old devil, so good to see you," said Yianni, struggling to sit up in bed.

"Don't move," said Tassos.

"It's not me that's weak; the meds only make me feel that way. The nurse had me walking while you were out. With any luck, they'll release me tomorrow morning."

"Don't push it," said Andreas.

Yianni frowned. "But we've got to set up that meeting if we hope to have any chance of finding the reporter before Monday."

"It's all taken care of," said Tassos. "I spoke to an old friend from Junta days, and he said he'd do what he could to set up the meeting."

"'Do what he could' doesn't sound very promising."

"The guy I spoke to was one of the Junta's fiercest opponents. They threw him in prison, and I was the only guard who made sure he was properly taken care of, which included protecting him from some of my colleagues who thought they could use him as a punching bag. Since then he's always thought of me as a brother. But more importantly, he's from Naxos and a legend on the island among the sort of people the reporter met with. To them, getting a request from my friend is a royal command."

"I think 'royal command' might be the wrong analogy, considering their politics," said Lila.

"Trust me, he'll make it happen. In fact, he's reaching out as we speak. He'll set it up for someplace where they'll all be comfortable, around siesta time so as not to interfere with their distinctly varied lines of work."

"What sorts of work?" asked Andreas.

"He said we've got a shepherd, a chef-restaurateur, an artist, a bookseller, and a farmer."

Yianni nodded. "And, according to Nikoletta's notebooks, each is firmly committed to different strongly held opinions. It should be quite a get-together. I can't wait."

"Like hell you'll be involved. Your pulse rate is moving up on the monitor just talking about it." Toni pointed at blinking lights above the bed.

"That's because my medication is wearing off, and having you so close to me is giving me intriguing thoughts."

"Flattery will get you nowhere."

"How about laid?"

Toni shook her head. "Please excuse his language. It must be his medication talking."

"I think it's our cue to leave," said Lila.

"No, we've got work to do," said Yianni.

"Your only job is to rest and get better. We'll take care of the meeting," said Andreas.

"But, like I said, I'm the only one who's read Nikoletta's notebooks."

"We'll read them tonight. Toni brought them here from your hotel room."

"I still think I should be at the meeting."

"Only if the doctors say so. And that's an order. I also think it's time we leave you two lovebirds alone."

"Toni, go with them. I'll be fine."

"Not a chance. When you leave, I leave, not before."

Yianni squeezed Toni's hand and winked. "More motivation for me to get out of here ASAP." He looked at Andreas. "Where are you staying?"

"At the home of a friend of Lila's family, about fifteen minutes south of Chora toward a beach area known as Plaka."

"That commute time assumes you know where you're going. From my experience with Naxos roads, you're in for a longer adventure."

"Use GPS," Toni told Andreas.

"You're wasting your breath," said Lila. "He's a man."

Andreas spread his arms. "What did I do to deserve this unprovoked attack?"

"You're right," nodded Lila. "It's not your fault you were born a man."

"Make that a Greek man," added Maggie.

Tassos patted Yianni on the leg and waved for everyone to leave. "I think I'd better retreat before this skirmish accelerates into an all-out separate bedrooms battlefield."

"Like I said, a Greek man. If you want to get his attention, feed him or threaten not to fuck him."

"Maggie, such language," said Lila, feigning horror.

"It comes from too many years hanging out with cops."

Toni looked at Lila. "I'll call you later and let you know what the doctor says."

"There's really no need for all of you to leave," said Yianni.

"Of course there is. You've just been fed." Toni smiled. "Now it's time for that other thing."

"What other—" Yianni's face lit up. "Bye, everybody."

———

A few minutes after his visitors had left his room, Yianni turned to Toni. "Well?"

"Well what?"

"What you promised."

"You've got to be kidding. I was joking. Here you are, wired up to a monitor and IV twenty-four hours after going through a car wreck, and you want to have sex? In your hospital bed, no less, when a nurse could walk through the door at any moment." She shook her head. "You *are* nuts."

"No, just excited. After all, I survived a near-death experience, with no seriously broken bones or internal injuries."

"But you have two broken ribs."

"I've had those before. Besides, if I'm discharged tomorrow, I'll want to have sex as soon as we're alone at the house, but you still might be afraid for me."

"Damn right."

"That's the brilliance of doing it here, while I'm hooked up to these machines. We can tell if I'm overdoing it and should stop."

Toni stared at him. "You do realize what you just said is among the most creative lines I've ever heard from someone desperately trying to get into someone else's pants? And in all my years of working in bars, I've heard a lot of them."

He smiled. "So, did it work?"

She leaned in and kissed him on the cheek, then on the lips. "Not totally."

"What does that mean?"

She kissed him again and looked up at the monitor. "Your pulse is beating faster."

"I'd certainly hope so."

She pressed her lips against his, opened her mouth and felt him press his tongue hard against hers. She glanced up at the monitor and mumbled, "Faster."

He kissed her more deeply and felt her hand slide under his blanket, beneath his gown, and down to where he was growing hard. She squeezed and slowly slid her hand up and down as she squeezed.

Again, she looked up at the monitor. "Faster."

"Yes," he whispered, "faster."

She pulled back from kissing him. "Uh-uh."

"What—"

Toni dropped her head beneath the blanket and brought her mouth to where her hand had been.

Neither noticed or seemed to care when the alarm went off on the monitor, and by the time the nurse responded, it was as if nothing had happened.

"Everything okay in here?" she asked.

"Yes, fine," said Toni.

"Are you sure?" she said, looking at Yianni.

Yianni nodded, closing his eyes. "I'm sure."

The nurse nodded back. "Funny thing about these monitors. In all the years I've been watching them, there's a certain pattern they follow when I leave young couples alone in the room. Congratulations, you two rang the bell." She smiled, stared for a few seconds at a red-faced Toni, and walked out.

"Busted," said a still-blushing Toni.

"Me too," said Yianni, sighing contentedly. "Thoroughly and totally busted."

Chapter Ten

Directions to the home of Lila's friend had Andreas turning left out of the hospital parking lot and following signs to the village of Vivlos. From there he made a right at a "big church" onto a paved road running toward Plaka Beach and a house identified by a white gate that opened by punching 1821# into an adjacent keypad.

With only a few brief wrong turns, they'd made it to the gate in less than twenty-five minutes.

Beyond the gate and a wide stone parking area lay an all-white stucco house set high above patches of pasture and farmland running out to the beach. The home paid clear homage to the traditional Cycladic cubist style, but with a modern flair most noticeably reflected in its oversized windows and broad terrace facing west toward the sea.

A housekeeper stood waiting for them at the front door. She explained the layout of the house, pointed out their respective bedrooms, and emphasized that at her employer's instructions the refrigerator had been fully stocked in anticipation of their arrival.

After offering many "thank yous" and "not necessaries" to the housekeeper, they went to their rooms to unpack. Lila took the opportunity to call her mother and check in on the children. That led to Tassaki taking the phone from his grandmother and describing in great detail, first to his mother and then to his father, all of the wonderful things he'd been doing with his *yiayia* and *pappou*.

By the time Andreas and Lila came out of their room, Maggie and Tassos were sitting on the main terrace reading the reporter's notebooks.

"How's the reading going?" said Andreas.

"This is interesting stuff," said Maggie. "The reporter's good at what she does."

"Which notebook are you reading?"

"The one covering her interview with the hacker."

"Anything jump out at you?"

"So far, based on the level of detail, only that he's likely telling the truth. Hard to imagine how he'd know all this if he hadn't planned the hits."

"So, if *you'd* paid him to do a hit, I assume you wouldn't be happy with all the publicity he's drawn?"

"For sure."

Andreas looked at Tassos. "Which one did you pick?"

"I passed on reading her interviews with politicians and hotel guys. I'm sure it's all politically correct bullshit. I took notebook number three, which includes her interview with the farmers Yianni and Popi met with before getting run off the road. Nothing exciting yet, but I just started reading."

Andreas looked at the remaining three notebooks. "Eenie, meenie, miney—"

"Here you are, folks," said Lila, carrying a tray of snacks out to the terrace.

The housekeeper followed with glasses and two large bottles of water.

"What do we have here?" asked Tassos.

"Only good things. Crudité, fruit, low-fat Naxos *anthotiro* cheese, and pita bread."

"Same food, different island," said Tassos, grabbing a carrot stick.

"Shut up and read," said Andreas, picking a notebook. "I'll take number five, her final day before disappearing."

Andreas handed another notebook to Lila. "Since you're here, come join in on the group read. Here's notebook number four, covering her time with the activists."

Lila took the notebook and a glass of water, found a comfortable chair, and sat down. "The housekeeper is preparing lunch, so happy reading."

Once settled in, each read silently, moving about only to get something to eat or drink from the table between them.

A half hour into their reading Tassos blurted, "Oh, my God."

"What is it?" said Andreas.

"I can't believe this guy is still alive."

"What guy?"

"The grandfather of the trio in Siphones."

"How do you know him?"

"It's a very long story."

Andreas rolled his eyes. "Is there any other kind of story you tell?"

"Do you want me to tell it or not?"

Andreas waved his hand at Tassos. "You've primed your audience, so just get on with it."

"I met him here during the Junta Years. He'd been shaped by an unimaginably hard life trying to survive World War II as a young boy in one of Naxos's poorest mountain villages. Starvation plagued those places, and you survived by doing whatever you had to do to feed your family. In his case, he became legend for his talent at finding ways to steal food and livestock from farmers and herders on the plains below." Tassos took a sip of water. "After the war he honed his foraging skills in a different direction, the artifacts market. Naxos was filled with unexcavated ancient sites, and he had a gift for finding them and their treasures."

"He must have made a fortune," said Lila.

Tassos gestured no. "He wasn't a businessman, just a thief. He'd find the treasures but sell them off to middlemen for virtually nothing compared to their true value to collectors."

"Dare I ask how you got to know him?"

"Not in the way you're thinking, wiseass. When I worked as a prison guard for the Junta on Giaros, I'd sometimes be detailed to another island, and when the Junta decided to build a major highway on Naxos running from Chora to Alyko, I spent a lot of time down in Alyko assigned to keep an eye on things."

"Where's Alyko?" said Lila.

"About a half hour south of Chora."

"What sort of 'things'?" said Andreas.

"They built the road to connect Chora and a big hotel project in Alyko overlooking the sea."

"The Junta was building a hotel?" said Lila.

"They encouraged a lot of hotel construction, but this was a foreign corporation's project. Anyway, I was there to make sure it wasn't disturbed."

"Disturbed how?"

"By trespassers intruding on the property while construction was underway. Mostly, we chased away herders with their animals and locals walking dogs."

"Why do I have the feeling this story has a lot more to go?"

"The farmer was working there, and he seemed at first like any other manual laborer, digging holes. He'd dig in one place, leave it open for a couple of days, and then cover it up and dig another hole somewhere else."

"Why?"

"Whenever I asked him that question, he always gave me the same answer. 'Keep your nose out of other people's business.'"

"Something we all know you can't do."

"Back then I wasn't as aggressive. Besides, I was a young man with a sweet Junta job and didn't need to risk pissing off someone who was doing something my superiors must have known about. No way he could be digging all those holes and not be noticed."

"Did you ever find out why he dug the holes?"

"I have a pretty good idea. Every night the same old man would walk his dog onto the edge of the property and I'd have to shoo him away. It became a ritual, and we'd talk for a bit before he'd head back home. One night he asked me why the caïques came in so late at night to the concrete pier just below the hotel construction. I said I didn't know anything about those boats, but they were probably there to unload supplies. He said, no, they were *loading*, not unloading, and always gone before dawn." Tassos reached for another carrot stick. "Years later, after the project had gone bankrupt and the Junta'd been overthrown, I heard from someone in the artifacts business that Naxos was filled with ancient burial sites—"

"Antiquities smuggling," said Lila.

"You win the prize," said Tassos. "The ancients buried their dead with whatever they'd need in their next life. Many of the treasures in the island's Archaeological Museum came from gravesites. Though it hadn't registered with me at the time, locals used to call the construction 'the gravesite project.'"

"So the holes the grandfather dug were on ancient gravesites?" said Andreas.

"Based on his history, I've no doubt that's true. But there's a lot more to the story. In later years he went back to farming. He'd done what he'd had to do to keep his family alive, but he didn't want his children and grandchildren following his ways. He became active in the conservation resistance to preserve the beauty and history of Naxos. He galvanized village opposition to expanding the airport, rallied locals to successfully challenge efforts to resurrect the failed Alyko hotel project, and openly supported the Case of the 33."

"Then the reporter was right about the old man, his son, and grandson being activists, and what Yianni was told about the grandfather was bullshit," said Andreas.

"I don't know about the other two, but it's sure BS about the grandfather."

"Why would they lie?" asked Maggie.

"That's something to ask them."

The housekeeper stepped out onto the terrace. "Lunch is ready. Shall I serve it out here?"

Lila and Maggie jumped up. "We'll help you," said Lila.

"Not necessary," said the housekeeper.

"We need a break," said Maggie, following Lila and the house-keeper inside.

"From what?" said Tassos.

"Don't worry about them. I'm still listening. Is there anything more you have to tell me?" said Andreas.

"Nope." Tassos jerked in his seat and reached into his pants pocket. "My mobile's on vibrate." He looked at the phone screen. "Perhaps I do. The call's from my friend who's trying to set up the meeting for tomorrow."

Tassos held the phone against his cheek with his shoulder, crossed his fingers on one hand, and reached for a pita with the other.

"A true multitasker," smiled Andreas.

Tassos nodded yes as he said into his phone, "Make me smile, my friend."

———

Tassos listened patiently as his friend described what he'd gone through to arrange the meeting. Apparently, word was out to many that the reporter had disappeared, and some of those that Tassos's friend had contacted now worried for their safety and that of their families.

"Who has them worried?"

"They're too worried to tell me," said Tassos's friend.

"Jesus."

"No need for you to worry, though. I convinced them they'd be much worse off if they didn't speak to you."

"How'd you do that?"

"By playing on their natural fears that the government is a police state capable of all kinds of merciless deeds."

"And they believed you?"

"Why not? I believe it. After all, do you forget where we met? I was a political prisoner under a fascist regime."

"But times are different now?"

"Are they?"

Tassos had been down this road before with his friend. "Okay, I get your point. Let's move on. What—not who—has them worried?"

"It's conjecture based upon gossip, but when you toss in an element of truth, even lies gain credibility. Here we have an Athenian journalist writing about big money angling to slice up the island for *private gain*, and Naxians remember how Athens media helped the thirty-three defeat a *public benefit* project backed by the local government to expand the port. The last thing modern-day privateers want is the national press focusing on what they have in mind for Naxos and its treasures."

"What are you saying?"

"Even among opponents and supporters of the port project, there were violent skirmishes. Passions run high in disputes over development."

"But we're talking about kidnappers and potential murderers?"

"I'm not suggesting there was anyone like that involved in the port dispute, but now we're talking about private projects capable of generating at least as much passionate resistance. You're a cop, do you have any doubt that among all the private projects percolating around here there aren't bad actors from dangerous places around the world looking to launder money made in the most mercenary of ways? For them to do physical harm in pursuit of monetary gain is not a reach at all."

"Do you have any particular projects or bad guys in mind?"

"Nope. For that you'll have to speak to the people I've pulled together for your meeting."

"Tell me about them."

"They're from different parts of the island. Some are native to Naxos, others expats, but all vigorously oppose unrestrained development."

"Who ever admits to being *in favor* of unrestrained development?"

"Good point. Come to think of it, I've never heard a politician say anything remotely like that, even those who love pouring concrete over any open space they can find. But the ones coming to your meeting actually live their lives keeping that commitment."

"I assume you know them all."

"Yes, and if they're locals, most of their parents and grandparents as well. The bookseller's late grandfather and I were together in resisting the Junta, though he never got arrested."

"Poor guy, he never got to meet me."

"I'm sure he regretted that. He was a lawyer, and his son

followed in his footsteps, but the grandson opted for bookselling as a better life choice."

"Hard way to make a euro."

"He has the benefit of a grandfather who left him several rent-producing properties to subsidize his lifestyle."

"Where's he live?"

"In Chora, above his bookshop. The others all live in villages out of town. The farmer raises olives in Eggares and runs an olive-press museum in the center of the village."

"What's his family tree?"

"Hers. She's a sixth-generation Naxian farmer. There's another woman in the group. She's an artist who lives in Halki and runs a very successful art gallery called Alex's Fishbowl. She's an expat. Been here for thirty years. One of the most articulate of those seeking to market the preservation of Naxos as a selling point for tourism."

"Interesting crew."

"It gets better. The chef-restaurateur has one of the best places on the island. It's less than a half hour out of Chora, down toward Alyko. We've set up the meeting in his taverna. He was a driving force behind the Case of the 33 and is still a strong voice among conservationists opposing the windmills and private exploitation of public lands."

"And the shepherd?"

"He's perhaps the most interesting. He's of one hundred percent Cretan blood, born and raised in the mountain village of Apeiranthos but married an American girl and now lives in Sangri by the Temple of Demeter."

"Why do you say he's the most interesting?"

"The list of names you gave me included his wife, not him, but when I called her she said she'd have to speak to her husband. He called me back to say he wanted to come instead of her. I was surprised because his roots and village aren't known for friendly cooperation with authorities."

"Do you think he's coming to cause trouble?"

"That's what I thought at first, too, so I asked him that straight out. He said he's coming because he's a close friend of the husband of the cop who was hurt in that pickup rollover outside of Koronos. He said he wants to do what he can to help find whoever's responsible."

"Sounds like he's suggesting what happened to the reporter and his friend's wife are related. Did he say why he thought that?"

"We're in Greece, friend. People see conspiracies in the number of raisins in a cereal box. Who knows what he thinks or the basis for his thoughts. That's why I set up your meeting, so you can be the super detective who ferrets out the answers."

"Just for the record," said Tassos, "I want you to know that you're just as ornery as ever."

"I think you mean *we're* just as ornery."

"I know."

"But I still love you."

"Me too," said Tassos. "Thanks for all your help, and stay well, old friend."

Tassos hung up but didn't move. He sat staring out to sea. *Where had all the years gone?* Each time he said goodbye to an old friend, his thoughts ran to whether that might be the last time they spoke. *Snap out of it, Stamatos. You've got a great woman, great friends, and a great life left to lead.*

"Would you please come back to planet earth and tell me what he had to say?" said Andreas.

Tassos rose from his chair. "Let's have lunch while I tell you."

———

Over a lunch of chicken *kalamakia*, beef *keftedes*, fried zucchini, *graviera* cheese, fresh bread, and a large Greek salad, Tassos shared what he'd heard from his friend.

"Sounds like an interesting group of people," said Lila.

"With strong opinions," said Maggie.

"And some real leads," added Andreas. "We're meeting at three, so we should plan to leave here by no later than two thirty."

Tassos motioned to the housekeeper. "May I have another *kalamaki*, please?"

The housekeeper paused as if confused, nodded, and went into the kitchen.

"Why don't we visit Yianni and leave for the meeting straight from the hospital?" said Lila.

"Good idea."

The housekeeper returned with a plate bearing a single straw and placed the plate in front of Tassos.

"What's this?"

"Your *kalamaki*, sir."

Andreas burst out laughing and said to the housekeeper, "I bet you're from Thessaloniki."

She nodded yes.

Andreas laughed again. "In Thessaloniki, if you ask for a *kalamaki* you get a *straw*. Down here you'll get chicken or pork on a skewer."

"Then what do they call meat on a skewer?"

"Souvlaki, which means the same thing to everyone."

"Just ask for souvlaki and avoid the problem," said Maggie.

Tassos shook his head. "I guess I'm still not too old to learn something new."

"What do they call *keftedes*?" asked Lila.

"Meatballs are meatballs everywhere," smiled Andreas.

Ring, ring.

"Not my phone this time," said Tassos.

"It's mine," said Andreas, pulling his phone from his pants pocket.

"Kaldis here."

Pause.

"Hold on, Adoni. I want to put you on speakerphone."

Andreas set his mobile on the dining table. "It's our head tech wiz back in GADA with news. I'm here with Maggie and Tassos. What do you have for us?"

"I heard about Yianni. How's he doing?"

"His hard head finally came in handy," said Andreas. "He's doing great. I'll tell him you asked."

"Thanks, Chief. Nikoletta Elia's editor just left. We examined his phone and analyzed the voicemail left by her possible kidnapper. The caller used a state-of-the-art scrambler. No way we could unscramble it, not even to say whether the caller was a man or a woman."

"Damn."

"But there's more."

"More bad news?"

"Depends on what you're expecting. We'd also examined the reporter's mobile and came up with the number of the last call she'd received and answered on that phone. It came through at about the same time as she disappeared from her hotel."

"Why didn't you tell us that before?"

"I did, in a voicemail I left yesterday for Yianni, before I heard what happened to him."

"Okay, go on."

"As a result of our examination of the journalist's phone, I have potentially significant news for you."

"Why is every cop so dramatic?" said Maggie.

"Because we strive for recognition of our small victories amid an ever-losing battle with the dark side," said Tassos.

"I like that," said Adoni.

"Just make your point, please," said Andreas.

"We came up with the same number as the caller who left the message on the editor's phone."

Silence.

"Dare I ask if you know whose number it is?" said Andreas.

"I have a name but no other information."

"What's the name?"

"Petros Zagorianos."

"Never heard of him." Andreas looked around the table and received a group shrug.

"It could be an alias. The phone was purchased at a shop on Naxos the day before Nikoletta disappeared."

"Do you know anything else about this Petros character?"

"Not a thing."

"Is that all you have on the phones?"

"Yeah. I hope it helps."

"It's a good start. Thanks."

Andreas clicked off. "Any thoughts?"

"Yeah," said Tassos. "Call Dimitri and see if he's ever heard of this guy."

Andreas dialed.

"Dimitri, it's Andreas. You're on speaker with my crew."

"Small world, I was just about to call you."

"I wanted to know if you ever heard of a Naxian named Petros Zagorianos?"

Pause.

"Dimitri, are you still there?"

"Did you say Petros Zagorianos?"

"Yes."

"I was calling to tell you we have an ID on the tourist who took a header on the rocks the night the reporter disappeared.

He was born on Naxos as Petros Zagorianos but emigrated to the U.S. as a child, and the name on his U.S. passport is Peter Zagori."

Andreas leaned in toward the phone. "When did he last enter Greece?"

"According to Immigration, the day before the reporter disappeared. He arrived on Wednesday. She disappeared early Thursday morning."

Andreas looked at Tassos. "The same day he bought the phone."

"What phone?" asked Dimitri.

"The one used to call Nikoletta the night she disappeared and to call her editor yesterday to say she was okay."

"But Zagori couldn't have called her editor. He was dead for nearly two days by then."

"I know," said Andreas. "Which means if we find Peter Zagori's phone, we likely find his killer."

"And whoever has Nikoletta," added Tassos.

"Any other info on Zagori?"

"Not yet, but based on your suggestion we ran him through Greek databases and he popped up with a Greek military record. He came back from the United States to serve his time in the army. That's all we have on him over here, but we've put in a request with the United States for anything they might have. I'll let you know as soon as we hear back."

"Thanks. How's Popi doing?"

"Stable is all we're hearing. The infection seems to be under control. They may not have to remove her spleen."

Andreas pumped his fist into the air. "Thank God. If you speak to her husband, please pass along our thoughts and prayers."

"Will do. Bye,"

Andreas shut off his phone and looked at Tassos. "What do you think?"

"That we've got one hell of a mystery to solve."

"And less than forty-eight hours in which to do it."

"Back to the books, boys and girls," said Maggie.

"Once we finish, let's go to the beach," said Lila.

"I can't go. We really have a lot to do," said Andreas.

"Sure you can. From what I've heard, until you meet with those folks tomorrow, all you have to do is think and toss around ideas. That can be done on a beach as well as in one of these chairs. Besides, a swim will clear your head and make all of us think better."

Andreas raised his hands in a sign of surrender. "Fine. Off to the beach it is. But I get to pick which one."

"Deal."

Chapter Eleven

Though their deal had Andreas picking the beach, when he passed on nearby Plaka Beach for a beach at least twenty minutes south, there were grumblings among his crew. Lila argued that Plaka was a perfectly exquisite sandy beach offering organized services for those who wanted them, and since neither she nor Andreas had ever been to that other beach, why risk messing up what remained of their day by heading toward the unknown?

Andreas did not relent. He drove back to Vivlos, turned right onto the main road, and followed it to its end before turning right onto a narrower paved road running between cedar-dotted sand dunes. Parked cars sat off on both the sides of the road. He turned left at what seemed more of a sandy path than a road, and followed it to where it opened up into an impromptu parking area separated from the beach by a line of cedars.

"Here we are, folks. Welcome to Alyko Beach."

Lila and Maggie hurried down to the beach, carrying bags filled with what they deemed essential for a day by the sea. Andreas and Tassos followed, carrying snacks, water, bamboo beach mats, and two beach umbrellas to shield them from the sun.

"Wherever you ladies pick is fine with us," said Andreas, glancing at a nodding Tassos.

"This place is gorgeous," said Lila looking south. "The beach must go on for half a kilometer with not a structure in sight."

"If you look south," said Maggie. "But up on that rise beyond the cedars to the north there's a church and what looks to be the skeleton of some sort of abandoned concrete and stone construction."

"But it's a small church," said Lila, "and the other structure looks to be only a story tall and is hardly noticeable up there off among all those cedars."

"I wonder what it is?" said Maggie.

Tassos looked at Andreas but said nothing.

"Frankly, I don't care. I'm just happy to be on a lovely white beach with crystal clear water that's utterly devoid of music, chairs, tavernas, and anything else man-made." Lila put her beach bag down ten meters from the edge of the water and, with a flourish suggestive of a conqueror claiming territory, said, "How's this?"

"Perfect," said Maggie.

Andreas gathered up rocks as Tassos scooped out a hole in the sand. They planted one umbrella in the hole, secured it in place from the wind with the rocks, and repeated the process for the second umbrella.

After they'd set up and spread out their things, Lila turned to Andreas. "How did you know about this place?"

"Tassos told me."

Tassos grinned.

"When were you here?" asked Maggie.

"Long before I met you, my love. I was but a young man of twenty serving my country." He nodded toward the structure on the hill north of them. "I was here when that was being built.

As you guessed, it's a long-abandoned project. A hotel project, to be precise."

Maggie nodded. "So, that's where you met that grandfather from Siphones."

"Yes. He was around forty then."

"And the beaches surrounding it sounded so idyllic I thought you'd like to see them," said Andreas.

Lila rolled her eyes. "I wondered why you agreed so quickly to come to the beach in the middle of a case that has you stressed out. It's not like you to risk relaxing, especially with Yianni in the hospital."

"I'm not stressed out," he barked.

"Yeah, sure. But at least admit that you brought us here so that you could check out that place." She pointed north.

Andreas shrugged. "Sure, we're here, so why not? Besides, it could be interesting for other reasons. I hear artists have done some extraordinary things with it."

Lila stood. "I'm going swimming. If you can bear to wait until I return before gallivanting off on your little expedition, I might join you."

Andreas lay back on his towel, staring straight up at the sky through a space between the umbrellas. "Lord spare me from doing good deeds unappreciated by mere mortals."

Lila kicked sand on his legs. "Like I said, wise guy, wait for me." She turned and ran toward the sea without waiting for a reply.

"I think the tag line to that exit was, 'or else,'" said Tassos.

"Don't I know it."

"Good," said Maggie smiling. "We've obviously trained each of you well."

———

Lila swam for twenty minutes, dried in the sun for ten more, changed into a one-piece bathing suit, and said to her husband, "So, are you ready for our hike?"

Andreas got up from his towel, grabbed a T-shirt, and slipped into a pair of sandals. "I thought you'd never ask."

"Are you guys coming?" Lila asked Maggie and Tassos.

"Nope, you two are old enough to go off exploring on your own," said Tassos, stretched out on a towel under an umbrella.

Andreas took Lila's hand and led her up toward the SUV.

"Why don't we just walk along the shore over toward the church?"

"While you were swimming, I noticed a pickup parked over by the church drive out to where we parked. It'll be a lot easier following that road than struggling past rocks and brush in bathing suits."

Their walk along the road to the church took five minutes, the last minute alongside a half dozen or so decrepit concrete shacks across the road from the church.

"What are those buildings?" Lila asked.

"My guess is they're part of the old hotel project, but from the shutters and doors, I'd say that at least some of them were used after the project was abandoned. For what purpose or by whom, I've not a clue."

They continued their walk, passing more faded structures and rows of unfinished stone and concrete walls. Andreas stopped at a still-serviceable concrete pier jutting out into the sea. "It's right where Tassos said it would be."

"Why didn't he come with us if he knows so much about the place?"

"He said it's been too many years for him to remember where that Siphones grandfather dug his suspicious holes."

"That doesn't sound like Tassos."

"I know," said Andreas. He shrugged.

"Maybe he doesn't want to be in a place that reminds him of his time in service to the Junta?"

"No, he came to grips with that long ago. My guess would be it's something far simpler. Like he's afraid to take the walk. Maggie said he's watching his weight but is reluctant to do more than minimal exercise."

"If I'd known that, I'd have insisted he come with us."

"I know; that's why I didn't tell you."

Lila went to smack him, but before she could, Andreas bolted toward a dirt path leading up to a wide promontory overlooking the sea.

"Ha ha, too fast for you."

"We'll see about that," said Lila charging after him. "You're in sandals and I'm in sneakers."

"Yeah, but I'm more afraid of you than you are of me," Andreas yelled, not turning or slowing down.

As they neared the top, the scope of the project they'd seen only part of from the beach came into view. One- and two-story stone skeletons tracked along the rim of the cape in an architectural theme reminiscent of the Roman Coliseum's penchant for archways.

They stopped.

"This is amazing," said Lila.

"I've never seen anything like it." Andreas turned to face the sea and swept his hand across the horizon. "I'd bet this view is what attracted the hotel project here in the first place."

"Why do we Greeks insist on selling our very souls?" Lila sighed. "But having said that, I must admit that compared to many of the modern-day hotel projects plaguing us, this one actually looks to have tried fitting in with its setting."

"Don't be so sure about that. It wasn't finished. Who knows what it would have looked like then."

"Sadly, you're right. But with any luck we'll never know." She took his hand. "Come, let's look around."

They left the shrubbery-lined path to walk between the perimeter buildings into a broad, open space covered in concrete. Unkempt gorse and other hardy greenery competed for random patches of available dirt.

"This must have been the intended main entrance and parking area," said Andreas. "Be careful where you step; parts of the concrete have collapsed. This entire area must be hollow below." He pointed to a hole just in front of them.

Lila poked Andreas on the arm. "Do you see what I see?" She swung around in a circle. "They're beautiful, they're stunning, and they're all around us."

Huge, colorful murals of mythical creatures—faces, birds, and omens—leaped out at them from almost every vertical surface. Long-abandoned concrete walls had been turned into gigantic canvases, one more challenging to the senses than the next.

"I've heard of this place, even seen photographs of some of the art, but I never imagined how overwhelming it is to see them here, in the surroundings that inspired their creation." She swung around again. "They were painted a few years back by a Balian street artist who lives in Athens." She pointed to a doorway leading into a skeletal maze of unfinished rooms and hallways. "There are more inside." She headed toward the doorway.

Andreas yelled, "Remember, be careful where you step." He watched her disappear inside. "I feel like I'm talking to Tassaki," he muttered. *But at least with him I have a shot at being listened to.*

He stood alone on the concrete, staring first one way and then another. He had no idea what he was looking for here that might tie into Nikoletta's disappearance, nor even a hint of where he should start to look for inspiration. He decided to take his mind off the investigation and just tag along with Lila. He followed the path she'd taken inside through an archway now doubling as the gaping, wide-open mouth of a sea monster. *Perhaps that's what happened to Nikoletta—she was swallowed up by some mysterious creature.*

So much for putting the investigation out of his mind.

He wandered from room to room, taking care not to step too close to the many holes, some of which promised to the inattentive a fall of a story or two. With all the tourists this artwork must draw, he was surprised no efforts had been made to repair or at least cover over the holes. But, then again, with the entire country still in the midst of financial crisis, there wasn't enough money available for far more pressing crumbling infrastructure projects directly affecting the daily lives of everyday Greek voters.

He stopped to look at a small mural obviously painted by a different artist trying to pass himself off as the original. An awkward impersonation, to say the least.

Impersonation…? Andreas stared straight ahead. *What if whoever attacked Yianni and Popi was trying to impersonate Nikoletta's mystery man?*

That could mean the telephone calls to Nikoletta and her editor were made by the man Nikoletta interviewed, and everything he told the editor was legitimate. *The hacker is keeping her safe from impersonators trying to harm her.*

Andreas felt he was onto something but needed more than instinct before pushing his theory. If his hunch was correct, then Nikoletta faced no danger from her "captor," but if wrong, she could die. Or already be dead.

Maybe the answer will come from what the Americans have to say about Peter Zagori. Given the calls from Zagori's phone, Andreas had no doubt he'd been killed by the hacker. But why? Certainly not for his mobile.

He nodded to the mural that had sparked his possible epiphany.

"Thanks for the inspiration whoever you are. Keep up the good work."

———

After another half hour of wandering through the ruins, Lila agreed it was time to rejoin Maggie and Tassos on the beach. They walked along the path past the church, every so often catching a glimpse of the beach below through a break in the cedars.

"I could use another swim," she said.

"I'm in need of one too. It's a warmer day than I thought." Andreas turned his head to glance at the beach and came to an abrupt stop.

"What is it?"

"Three men are surrounding our umbrellas, and Maggie's standing between them and Tassos."

"Is something wrong?"

"I don't know, but I'll meet you there." Andreas jumped into the brush, slipping and sliding along the rocks until he'd made it down to the beach. He kicked off his sandals and broke into a trot, aimed straight for his friends and some very loud music. The closer he came, the louder the music. He watched one of the men grab Tassos's umbrella and throw it toward the sea.

"*Whoa, there,*" yelled Andreas. "Let's calm things down, fellas."

The man who tossed the umbrella responded in English. "Fuck off, mate, unless you want some of what this old asshole's gonna get." The man stood about as tall as Andreas and had the bull-like build of Yianni.

Andreas changed course to pick up the umbrella, saying in English as he did, "You're obviously not from around these parts, but that's not the way we talk to strangers in Greece." He collapsed the umbrella and wrapped it tightly shut as he walked toward the men.

"I said fuck off." The man pointed to his two friends, each the size of a professional rugby player. "Take care of him. I'll take care of the old fart and his pig of a woman."

Maggie swung around to face Tassos, saying in Greek, "Don't you dare let him goad you into a fight."

"Yeah," said Andreas, in English, "give me a chance to reason with these fellas." He stopped five meters from the men. "Why don't you go back to your blanket and sleep off whatever has you all fired up? Honest, that's a much better choice than what you'll face if you insist on taking this route."

"I said, take care of him," growled the man. "Do it *now*."

"Oh, so you're in charge. Just for the record, permit me to explain whom you and your friends are about to assault. We're both Greek policemen, so no matter how what you have in mind turns out, you and your buddies are in for a mass of hurt."

"Cops? I love beating up cops."

"Nah, be honest, you like your buddies to beat up cops. You only have the balls to go after old men and women, and only then when you're drunk enough to think you have the courage. Like now. You're a…uh what's the word?" He looked at Maggie.

"Pussy."

The leader swung around toward Maggie.

"Hey!" Andreas put a little heat into his voice to catch the guy's attention. "Like I said, no balls, only guts when you're high enough to go after easy targets. Why don't you try me, asshole?"

The leader paused for an instant to look at his friends, then charged at Andreas as if headed into a scrum, arms spread wide and eyes glaring. A pace before the raging man reached him, Andreas slipped to the man's right, causing the man to stumble and giving Andreas the opportunity to drive the pointed end of the umbrella into the side of the man's right knee, sending him crumpling to the sand. The man clutched his leg and howled, just as Andreas delivered another pointed shot to the man's left shin, followed by a haymaker from the umbrella's blunt end to the man's jaw.

Andreas stepped back. "Are we done yet?"

The man growled and lurched along the sand toward Andreas.

"Not yet, huh? Well, have it your way." Andreas stepped back as the man tried to get up. Andreas stepped forward with his left foot, as he brought his right foot forward and up in a fierce pendulum shot of a kick to the man's balls.

As the man lay writhing on the ground, Andreas turned to his mates. "Here in Greece we prefer football, though you might call it soccer. Now, would you two mind removing your buddy from our area of the beach?" The two men looked at each other and charged at Andreas. He stepped back and braced for their attack.

CRACK!

The sound echoed across the beach, stopping the two men in their tracks.

"Okay, assholes, I've had all that I can take from your loud-ass music and bullshit machismo." Tassos stood with his gun aimed at the chest of the bigger of the two men. "If you aren't off this beach with your hurt buddy in two minutes, I'm going to start taking target practice at your kneecaps."

The men stood frozen in place.

"I said *move*." Tassos fired another round at their feet.

One tossed everything of theirs into a blanket and ran with it Santa Claus-style toward the parking area while the other helped their staggering leader struggle along after.

Andreas watched to make sure they'd left before turning to Tassos.

"That was a highly inappropriate use of a firearm."

"Yeah, tell me about it."

Maggie said, "I wondered why you seemed so calm when they threatened you for asking them to turn down their music. For a moment, I thought you'd forgotten your English."

"Yeah, I should have shot their music box instead. That would have ended the confrontation right there."

"I remember the days when you wouldn't have needed the gun to take care of those three," said Andreas.

"So do I, but times change."

Andreas nodded. "They sure do. And by the way, why didn't you pull your pistol and put an end to it all before I had to fight the guy?"

"I figured he needed his ass kicked and you needed some practice."

Andreas shook his head. "Those three weren't the only assholes on this beach today."

"Yeah, it was their bad luck we all happened to end up in the same place on the same day."

Same place, same day. Andreas froze. "That *can't* be."

"What can't be?" said Tassos.

"That dead Greek-American, Zagori. He couldn't have been in the bar the night Nikoletta met the hacker. He wasn't even in Greece until days later!"

"Maybe it's just a coincidence the two men resembled each other?" said Maggie.

"We hate coincidences," said Andreas.

"But this time, maybe it is?" said Tassos.

"Meaning that lead's a dead end. Damn it."

"*Is everything all right?*" shouted Lila running toward them. "I heard shots and saw three men hurrying off like fleeing thieves."

"It was just another drunken tourist episode," said Tassos.

"Yep," said Andreas. "The kind that comes to our country on

holiday thinking they can do anything they want, and too many of us let them do just that." He nodded toward Tassos. "Unluckily for those three, Tassos isn't one of them."

"All this excitement has me hungry," said Maggie. "What do you say we get something to eat?"

"Good idea," said Lila.

"Just one question," said Maggie, looking at Andreas. "What was that bit about *old men and women*?"

He smiled. "I just used that for dramatic effect."

"I would certainly hope, because I was a pretty good footballer myself."

"That's good to know. I'll keep it in mind."

Tassos nodded. "I also learned something today,"

"What's that?"

"Always bring an umbrella to the beach."

Chapter Twelve

After leaving the beach, they followed the highway north toward Chora. A few minutes later they entered the area of Kastraki, passing between fields of hay, olives, and pasture, all bordered in the distance by clusters of modern white villas. Beyond a row of beach pines, Andreas turned right into a dusty parking lot and stopped beside a pale ochre roadhouse cloistered by olive, fig, apricot, and pomegranate, well-tended gardens, and a veranda draped in bougainvillea, hibiscus, and grape.

"What's this place?" asked Lila.

"Tassos's friend said it might be the best taverna in the Cyclades."

"It's where our meeting is set for tomorrow," said Tassos. "I figured since we're in the area, why not take a peek at it?"

"As long as the food is good, I don't care about your ulterior motives," said Lila, opening her rear door and sliding out.

"Ditto on that," said Maggie, getting out the other side.

Andreas looked at Tassos. "Hardly a serious wisecrack from the crew in the back. I guess they really are hungry."

"They're not alone in that. And that's not a coincidence; it's a fact."

Andreas shook his head. "I still can't believe a Zagori look-alike was in that bar nights before the real Zagori arrived on Naxos."

"I admit it's freaky. But what other explanation is there other than coincidence?"

"That's what I'm asking you."

"Perhaps lunch will inspire me."

They caught up with Lila and Maggie waiting just inside the entrance to a large empty room next to an open kitchen. A bearded young man said hello and led them out onto an even larger L-shaped veranda where diners happily chatted away at traditional taverna chairs and tables painted terracotta and olive.

"I think I'm going to like this place." Lila pointed to a small ceramic tile depicting a fish and olives mounted onto a concrete pillar supporting the veranda's beam and double-slatted roof. "I love the little touches."

"Yeah, I was thinking the same thing," said Tassos.

Maggie poked him. "Nobody likes a smart-ass."

"That's okay," said Lila. "We know he's only trying to hide his sensitive side."

The young man showed them to a corner table on the side of the veranda farthest from the road.

"I suspect that big room next to the kitchen is for use in the winter," said Lila.

Tassos nodded. "A lot of tavernas are like that. Summers, everyone wants to sit outside, winters it's back inside."

They ordered off the menu and from a wall-mounted chalkboard listing specials, each picking a dish for the table to share. As courses like mussels in wine, grilled figs with local cheese, deep-fried little fishes, and sardines stuffed with capers and cherry tomatoes drew praises of "best ever," "fantastic," and "amazing," they expanded their order to mackerel and fava, shrimps in lemon, rabbit in tomato, oven-cooked chicken with potatoes, and a few repeats. All accompanied by the house's homemade wine.

At the end of the meal, after the plates had been cleared and desserts refused amid myriad I-must-watch-my-waistline excuses, a man in his late thirties came to their table carrying a tray filled with fruits.

"These are from our garden. Compliments of the house."

"Thank you," said Andreas. "This had to be one of our best meals ever. Our compliments to the chef."

The man nodded. "I thank you. Praise like that is what keeps me cooking."

"You're the chef?" said Lila.

"Yes and an owner."

Lila smiled. "I agree; it was a wonderful meal."

Chef nodded. "Thank you, *keria*."

"May I ask you to sit with us for a moment?" said Andreas.

Chef looked around the room. "For a minute, I can." He pulled up a chair and sat next to Andreas.

"Since we're talking, I thought I should introduce myself so that tomorrow you don't wonder why I hadn't."

"Tomorrow?"

Andreas extended his hand. "My name is Andreas Kaldis. I'm chief of GADA's Special Crimes Unit. We're part of that meeting taking place here tomorrow at three, but I want to assure you our reason for being here today has absolutely nothing to do with any of that. We're here solely because of the food. We kept hearing this is the best taverna on the island, so after swimming at Alyko Beach, we decided to come here."

Chef nodded thanks to everyone at the table. "Now, it's my turn to compliment you on your choice of Alyko. It's my favorite beach. Let's hope it doesn't change."

"We all agree with that," said Lila.

"I assume you saw what remains of the Junta's abandoned hotel project?"

"Yes," said Andreas.

"It's a tragedy what we Greeks do with God's gifts of natural beauty."

"My thoughts exactly," said Lila.

"Thankfully, the courts stopped it from going forward," said Andreas.

Chef winced. "For now."

"What do you mean?" said Andreas. "Didn't the Supreme Court decide it was government land and couldn't be built upon?"

"I'm sure you know better than I that nothing is certain these days. With our government desperate for money, there's no telling what might happen if the right deep-pockets foreign investor decides to offer an extravagant sum in exchange for permission to build there."

Maggie crossed herself. "I pray not."

Andreas leaned forward. "Is there any talk of such a deal in the works?"

"Not that I know of, but those who'd like to make it happen aren't likely to let me in on their plans."

"The whole project would have to be demolished, from the ground up," said Andreas. "Correction, make that from *below* ground up. Its concrete base is collapsing."

Chef nodded. "Every once in a while a herder complains to me of a goat falling into one of those holes. They're deep. Much deeper than you'd think necessary for a hotel project."

"I wouldn't know," said Andreas, "but hotels put a lot of their support services underground."

"Not sure how much of that they did back in the early 1970s," said Chef, "but if you ask the locals, they're convinced all that concrete covered open space was just that, a cover for smugglers digging for antiquities deep below the surface."

Andreas glanced at Tassos. "Yes, I've heard those rumors. Do you think they're true?"

He smiled. "You're a police officer. If I started talking to you about the number of locals and others who have personal collections of artifacts found around that hotel site, you'd be duty-bound to send the minister of culture a memo, which, if I were lucky, would *only* get me disowned by my family and run off the island."

Andreas patted Chef on the shoulder. "I understand, but don't worry, there will be no such memo."

A bearded younger man came to the table. "Excuse me, but they need you in the kitchen."

Chef stood and Andreas quickly did the same.

"Thank you for a wonderful meal."

"You're welcome. See you tomorrow."

"For sure."

Andreas sat down and watched the man walk back to the kitchen. "What do you think, Tassos?"

"I think he's telling the truth."

"I meant about someone resurrecting the hotel project."

"I agree with him. There's no telling what might happen in this economy. But it would be interesting to know if anyone's expressed an interest in reviving the project."

"I'll ask my father," said Lila. "Perhaps he knows or knows someone who would."

"Any excuse to call home to speak to the kids," said a slightly tipsy Maggie.

Lila laughed. "No guilt feelings here. I'm sure they don't even realize we're gone."

"Besides," said Andreas, "it leaves my lovely wife more time to have me all to herself."

Lila pulled her phone out of her bag and hit a speed dial button. "Be still my heart."

"I see the wisecracks are back," said Andreas.

"Just in time for the trip back home," said Tassos.

"Lucky us."

———

By the time Lila and Andreas finished checking in on the children and explained to Lila's father what Andreas wanted to know about the hotel project, they were back on the road heading home, and the sky had taken on the distinct burnt-orange tones of another magnificent sunset.

"We should bring the kids here," said Andreas.

"After spending this weekend with my parents, who no doubt will spoil them rotten, I think it's safe to say we'll have been knocked out of first place on their preferred holiday escorts list."

"Grandparents have a knack for doing that," said Andreas.

"Especially with your mother joining in on triple-teaming us," said Lila.

"God bless them all," said Maggie, crossing herself.

"I wonder how Yianni's doing," said Tassos.

"Toni texted me that everything's looking good," said Lila. "They might release him as early as tomorrow morning."

Maggie crossed herself again.

"What about Popi?" said Andreas.

"No word yet, other than hopeful."

Andreas exhaled. "Bastards."

Ring.

"That's mine," said Lila. "It's my father."

"Hi, Dad."

Pause.

"I'd put you on speaker but the reception's a bit sketchy here, and Andreas is driving, so tell me what you have for him and I'll pass it on."

She listened intently for several minutes.

"Thanks, Dad. Love you too."

Lila put her phone back in her bag. "He said you can call him later if you like, but here's what he's learned. Years after the Belgian entity that owned the project declared bankruptcy, a Lichtenstein company claimed ownership of the Belgian's shares and the right to continue the project. The person behind that claim was a Greek shipowner known to my father. He got tied up in court for years on any number of grounds and ultimately got nowhere with it. My father has no doubt that if someone offered him the right deal in cash, a partnership, or some combination thereof, he'd take it in a heartbeat. My father also said that whoever tries to develop that site faces serious public opposition from both local and national community activists on the order of what's stymied the redevelopment project at Athens's old international airport."

"Do you mean there actually are people out there who dare distrust the intentions of our elected leaders?" smirked Tassos. "Next thing you know, they'll be losing faith in God to deliver us from evil."

"*Tassos,*" said Maggie, "how *dare* you equate God's love to those minions of the devil who deceive and mislead us with false promises?" She crossed herself three times. "Especially after being spared who-knows-what horrible fate back on that beach."

Silence.

"Is everything okay?" said Lila softly. "I've never seen you act so seriously."

"I'm not *acting.*"

Lila leaned in toward Maggie. "You're calling out to God and crossing yourself far more than I've ever seen you do before."

"How dare you criticize my right to practice my religion as I see fit?"

Tassos and Andreas glanced at each other.

"Maggie. I repeat: Is everything okay?"

Maggie shut her eyes, drew in a breath, and exhaled. "I don't want to talk about it."

Lila nodded. "Okay."

Maggie looked out her side window.

Not a word was spoken for more than a minute.

"Beautiful sunset," said Tassos.

"A beautiful, blinding sunset," said Andreas, pulling down the sun visor as he turned west at Vivlos, aimed straight into the setting sun.

Maggie coughed. "Sorry I raised my voice."

"No need to apologize," said Lila. "You're among friends."

"I know." Maggie dabbed at her eyes. "And I love you all dearly." She turned back to the window. "I think I had too much to drink."

She said nothing more.

———

When they reached the house, Maggie hurried inside ahead of the others, closely followed by Tassos.

Lila and Andreas hung back, as if admiring the fading sunset.

"What do you think?" said Lila.

"She's definitely edgier than I've ever seen her."

"Do you think it's her health?"

Andreas shook his head. "I don't know, but I pray not."

"Maybe she's worried about Yianni?"

"I wouldn't think so. He's out of danger. But, again, I don't know."

"She needs someone to talk to about whatever it is."

"Greeks aren't big on that sort of thing."

"I know that. I meant a friend, not a psychiatrist."

Andreas took Lila's hand and headed toward the door. "She has you, she has me, and most of all she has Tassos. When she wants an understanding ear, she'll have it."

———

Tassos closed their bedroom door and spoke softly. "What's bothering you, Maggie?"

She sat on the bed, looking at the floor. "Nothing."

"That's reassuring. I thought it might be something serious, like you've given up on your plan for achieving world peace."

"It's not funny."

He sat down next to her. "I know." He put his arm around her shoulders, drew her to him, and kissed her on the forehead.

Maggie leaned in against his chest and cried uncontrollably, finally sniffling to a stop after a succession of deep breaths. All the while, Tassos never uttered a word or softened his embrace.

"Thank you," she sniffled.

"No reason to thank me. I'm here for you the same as you've always been for me. All that matters is that something serious is bothering you. Do you want to tell me what it is?"

Maggie shut her eyes. "Perhaps I've been on the job too long. Seen and heard too much."

"Is this about Yianni or the other cop?"

"No." She opened her eyes and sat up straight. "It's about you."

"Me?"

Maggie paused. "You've been a bit down since your heart incident. The doctors say you're fine, and you've been following their instructions better than I ever hoped, but your mood worries me. You're not back to your old self. It's as if you're counting down how many years you have left, rather than living them." She sighed, followed by a deep swallow. "On the beach today when those three animals were ready to hurt you, I felt helpless to protect you."

"There was no need for you to protect me."

"I didn't know that. All that I knew was that the one person on earth who means more to me than my own life could have been killed today over loud music on a beach."

"This does not sound like you at all."

"I know. As I said, perhaps I've seen too much and realize how, in an instant, a fit of temper can wreck more lives than just the victim's."

"What do you want me to do? Resign from the force?"

"No, that wouldn't change you. You'd still be the same aggressive grump you've always been, just without a gun and a badge."

"Well then, what is it you want me to do?"

Maggie grabbed his free hand. "Promise me you'll learn to let these lesser offenses to your sensibilities slide by. You can find a reason to get into a fight these days almost anywhere you look, and that's before anyone even begins talking politics."

"You're saying you want me to be more laid-back?"

She sighed. "Yes, I guess that's right. I miss your old self."

"Fine. But you'll have to promise to do something for me in return."

Maggie cocked her head. "Why do I sense what's coming?"

Tassos leaned in and began kissing her on the neck.

"Because you never miss a thing."

———

"Hello."

"Yes?"

"Is this Detective Kouros?" The voice was deep but tentative.

"Yes, who's this?"

"Popi's husband."

Yianni's heart jumped. "Is she okay?"

"She's out of her coma."

"Thank God. My thoughts and prayers have been with you both."

"Thank you."

The line remained quiet for so long Yianni thought they might have been disconnected.

"I got your number from Dimitri and meant to call you before, but things just...well...I guess all I can say is I didn't."

"No problem. I'm glad that you called now with good news." More silence.

"How are *you* doing?" Mamas's voice still sounded tentative.

"With any luck I'll be out tomorrow and back to catching the bastards who put us in the hospital."

"It's why I called you."

Yianni paused. "I don't understand."

"I think I can help you find them."

Yianni swallowed. "I, uh, understand how upset you are. Believe me, I do, but this is a police matter, and I don't think it's a good idea for you to be involved in hunting them down. As much as I agree with your motives, and I don't doubt you'd be a great help, tempers could flare and you might get yourself in some serious trouble."

"I know." He seemed struggling to restrain his voice. "When I thought Popi might not survive, I promised myself that if she passed away I'd hunt down and slaughter everyone responsible, one by one."

Yianni had no doubt the man meant it.

"But when she woke up, I felt reborn. Like I had a new reason for living. I realized then that going after the ones who'd tried to kill her would only put her and our future in danger again. That's when I decided to leave retribution to you."

"A wise decision." Yianni exhaled. "The police found the truck and car involved in attacking us."

"The drivers were hired that morning to run a motorbike off a mountain road, but when you ended up in Popi's pickup, their instructions must have changed."

Yianni stared at the phone for a moment. "Wait. How do you know all this?"

"Yesterday, someone I know from Naxos visited me in the hospital. He said he had something he had to tell me in person." Mamas paused. "I'm sure I don't have to tell you, Detective, that there are some very nasty people out there, and the one who came to see me is among the worst. But we grew up together. Our families have known each other for generations."

Yianni heard Mamas swallow.

"He'd been offered a huge fee to kill a cop on a motorbike. But it had to look like an accident and happen that day. He was told he'd find the cop at a hotel west of the airport and should follow him until he found the right place to run him off the road. He said he turned down the job. Even at that price, it wasn't worth the risk of killing a cop."

"I wonder what's the going rate for two cops in a pickup?"

"He said he didn't know for sure what happened after he turned down the offer, but he guessed someone involved in the plan saw you in a pickup and the plan changed."

"Why would such a bad guy tell you all this?"

"Self-preservation. He knew if I somehow thought he'd had anything to do with what happened to Popi, he was a dead man. As soon as he heard about the crash, he knew he had to tell me. He did it in person because he knew I'd need to look him in the eye to believe him."

"Do you believe him?"

"I believe he wouldn't do anything to harm Popi."

"What's his name?"

"I promised I wouldn't say."

Yianni decided not to push the point. "Does he know who was involved?"

"He knows who *tried* to hire him."

Yianni clenched a fist. "Who?"

"He's a local, another of the nasty ones. His name is Spyros, but everyone knows him as Honeyman."

"What's a Honeyman?"

"It's his nickname. He works a honey-selling routine on tourists out of the back of his old pickup truck. He's quite a fast-talker, convincing tourists that the supermarket honey he's selling them at three times the price comes from his own bees."

"Happens everywhere," said Yianni.

"But for him it's just a cover for how he makes his real money. He drives all over the island selling his honey, picking up bits of information here and there, and selling it to whoever might be interested."

"Sounds like a spotter for burglars."

"More likely he's one himself. Among other things..." Mamas's voice sharpened, "But being involved in a murder plot is way beyond anything I've ever heard said about him before. Considering the risk, there must be some real money or pressure involved."

"I take it you don't see him as the top dog in this?"

"No way. He likes to hear himself talk, and he thinks he's clever, but he's a small-time grifter. He did it for somebody else."

"Where can I find Honeyman?"

"Hard to say. He's always on the move, likely up and out of his house before dawn and not back until after dusk. Dimitri should be able to find him. Come to think of it, your best chance at catching him might be at night when he's home."

"Where's his house?"

"I couldn't give you understandable directions, certainly not for finding it at night, but Dimitri will know how to get there."

Yianni hesitated. "One question. What do you think the chances are that Honeyman knew the taverna we were headed to was Popi's favorite?"

"He could have found that out from any number of people. Popi always talked it up as her favorite place on the island. How's that important?"

"I'm trying to figure out how Honeyman knew when, and which way, we'd turn coming out of Siphones. Hard to imagine he'd leave something that important to chance."

"I don't think he did. One of his usual places for parking his pickup and setting up his honey operation is along the road running past Siphones. Your only choice out of Siphones is to head south toward roads connecting back to Chora or north toward Koronos. All he had to do was wait until he saw which way Popi was headed and call the drivers. My guess is they expected you to head toward Koronos and were waiting up that way, but if you'd gone south, they'd have tried to chase you down from behind."

Yianni shut his eyes, drew in a deep breath, and thought back to when they left Siphones…and of that old pickup parked off to the side of the road.

He exhaled and opened his eyes. "I think it's time to arrange for Naxos's finest to pay an official visit on Mr. Honeyman."

Mamas's voice lightened up, "I was hoping you'd say that." He paused. "I'm sure Popi is too."

Chapter Thirteen

In the moonlight, to the tempo of what seemed a million cicadas, the SUV and a marked police car crept lights-out down a rutted donkey path toward a ramshackle stone farmhouse at the bottom of a hollow. Not a glint of light came from the farmhouse. Beyond the house, parallel rows of beehives ran off in the direction of a long-neglected shepherd's hut.

The vehicles stopped thirty meters from the house, and two men got out of each vehicle. Two approached the front door, and two went to the rear. The men at the front stood to each side of the door as the taller of the two knocked twice on the door.

"Spyros, it's Chief of Police Dimitri. Open up."

No answer.

He banged on the door three times. "Police, open up."

No answer.

He banged away, shouting all the while. "Spyros, it's the police. Open up. We know you're in there."

The front door opened. "Easy guys, it's me," said Tassos. Behind him stood a uniformed Naxos cop holding a teenaged boy by the arm. "This one tried scooting out the back door."

"Who are you?" asked Andreas.

The boy said nothing.

"I said, who are you?"

Dimitri interrupted, "It's Spyros's son." He looked at the boy "Why did you run?"

No answer.

"Do you want to go back to bed or be arrested? A simple choice. Now tell me why you ran?"

The boy shuffled his feet. "I was afraid."

"Of what?"

"Of you."

"A guilty conscience over some crime you committed that you thought we knew about, perhaps?" said Tassos.

The boy looked down at the floor.

"Where's your father?" said Dimitri.

"I don't know."

"And your mother?"

"She's in Athens with my sister."

"Doing what?"

"I don't know."

"What's your father doing?"

"I don't know."

Tassos whispered to Andreas, "My guess would be off doing a little while-the-cat's-away-the-mice-will-play action."

"When will your father be back?" said Andreas.

"I don't know."

"You've got that 'I don't know' bit down pretty well," said Tassos. "Why don't you tell us what you do know about where your father *might* be."

"I don't know."

"When's the last time you saw him?"

The boy hesitated.

"Remember the choice I offered you," said Dimitri. "Back to bed or back with us."

"Two days ago."

"Do you mean the day before yesterday?" said Andreas.

He nodded. "In the morning."

"When did your mother and sister leave for Athens?"

"Three days ago."

"Are you alone?"

He nodded.

Dimitri said to his cop, "Check out the house to see if anyone else is in here."

Tassos walked to the back door and stared out at the beehives. "Didn't Popi's husband tell Yianni that Honeyman's game was to buy honey at the supermarket and resell it to tourists as his own?"

"Yeah," said Andreas.

"Then why all the hives?"

Tassos looked at the boy. "Does your father raise bees?"

The boy gestured no. "My sister is allergic to bee stings. She almost died from a bee sting, so mother made him give up the bees."

"Is that when he started passing off store-bought honey as his own?"

The boy nodded.

"I have to admit, his improvised method for supporting his family earns my grudging respect," said Tassos.

"Don't get too carried away with the admiration," said Dimitri. "Honeyman has been passing off store-bought honey as his own since before he was his son's age. He found that a lot easier way to make money than raising bees." He looked at the boy. "That's the same sympathy pitch his father gives to any tourists who happen to discover they've been hustled and come back looking to complain."

Tassos looked at the boy. "Ah, so the little rotten apple doesn't fall far from the tree." He motioned for Andreas to follow him as he walked to the back door, headed toward the hives. "Come. Let's see what we have here."

"Bees," said Andreas. "And they sting when their rest is disturbed."

"What troubles me," said Tassos, as he approached the first row of beehives, "is that even with the bee shortage in Greece, these hives are worth money, and I can't imagine why he wouldn't sell them, rather than leaving them to rot."

Tassos held his flashlight up to the first hive in the row. He stepped forward and tapped on the hive. Nothing happened. Next, he shook the hive. Nothing happened.

"So far so good," he said.

"They're just waiting to ambush you for taking off the top," said Andreas.

"We shall see. Here, hold the light so I can lift the lid."

Andreas took the light and Tassos lifted off the top.

"No bees."

Andreas stepped forward and shone the light down into the hive. "What's down there? I can't see in."

"I have a buddy who raises bees on Syros. I'll have to remove the feeder section to see into the body of the hive." Tassos pulled and tugged at the top section. "My buddy uses a pry bar to do this." He kept tugging until the feeder came off.

They looked inside.

"What the hell is this?" said Andreas, holding the light.

"It should be filled with frames that hold the honeycombs. Instead we've got a different kind of honey." Tassos reached in and pulled out a piece of ceramic.

"A potsherd." He reached in again and pulled out another piece. He held them both up to the light. "They look to be from the same urn." He took the light from Andreas and stared into the hive. "From my onetime experience in this business, I'd say that this hive contains all the pieces of at least one very old urn." He carefully put the pieces back in the hive and replaced the sections.

Tassos aimed the light at the rows of hives. "If all those hives are stocked like this one, I'd say we've hit upon a serious antiquities-smuggling operation."

"How would that tie into Honeyman arranging for a hit on Yianni and Popi?"

"It may not."

"Another coincidence?" said Andreas.

"I'm just as suspicious as you are of coincidences, but it's a possibility. After all, I haven't seen or heard anything that ties the reporter, Yianni, or Popi to antiquities smuggling. Have you?"

"No." Andreas waved his hand at the hives. "But here we've got this honey seller sitting atop a fortune in illegal antiquities, organizing a frantically ill-conceived hit on two cops looking to find a missing newspaper reporter writing a story about tourism versus preservation. It makes no sense."

"Maybe Honeyman is more than just a honey seller. Perhaps he's a *really* bad guy." Tassos paused. "Possibly even Nikoletta's mysterious guy?"

"Wouldn't that be a fateful twist?"

"Is a fateful twist any different than a coincidence?"

"Let's go back inside and talk to the kid some more. Then I'll answer your question."

"I'll meet you later. I want to check out that shepherd's hut."

"For what?"

"Who knows what other wild coincidence or fateful twist might be lurking in the shadows?"

"Good point," said Andreas, turning back toward the house. *Who knows, indeed?*

Their efforts at getting the boy to talk began with wading through the boy's defensive barrage of "I don't knows" and "I haven't spoken to my father in two days." Once the boy admitted that his father had never left him alone this long before, it didn't take much to convince him his father might be in serious trouble, and by keeping quiet he wasn't helping him.

The boy knew all about the beehives but swore nothing in them was his family's. His father had told him he ran the beehives as a hotel for other people's property—he called the items *guests*—and also provided transfer services for guests requiring a pickup from or delivery to a plane, boat, or other place on the island. He'd transport the *guests* hidden beneath a tarp in the back of his truck. Sometimes the boy helped his father transfer guests from the truck into the hives. At other times he'd help move guests out of the hives, either back to his father's truck or into a stranger's vehicle, but no matter what, his father would smile and say, "Sure beats beekeeping."

The more the boy talked, the more noticeably anxious he became for his father.

"When's your mother coming back from Athens?" asked Andreas.

"I don't know. When she left she said next week."

"Does she know you're alone here?"

"No, I didn't want her to worry."

Andreas nodded. "Is there anyone you can stay with until she's back?"

"My aunt."

Andreas looked at his watch. "It's about a half hour before dawn. We'll call her after sunrise."

"You've been most helpful," said Tassos. "I have just one more question."

The boy tensed.

"How did you know which *guests* went in which hive? And which guests belonged to the strangers who came to collect them?"

The boy pointed at a loose-leaf notebook on a shelf behind the kitchen table. "It's all in there."

Tassos pulled it off the shelf, opened it, and spent a minute quickly looking through it. He smiled. "It sure is. Thanks, son, you can go back to bed now."

The boy hurried out of the room.

"What's in the notebook?" asked Dimitri.

"Separate ledger pages for each hive, recording guests, dates of check-in and checkout, and initials, which I suspect represent who was paying rent on the particular hive."

"Any way to put a name to the initials?" said Andreas.

"Not as far as I can tell."

"Maybe we'll find a key somewhere else in this mess?" said Dimitri.

"I'd like to think so," said Tassos, "but the truth is there's only a half dozen or so sets of initials, so he probably doesn't need to keep a list in order to know the names that go with them."

"I guess we'll just have to find Honeyman and sweat him." Andreas looked at Dimitri. "But until then, and until the Ministry of Culture gets its people here to catalog and take custody of all this, you better keep some cops here. It would be a real embarrassment if any of what we found disappeared while in the hands of the police." He spread out his arms, stretched, and yawned. "Make that a *career-ending embarrassment* for everyone involved."

"It's going to be a busy day," said Dimitri. "And you've got that meeting at 15:00."

Andreas nodded. "Plus Yianni's checking out of the hospital this morning."

"Don't worry about picking him up. I've arranged for an ambulance to take him to your house."

"That's very kind of you."

"It's the least I could do for you after all you've done for me."

"What have we done for you?" asked Andreas.

"I agree that losing any of these artifacts would be a surefire career-ender. But on the other hand, finding them should put us all in line for serious promotions."

"I don't want one," said Andreas.

"Me either," said Tassos. "But I'll tell you what. If you take responsibility for protecting all this stuff and coordinating things with the Culture Ministry so that I can get out of here and back to bed, you can have my promotion."

"Mine, too."

Dimitri smiled. "Deal."

———

Yianni refused to leave the hospital in an ambulance. He said he was fine. Toni told him to get over his macho stubbornness and think of it as a limo or else she was going straight back to Mykonos. They compromised on Yianni sitting up front with the driver.

When they arrived at the house, Lila and Maggie were waiting for them outside the front door. "We had to put the brass band on hold," Lila said, exchanging cheek kisses with Yianni and Toni, "because the men of the house are sleeping."

"They were up until after dawn," said Maggie.

"I know," said Yianni. "I spoke to them on their way back to the house."

Toni poked Yianni in the arm. "This one kept waking up all night to check his messages."

"They promised to message me once the raid was over. How could I sleep?"

"There's a bedroom waiting for you two whenever you'd like it," said Lila.

"I'll take you up on that offer," said Toni. "After two days of dozing on a hospital chair, I could use a bed."

"What time do they plan on leaving for the meeting?" asked Yianni.

"We're leaving at two thirty," said Maggie.

Yianni perked up. "You're going with them?"

"So am I," added Lila. "Each of us read a different notebook, so we all have to be there."

"I read two," said Maggie. "Besides, the restaurant we're meeting at is terrific."

"It'll be like a family outing," said Maggie.

"Well, I guess that settles it," said Yianni.

"Settles what?" asked Toni.

"We're all going."

"No you're—"

Yianni cut Toni off. "Nonnegotiable. As Maggie said, it's a family outing, not a police action. Besides, I'm the only one who's read all of the notebooks and spoken to people named in two of them. I have to be there."

"Your health is more important. And need I remind you again: *You just got out of the hospital.*"

"And now I'm going to take a nap. I'll be fine."

Toni shot him the middle finger and glared. "Fine, but if that meeting puts you back in the hospital, get yourself another nursemaid."

Yianni leaned over and kissed her on the cheek. "Never."

———

Yianni sat in the front passenger seat next to Andreas, while Lila and Toni occupied the far rear seats and Maggie and Tassos had the middle row.

Andreas glanced at Yianni. "Are you comfortable?"

"Yes."

"Are you sure?" asked Maggie.

"*Yes*," said Yianni. "Please stop worrying about me. I'd be more concerned about how we're going to play this. If we're not careful, it could turn into the opening line to a bad joke. 'Three couples walk into a restaurant…'"

"Or a caper movie starring Charlie's Angels and the Three Stooges," quipped Maggie.

"Okay, children, behave," said Andreas. "This is how we're going to play it. I'll introduce each of you and explain why you're there. Yianni, Tassos, and I will do most of the questioning. If any of you have a question or think there's something we missed, don't just blurt it out. Let me know what's on your mind. There may be a method to what you see as our utter stupidity."

"Or there may not be," added Yianni.

"As I can attest," said Tassos.

"Thank you, gentlemen, for demonstrating another point I want us all to keep in mind. The key to this afternoon is *to remain serious.* That means, staying on message. The message being: *We need your help to save a young woman's life.*"

"I guess we're done with denying she's disappeared," said Yianni.

Andreas nodded. "That's a secret I think it's safe to assume is long out of the bag among many Naxians and certainly is with those we'll be meeting. Besides, it's Sunday afternoon, and we only have until noon tomorrow before the whole world knows."

Yianni adjusted himself in his seat. "I know you've been talking among yourselves about the notebooks, so it would be helpful to me if you'd each give a quick rundown on what you found significant in whatever notebook you read. That way, I'll know if I missed something or have something to add to your take."

"Sure," said Andreas. "Maggie, since you read the notebooks covering Nikoletta's interview with the hacker, and with the mayor and hotel association guy, why don't you start?"

One by one they described their respective notebook's high points and what they thought significant. When they'd finished it was close to two thirty, and they were less than a kilometer from the taverna.

"Well done, class, and we're right on time. Now remember what I said: Stay serious, and stay on message."

Chapter Fourteen

Andreas parked behind the taverna at the edge of an olive grove. His party entered single file through an open back door and found their way onto the veranda, where three men and two women sat on the far side of a long table spanning the rear of the space.

Timeliness was not a traditional Greek trait, yet the five they'd come to meet were all there, and from the number of bottles, plates, and cigarette butts in front of them, had been there for quite a while. Andreas took that to mean they'd been meeting among themselves in preparation for their meeting with him. A prudent thing to do.

"Welcome," said Chef from his seat between two men and two women. "Please excuse us for not standing, but we're sort of wedged in here."

"No problem," said Andreas, walking up to a chair directly across from Chef's extended hand. "Sorry we're late."

"You're right on time." They shook hands and Chef turned first to the women seated next to him to Andreas's left and then to the men seated to Andreas's right. "This is Chief Inspector Andreas Kaldis, head of GADA's Special Crimes Unit. He requested this meeting." Chef turned back to Andreas. "Perhaps you'd like to introduce your colleagues to us, some of whom I've already met."

"As very satisfied customers," added Andreas. "My pleasure, but before I do, please allow me to express my gratitude to each of you for taking the time to come here today. We truly need your help, or rather the reporter to whom each of you spoke, Nikoletta Elia, needs your help."

He paused. When no one asked *why* their help was needed, he knew they were indeed already aware that Nikoletta had disappeared.

"I've brought five colleagues with me, because the situation we're facing is serious and urgent. I trust you'll keep what we talk about this afternoon in strict confidence, as the safety of the reporter may depend upon our discretion."

He pointed at Tassos. "This is Tassos Stamatos, chief homicide investigator for the Cyclades. And this is Detective Yianni Kouros, who works with me at GADA." Both men nodded to the group and sat to Andreas's right.

"Maggie," he said, "is my personal assistant at GADA. And Toni is an expert at recovering missing items and persons. Finally," he nodded at his wife, "Lila Vardi specializes in the study of erratic behavior." As they sat to Andreas's left, he made a mental note to compliment Lila and the others for keeping a straight face at her introduction.

Chef introduced those seated on his side of the table: Farmer, Artist, Bookseller, and Shepherd.

Except for Andreas and Chef, no one had said a word since Andreas and his group walked onto the veranda. Nor had anyone asked about Yianni's bandages, which Andreas took to mean they already knew how he'd earned them.

Andreas looked at Farmer. "May I start with you, Miss?"

"It's Ms."

"My apologies. I believe you were the first of this group to speak to the reporter."

"We're not a group. We're each independent of the other, with independent views, principles, and goals."

"I did not mean to suggest otherwise. Did you have the occasion to discuss any of that with the reporter?"

"The reporter is a woman with a name. You should use it."

Andreas forced what he hoped looked like a sincere smile. "I'm actually working quite hard at trying to save Nikoletta's life, so if you'd meet me halfway on this back-and-forth over what you two talked about, it might be of great help in that endeavor."

"Are you suggesting I'm not cooperating?"

"Oh, shut the fuck up, already, and answer the man's question," growled Artist. "This isn't an equal rights confrontation; it's an attempt to save a sister's life. So stuff the bullshit and get to what you talked about with her."

"Go to hell," said Farmer.

This was not working out as Andreas had hoped. "Uh, folks, could we try kickstarting this again? Please remember why we're here." He stared straight at Farmer.

She stared back. "Nikoletta wanted to know how I felt about the island's expanding tourism. I said I wasn't against it as long as it was measured and in keeping with the environment. She told me that was a wonderful phrase to crochet on a pillow, but what did I *really* think?"

Andreas nodded and said nothing.

"That's when I told Nikoletta that strangers were buying up some of our finest virgin beachfront property in areas where development was forbidden."

"What sorts of strangers?" said Andreas.

"I don't know. They're using foreign companies."

"How do you know this?"

"I come from an old Naxian family with relatives everywhere, and many with beachfront property were approached."

"Why do you think strangers are trying to buy up that kind of property?"

"Because they see the writing on the wall. Naxos is gaining in popularity, and they're betting that sometime soon mounting pressure for development will make the government ease up on restrictions."

"Let's hope that day never comes," said Lila.

Andreas glanced at Lila, and she looked back at him.

Farmer smiled at Lila. "Exactly. Stand your ground."

Andreas swallowed. "What else did you and Nikoletta talk about?"

"That's about it."

"Did you give her the names of those buying or attempting to buy the properties?"

"She asked, but I said I didn't remember."

Andreas paused to compose his next question. "Does that mean you remember now?"

She spread her hands out in front of her. "Is it important?"

"It might help save her life."

"How?" asked Bookseller.

"If I knew that," said Andreas, "I wouldn't be asking for the names."

"But naming names is frowned upon on this island."

"Snitching is frowned upon just about everywhere," added Chef.

"In some of our villages it can lead to a vendetta," said Shepherd.

Andreas held up his hands. "From the way everyone's reacting, am I correct that all of you know of this effort to buy up properties?"

At first no one responded. Then, one by one, each nodded yes.

"So, how many different buyers are we talking about?"

Silence.

"Come on, at least tell me that."

Bookseller raised his hand. "I can't say for sure, but my father's a lawyer and his clients have received offers for their property from a lot of different foreign companies."

Andreas suppressed a sigh at the continued vagueness.

"But they all had one thing in common."

"What's that?"

"The same local approached each of them on behalf of a different foreign company."

Andreas leaned in toward Bookseller. "Could you please give me that person's name?"

Bookseller looked at his colleagues, but none reacted.

"I assume from their silence that no one disagrees with your telling me."

"I don't know his full name, but everyone calls him Honeyman."

Andreas hoped his poker face had held up as he turned to Farmer. "Is that the name you couldn't remember for the one who approached your relatives?"

"Yes, Spyros the Honeyman. That's the one." She smiled.

"Why are you smiling?"

"All the locals know he's a fast-talking con man, and they'll have nothing to do with him. Which means whoever's buying isn't local. No Naxian would ever use him as their intermediary."

Andreas paused. "Did Nikoletta ask all of you what you knew about people trying to buy and develop beachfront property?"

All nodded yes.

Why then, Andreas wondered, *had not a word about any of this appeared in Nikoletta's notebooks?*

Where to go next with the questioning? And, more to the point, what else could Nikoletta have not recorded from her interviews?

"Chief?" said Shepherd.

"Yes, sir."

"I'm a close friend of Popi's husband."

"Yes, I know."

"He told me what happened, and that got me to thinking about the really bad guys on this island. There's the one the reporter wrote about and the ones who tried to kill Popi and you." He nodded at Yianni.

Yianni nodded back.

"It's said bad things come in threes. Well, I have a third for you, Petros Zagorianos."

Yianni raised an eyebrow. "Do you mean Peter Zagori? The tourist who died in a fall from Grotta?"

"Yes, but he's no tourist. He's from a village close to mine. He was a bad kid and a worse adult. He went to America, changed his name, and became a hired killer. His family actually bragged about it. It's that kind of family."

"Are you saying everybody knows he's a hired killer?" said Andreas.

"No, just those from his village and some in a neighboring village that shares its Cretan roots."

"May I ask the name of Zagori's village?"

"Filoti."

Andreas stared at him. "I think I know the place. We spent most of last night there." *With Honeyman's beehives.*

———

The rest of the afternoon was interesting and, when food started coming out of the kitchen, tasty as well, but Andreas's thoughts focused on Honeyman. In less than twenty-four hours of poking into the background of this seemingly simple local grifter, Spyros had been exposed as central to a high-end antiquities-smuggling operation, the island's front man for a host of clandestine real estate ventures and a broker for contract killings. *How could an experienced investigative reporter like Nikoletta not have discovered at least some of those same things?* Perhaps she had, possibly much more. All of which kept leading Andreas back to the same question. *Why didn't she put any of this into her notebooks?*

Andreas excused himself from the table and went back to the SUV. From there he called Dimitri and asked him for the Athens address of Honeyman's wife and daughter. If Honeyman was there, they'd arrest him on the spot. If not, they'd keep an eye on his family until they found him. Attempted cop killers earned that kind of attention. Besides, characters this dirty could be involved in anything, and with Honeyman's fellow villager and contract killer Peter Zagori's body turning up at the scene of Nikoletta's disappearance, Andreas had no doubt Honeyman was somehow tied into whatever happened to the reporter.

By the time he returned to the taverna, Andreas had heard back from Dimitri with the address and passed it along, together with instructions, to the GADA officers he wanted to make the arrest. All they needed now was luck. Inside, the meeting was breaking up. Andreas joined in thanking everyone for coming and offered his help should the day ever come that one of them might need it.

Artist hugged Lila. "Please do stop by my studio in Halki. I'd love to introduce you to some of the other board members of our environmental organization. I sense we share the same sensibilities."

"That's very flattering," smiled Lila.

"And she's speaking for both of us," said Farmer.

"You're on the same board?" said Andreas.

"Of course, why else would I let her speak to me the way she does? It livens up our meetings."

"Don't believe it. She's a royal pain in the ass," said Artist, taking Farmer by the arm and tugging her toward the door.

Lila smiled. "It still will be my pleasure."

"I hope we helped," said Bookseller.

"You certainly did. Thank you," said Andreas.

"I want you to catch the bastards who did this," Shepherd told Yianni.

"You can count on it, if only for Popi's sake."

Shepherd shook Yianni's hand, nodded to Andreas, bowed to the women, and followed Bookseller out the door.

Andreas turned to Chef and smiled. "I really owe you a big-time favor. We couldn't have accomplished this without you."

"It was the right thing to do. You were vouched for by a man we all respect, and we agreed before you got here that since we'd shown up, we had to follow through and do what we could to help, even if some of us were less than thrilled at the notion of helping the police."

"Understood," said Andreas. "But I meant what I said: If there ever comes a day when you need me for anything, don't hesitate to ask."

"Well, now that you mention it, there is one thing."

So soon? Andreas wondered what was coming.

Chef handed a paper to Andreas. "You can pay the lunch bill."

———

Once in the SUV and headed back to the house, Andreas brought Tassos and Yianni up to speed on his efforts to track down Honeyman.

"I'm sort of getting used to driving this road," said Andreas, glancing off to his left.

"Too bad you don't get to see the scenery," said Lila. "It's amazing just watching the shadows play off against the hills and valleys. So many shades of color."

"My favorite part," said Toni, "is that elevated stretch of road bound by a long line of eucalyptus trees framing everything between us and the sea."

"My favorite part is the food," said Tassos.

"That explains why you were so quiet during our meeting," said Andreas.

"I thought you handled it quite well and saw no reason to speak."

"That generally means we both missed something."

"Speaking of missing something…" said Yianni.

"What's that?" asked Andreas.

"With all these folks talking to Nikoletta about foreign efforts to buy up beachfront property, why's there no mention of any of that in her notebooks?"

"That bothers me too," said Andreas.

"What do you mean?" asked Toni.

"Just that," said Yianni. "There's not a word about any of that in her notebooks."

"That can't be true," said Toni, leaning forward.

"I've read them all and, believe me, there's no mention."

Toni shook her head. "While Andreas was outside and the rest of you were chatting among yourselves, I was talking to Artist and Farmer. Artist said she noticed that none of us was taking notes. I said I hadn't noticed. She asked me if we were recording the meeting, and I said not that I knew of. She said that was good, because she wouldn't want what she'd said to Farmer recorded on audio for posterity. All of us laughed. That's when Farmer said how impressed she was at the reporter's thoroughness as a note-taker, taking down almost every word."

"We already knew that," said Yianni.

Toni bristled. "Well, then you probably already know this too, *Detective*. The artist said Nikoletta was not only thorough but organized. She brought two notebooks with her, and when she started asking questions about the efforts to buy up property, she switched to the second notebook. When she'd finished asking those questions, she went back to her first notebook. And while Artist was telling me all of that, *Detective*, Farmer was nodding in agreement."

"*Another notebook?*" said Andreas.

"I never saw a sixth notebook," said Yianni. "Where the hell could it be?"

"I don't know," said Andreas, "but I'm going to have Dimitri leave us a car at the house. Tassos and I will use that one and leave the SUV for the rest of you."

"Hey, what about me?" said an irritated Yianni.

"You've done enough for your first day out of the hospital. Rest up, because tomorrow could be D-day for us all."

"Where are you two planning on going?" said Maggie. "Tassos isn't exactly up to storming beachheads."

"Don't know yet, but the logical place to start looking for the missing notebook is back at Nikoletta's hotel."

"A *sixth* notebook," said Yianni. "I can't believe it."

"Believe it, Detective." Toni leaned across the middle seat and patted him on the head. "Whether or not you apologize."

———

The battered blue-and-white police cruiser had seen better days, but Andreas was happy to have it. The dents and scrapes gave it the sort of character that made other drivers hang back out of fear that they might be its next victim.

"So, what do you think happened to the sixth notebook?"

Tassos looked out the passenger side window. "The obvious answer is someone took it from her hotel room."

"Before or after she disappeared?"

"Could be either, though if after, the night security guy is the chief suspect."

"Dimitri's asking the hotel owner to bring him in early so we can question him."

"What if no one took it?"

Andreas slowed down to allow a half dozen hobbled goats to cross the road. "Then Nikoletta must have done something with it."

"Like what?"

"Hidden it, lost it, given it away, taken it with her, or destroyed it. If we find it, or find her, we might find out."

"I wonder what's in it?"

"Don't we all."

Ten minutes later, Andreas pulled up in front of Nikoletta's hotel. "Time to see where this new twist takes us."

"Speaking of twists, I already feel like a pretzel. This damned seat doesn't go back."

Andreas looked back and laughed. "It will if you move the case of water from behind it."

"Son of a bitch," said Tassos, wedging his way out of the seat.

"I'm sure Dimitri put it there because he thought we might need the water."

Tassos opened the rear door and lifted the case onto the back seat. "Well, it's enough to last us for a week. I hope he doesn't think we'll be driving this piece of crap for that long."

"Chief Inspector Kaldis?"

Andreas turned to see a tall, slim man standing outside the hotel entrance. "Yes?"

"I'm the owner of the hotel. Welcome."

The three men shook hands.

"We'd like to speak to your night man, Anargyros."

"I tried to get him to come in earlier, but he can't make it before eleven."

"Damn," said Andreas.

"Perhaps there's something I can help you with? Come, let's go into my office."

As they walked by reception, a dark-haired, perky young Greek woman smiled. "Hi."

Tassos and Andreas smiled back.

Once inside his office and seated around his desk, the owner said, "So, what can I do to help you?"

"How long have you known Anargyros?"

"Many years."

"Do you trust him?"

"If I didn't, he wouldn't be working here."

"I understand he has a drug problem."

"*Had.* He's worked hard at beating it."

"Does he have access to your guest rooms?" said Tassos.

"He knows where the keys are, so I guess the answer is yes."

"Who else has access to those keys?" said Andreas.

"Theoretically anyone."

"How's that?" said Tassos.

"When guests go out of the hotel they're required to leave their keys with us, and we place them on top of the reception desk for them to pick up on their return."

Andreas leaned forward. "So, after she left the hotel at four that morning, anyone could have picked up her key and gotten into her room, assuming they got past Anargyros?"

"As a matter of fact, not that night. When Nikoletta ran out, she took her key with her. We had to have a new one made."

Andreas slouched back in his chair. "Damn."

"What are you looking for? If you told me, perhaps I could be of better assistance."

"We think someone took something from her room."

"What sort of thing?"

"A notebook," said Tassos.

"Let's speak to my receptionist. If anyone on the hotel staff knew what happened to it, she would." He picked up his phone. "Marine, could you please come in for a moment."

Five seconds later the perky woman stepped into the room. "Yes, sir?"

"These gentlemen are with the police, and they are looking for a notebook that belonged to Nikoletta Elia."

"What sort of notebook?"

"The size we used in school," said Tassos.

"Way back in the days before computers," smiled Andreas.

"About this size?" said Marine, making a shape with her hands.

"Yes."

"No, I never saw a notebook."

Andreas exhaled. "Well, thanks anyway."

"But she did ask me to send off a package for her of about that size."

Andreas and Tassos sat up in their chairs.

"When?" asked Andreas.

"A day or two before she disappeared."

"She disappeared early Thursday morning," said Andreas.

Marine thought for a moment. "She gave me the package on Tuesday afternoon. Said it had to get to Athens right away."

"And you mailed it?" said Tassos.

"No, she wanted it sent by air courier that evening, no matter what the cost."

"Where did she send it?"

"I'll have to check my calendar. That's where I keep a record of such things."

The owner motioned for her to get it.

"You run a tight ship," said Andreas.

"We try."

Marine returned with a large calendar. "Let's see. Last Tuesday. Oh, here it is."

She put the calendar down on the desk between the two policemen and pointed with her finger to an entry. "That's the name and address."

Tassos read the name out loud. "Giorgos Pappas."

Andreas's jaw tightened. "Nikoletta's editor."

Chapter Fifteen

"Pappas? It's Kaldis here."

"Have you found Nikoletta?"

"Not yet."

"Then why are you calling me? I don't need stroking."

"What you need is a hard kick in the ass, but I'd rather deliver that to you in person."

"What—

"Just shut up and listen. In your moments of deep concern over the fate of your reporter, did you happen to forget to tell me a few things?"

"What *things*?"

"Let me be clear about this, Giorgos. From the way you're reacting, you might want to consider hiring a lawyer before getting yourself into deeper trouble than you're already in."

"Is that a threat?"

"If you're guilty of what I have in mind, you'd better believe it is."

"Would you mind telling me what you're talking about?"

"Let's start with that notebook you neglected to tell me about."

"What notebook?"

Andreas said nothing.

"I said what note—Wait, are you talking about the one Nikoletta sent me a couple of days before she disappeared?"

"Brilliant. Amazing how you figured that out all on your own."

"Just hold on a minute. It never entered my mind that it might be relevant to her disappearance."

"Bullshit."

"Like hell it is."

"Then convince me why you didn't think it relevant."

"Fine!" he yelled. "When Nikoletta's interview story broke, I wanted her back in Athens to work on our planned follow-up series, but she insisted she needed more time to finish her tourism piece. I told her to forget about it and get her ass back to Athens. Frankly, I thought she was looking for a way to extend her stay on Naxos at the paper's expense. Underpaid reporters have been known to do that sort of thing."

"You're not convincing me."

"I agreed to give her more time, but then my publisher started busting my balls to get her back in the office at work on the series. He'd never liked the tourism piece, said death and disaster sold newspapers. I told her the only way she could stay on Naxos was if she gave me something to convince our publisher that her time spent there was worthwhile. She said she couldn't divulge her sources on the tourism piece but that she'd come across something that might just do the trick. She learned about a local character who has a hand in just about every hustle on the island. He's a small-time grifter, and his story wasn't part of her tourism piece, but it's the sort of roguish tale people like to read. I thought it might appeal to our publisher. I told her to get me what she had right away, and she promised to send her notes to me by courier."

Andreas had a pretty good idea of the answer to his next question. "And the rogue's name is?"

"Unknown. She just called him Honeyman."

"How could you possibly have thought none of this might be relevant to her disappearance?"

"If I had, I'd have told you."

"Did she send you her notebook, then?"

"I received a package from her late that afternoon, just as I was heading off to a dinner party with my wife."

"Did you read her notes?"

"No, I forwarded them on to my publisher. I wasn't about to get in the middle of a brouhaha between him and Nikoletta. I'd let him make the call."

"What did he say after he read them?"

"I don't know if he ever did read them. She disappeared and all we've focused upon since then is finding her, not her stories."

"Do you have a copy of the notebook?"

"No, like I said, it was late and I was running out of the office so I just routed it on to my publisher."

"Do you have his number?"

"Of course, but why do you want to contact him?"

"To find out what he did with the notebook—and to read it."

"Good luck with that."

"What do you mean?"

"He's big on protecting journalists' sources, and if Nikoletta's notebook could possibly expose her sources, he's not going to agree to turn it over without her consent."

"A rather interesting dilemma, isn't it? She may die because he wants her consent to turn over what could possibly save her. And you guys complain about how fucked-up the government is." Andreas struggled to control the outrage in his voice.

Andreas heard Pappas breathe in and exhale. "You can try, and I hope you convince him." He gave Andreas the number. "Good luck."

Andreas hung up without saying goodbye. He looked at Tassos sitting next to him in the police car. "Did you hear that bullshit?"

"Somebody is either very stupid or thinks we're very stupid." Tassos shook his head. "Pappas harangues you to find his allegedly kidnapped reporter, yet never bothers to tell you that two days before she disappeared he received a notebook from her containing her notes on a story involving a *rogue* from the same island on which she's gone missing."

"Hard to believe what he said is true. So hard, in fact, that it could get one to thinking it must be true."

"I consider the part about his publisher busting his balls to be a particularly novel way of attempting to justify withholding evidence."

"Let's see what his publisher has to say." Andreas dialed the number Pappas had given him. The call went into voicemail. Andreas identified himself and asked that he please call him back immediately, as it concerned his missing reporter.

"When do you think you'll hear back from him?"

"That depends on whether Pappas gets to him first. Curiosity should have him calling me right back, but in this instance, maybe not."

"What do you think the chances are that this whole thing's been staged to sell newspapers?"

"But for the attempted hit on Yianni and Popi, I'd have seriously considered that possibility. I don't see that now."

"So, what's next?"

"We wait"

"For what?"

"I don't know."

———

Andreas drove down to Chora's harbor and, after searching unsuccessfully for a legal parking space, parked in a spot marked NO PARKING ANYTIME.

"Ah, the advantage of driving a blue-and-white," said Tassos.

"Why not? We're on official business waiting for the telephone call that could break our case wide open."

"This place looks good," said Tassos, steering him into a taverna close by the harborside piazza.

They sat where they could watch the children at play in the square, darting every which way on their bikes, scooters, and skateboards.

"Watching kids play always makes me miss my own."

"You'll be back with them soon enough," said Tassos.

"Doesn't it amaze you how when children get to play on their own, away from grownups, it looks like sheer chaos, yet they somehow manage to adhere to an overriding pattern of order that keeps their play from ending in disaster? What do you think it is? Some instinctive thing, like birds knowing how to fly in formation?"

"Whatever it is, it's not a lasting influence, because by the time they're fully grown they've learned it's every man for himself."

"You're one hell of a cynic."

"As if you're not."

Andreas shook his head from side to side. "Just enjoy the moment."

Ring, ring.

"So much for the moment."

"This could be the call we're waiting for." Andreas pulled his phone out of his pocket. "It's Dimitri." He held the phone so Tassos could hear.

"Hi, what's up?"

"We found Honeyman."

"Terrific, where is he?"

"Not sure right now, but when my cops found him he was facedown at the bottom of an abandoned quarry, with one end of a rope tied around his neck and the other end tied to a slab of marble."

"Oh, shit." *So he never made it off Naxos.*

"It's not clear yet when he died, but hikers saw him late this afternoon. As far as we can tell, he and his slab were tossed off the top of the quarry a hundred meters or so above where they found him."

"What are the chances it's a suicide?" said Andreas.

"I can think of a lot less terrifying ways than a header off the top of a cliff with your neck lashed to a slab of marble. Besides, his hands were tied behind his back."

"Well, at least this one wasn't staged to look like an accident."

"Is that good or bad?" said Tassos. "It could mean that whoever's behind this is now desperate enough to use amateurs to eliminate loose ends."

"The question is, was our mastermind desperate enough to step out of the shadows in order to take out Honeyman?" Andreas paused. "Hmm...if someone from Naxos killed Honeyman, what do you think the chances are that Honeyman knew who killed him?"

"Pretty good," said Dimitri. "It could have been the same guys he'd sent after Yianni and Popi. Wouldn't that be poetic justice?"

"If they're locals known to Honeyman, would they be known to you too?" asked Andreas.

"If they're the blunt, slash-and-burn sort of bad guys who bounce in and out of prison and not some sophisticated pro like Nikoletta's, I'd say the chances are pretty good."

"Well, then, to quote one of my favorite movies, I think it's time we rounded up *the usual suspects.*"

———

With an assist from GPS and a call to Dimitri, Andreas and Tassos found their way back to Honeyman's house. It was close to midnight, but lights were on inside the house, and as the car rocked its way along the old donkey path, a uniformed cop stepped out of the house, trained a light on their car, and waved for them to park next to another marked cruiser.

Once inside, the cop told them it was his partner's turn to keep an eye on the beehives while he watched the empty house. He complained about how this extended guard duty detail was already straining the Filoti Police station's ability to provide normal coverage to large areas of the island. Andreas assured him that the Ministry of Culture had promised to take possession of the items in the beehives on Monday.

The cop looked at his watch and pointed out that, as of two minutes ago, it was Monday.

Andreas smiled and told him to go hang out with his partner if he wanted to, because he and Tassos had some reading to do.

Andreas took Honeyman's ledger from its shelf in the kitchen and set it on the table. He carefully read through the ledger sheets, jotting down each set of initials, hoping to find a clue to someone's identity. He found six sets of initials—JSS, GTS, AKS, KSM, RIM, and BZ—but no clues or key to the abbreviations. A handful of beehives had apparently been hiding treasures for almost two and a half decades. Over ensuing years, other beehives came online, until every beehive had replaced its bees with antiquities. It looked like Honeyman had started off small and expanded his business significantly. A regular entrepreneur.

Andreas shook his head. "The same initials listed twenty-five years ago are listed in the new entries."

"I've heard that honey prolongs life."

Andreas waved off Tassos's attempt at humor. "Honeyman's clients didn't just show up one day and say, 'Hi, I have pilfered antiquities I'd like for you to hide in your beehives.' I'd bet my pension they've been involved in antiquities trafficking for a lot longer than Honeyman's run his business."

"Your pension? That's not much of a bet, but I still wouldn't take it."

"If I'm right, then there must be others who worked with Honeyman's clients before they came to him, which means there could be people out there who know the names tied to those initials. We just have to figure out how to find them."

"Assuming they're still alive." Tassos yawned.

"Getting a bit tired, are we?"

"It's been a long day."

"I'm feeling it myself. I must be getting older."

"With every passing day. My gardening keeps me young. That and chasing bad guys."

"Perhaps I should become a farmer," said Andreas.

"You could do worse, and no better place to learn than Naxos."

Andreas sat up in the chair. "That old farmer in Siphones. The one you know. He was with his son and grandson the afternoon Yianni and Popi were attacked."

"He's still perky enough to teach you a few things, I guess." Tassos yawned again.

Andreas smacked his hand on the table. "Stop that before you get *me* to yawning. If anyone knows who belongs to these initials, it's the grandfather. You told me he's been involved in antiquities smuggling on Naxos since before the Junta."

"But didn't his son say he's senile?"

"That's a convenient way to keep people from bothering him, but it doesn't mean he *is*. I think Yianni, you, and I better pay him a visit first thing in the morning."

"For a farmer, that's dawn."

"Okay, let's say nine."

"But that doesn't give us much time if the newspaper's going public with the story at noon. If that happens, we'll go from the few on Naxos who are aware and the many here who suspect she's disappeared, to all of Greece knowing she's vanished and spook the kidnapper for sure."

"Maybe not. I plan on having a talk with Pappas first thing in the morning." Andreas smiled. "Which to this cop means dawn."

———

"Hello." The sleepy voice came through the phone with a mix of confusion, anxiety, and budding rage.

"Good morning, Giorgos. Wakey, wakey, today's a big day."

"*Kaldis?* Have you gone mad? Do you know what time it is?"

"Of course I do. It's time for you to get your ass out of bed and convince your publisher to extend his noon deadline until midnight."

"You *are* mad. How the hell do you expect me to do that?"

"I know what I'd have told him if he'd bothered to return any of the many messages I left for him."

"And what would that be?"

"Simple. If he sticks to his noon deadline and tells the world Nikoletta has disappeared, I'll call a press conference to announce that your distinguished publisher is in possession of documents that could help the police locate his missing reporter but refuses to turn them over."

"With his power and connections, you wouldn't dare."

"Try me."

"Do you have any idea who you're dealing with?"

"The question is, does he?"

"You'll be making an enemy for life."

"Tell him to get in line." Andreas paused. "Are you done yet with this who-has-a-bigger-one ping-pong match?"

Pappas cleared his throat. "What is it you really want?"

"Like I said, I want him to hold off until midnight. Of course, if he's dead set on going ahead at noon, he could outmaneuver me by simply turning over the sixth notebook, but I don't think either of us believes he'll do that. Do we?"

"I've no idea what he'll do." Pappas paused. "Just so you know, I told him about our last conversation and urged him to cooperate, but he said his commitment to preserving his reporter's sources is sacrosanct."

"As is my commitment to preserving his reporter's *life*. Have a nice day."

Andreas hung up and looked at Tassos. "How did I do?"

"Like someone who went out of his way to turn his and his family's past, present, and future into the most-favored targets of the most powerful publishing family in Greece."

Andreas smiled. "Good, then he got the message."

"When are we leaving for Siphones?"

"Let's give Yianni another hour of sleep. He needs the rest, and we need him with us to make the introductions."

"Great, then there's time for breakfast."

"Is that all you care about?"

"No. Since Maggie put me on this strict diet, I think of other things."

"Like what?"

"Lunch."

Andreas smacked his forehead and sighed. "Why do I keep feeding you these straight lines?"

"Hey, it's a skill."

Ring, ring.

"Who the hell would be calling me at this hour?"

"Now you sound like Pappas. Maybe it *is* Pappas?"

Andreas looked at the screen, gestured no, and put the call on speakerphone. "Hi, Dimitri, what's up?"

"Obviously, you are. I was prepared to leave you a message."

"The early bird gets the worm and all that."

"Well, it seems likely there's something much larger than a worm we're looking for."

"That sounds ominous."

"Because it is. The preliminary autopsy's in on Honeyman. He died before hitting the bottom."

"Mercifully, I hope."

"A bullet to the head."

"It beats flying wide-awake off the top of a cliff wearing a rope necktie anchored to a slab of marble," said Tassos.

"Why do I sense you're just getting to the *ominous* part?" said Andreas.

"Last night we began rounding up the usual suspects, as you called them. A couple of hours ago, we found two ripe ones in a stolen car down behind the airport. Each with a bullet through his head."

"Don't tell me. The bullets match the one pulled out of Honeyman," said Andreas.

"Too soon to tell, but since it looks as if they've been dead for about as long as Honeyman, I wouldn't be surprised if they match."

"I'd be surprised if they don't," said Tassos. "Sounds like whoever got rid of Honeyman also took out the other two."

"One of the victims was at the top of our list of likely drivers in the attack on Popi and Yianni."

Andreas bit at his lower lip. "So, what do we have here? A sophisticated killer who kills Honeyman and then hunts down the other two? Or an amateur who somehow knew the two well enough to lure them to a convenient place for eliminating them as potential witnesses?"

"Or some combination thereof," said Tassos. "My guess is it's closer to your amateur scenario, because with the police hunting for them, it's hard to imagine how their killer would have been able to find them if they didn't want him to."

"But couldn't Nikoletta's computer guy have found them?" said Dimitri.

"Unless he's wired into the local bad-guy network, somehow used his skills to get a GPS reading on them, or has superhuman powers, I don't see how he could," said Andreas. "Besides, none of this bears the mark of a master at work."

"Perhaps he's just trying to confuse us by appearing sloppy," said Dimitri.

"I don't see it that way," said Andreas. "I'm into believing there's a new player involved. But I'm not sure what team he's playing for."

"What's that supposed to mean?" asked Tassos.

"Are these killings because of what *else* Nikoletta might write about her hacker? Or did her activist research trip a different alarm among some very bad people?"

"Or are they dead because of something completely unrelated to anything we know or imagine?" said Tassos.

"That too," said Andreas, drawing in and letting out a deep breath. "But since we'll never know if it's something unknown until we've eliminated the known, I say we go with what's tied to the highest body count. Namely, Honeyman. More specifically, his involvement in antiquities smuggling and development-project buyouts."

"In other words, it's off to Siphones," said Tassos.

"Yes."

"Right after breakfast?"

Andreas nodded. "But be sure to make it a big one. It's shaping up to be a long day."

Chapter Sixteen

By the time Toni, Lila, and Maggie sat down to breakfast, the men had left.

Lila picked up her coffee cup. "Well, we've got a car and the day all to ourselves. What would you like to do?"

"I'd like to see more of the island," said Toni.

"Me too," said Maggie.

"Sounds good to me." Lila took a sip. "We could stop by and say hello to the women we met yesterday."

"They're an interesting pair," said Toni. "The farmer not only grows olives but runs a museum dedicated to the history of olive-growing in Eggares. And then there's the artist's gallery in Halki."

"Both are lovely villages," said Lila, "and I'm sure they'll have suggestions on what else we should see."

Maggie reached for a croissant. "What time do you want to leave?"

"In about an hour," said Lila.

"Finally," said Maggie with a smile. "A day away from intrigues and mystery."

Toni raised her cup. "And hospital rooms."

———

Andreas, Tassos, and Yianni made it to Siphones by eight thirty a.m. They stood on the side of the road above the abandoned village and saw no one.

"The broken plaque with the mysterious inscription is up there." Yianni pointed to the right.

"No one's here yet, so we might as well take a look at it," said Andreas, walking toward the marble cross. "Who knows? Maybe we'll be struck with some brilliant insight that solves Popi's mystery and makes her day."

Looking at the cross, Andreas said, "So, where's the plaque?"

Yianni pointed to broken pieces of marble in the grass by the base of the cross. "I've written it all down in my notebook."

Andreas crouched and read the inscription aloud:

"TRIBUTE DEDICATION TO SAINT CYPRIAN.
OH SAINT MIRACLE WORKER
I WILL NEVER CEASE TO THINK
OF THE MANY MIRACLES YOU'VE DONE FOR US
FAITH IS TAKING ROOT IN MY HEART
EXHILARATION OVERFLOWS
AS DOES MY GRATITUDE TO YOU
TO THE WALKER PASSING BY
HE MAY BRING FAITH THAT SAVES US
FROM EVERY CALAMITY
FROM CHRIST YOU TOOK YOUR JOY
TO HEAL THE WOUNDS FROM THE DEMONS
AND FROM THEIR WORKS OF MAGIC
PUT ON THE FAITHFUL WHO CALL ON YOU
TO UNBIND ALL THOSE WITH LOVE
WITH A FAITH THAT IS VAST."

"Sure sounds mysterious to me," said Tassos. "I know some pray to Saint Cyprian to break curses and spells, if you go in for that sort of thing, but you have to read an extremely long prayer to invoke his assistance."

"I don't have a clue to what it means," said Andreas.

"Maybe the grandfather knows something about it," said Yianni.

"I've more important questions to ask him," said Andreas.

"Speak of the devil," said Yianni. "Look who's pulling up."

"Let's hope not," said Tassos, crossing himself.

A sun-bleached maroon Toyota pickup stopped by the side of the road across from their police car. The father got out the driver side, the grandfather the passenger side. One grabbed a hoe from the bed of the pickup, the other a shovel, and together they walked away from the cops alongside a stretch of goat-wire fencing strung parallel to the road.

"I wonder where the boy is," said Andreas.

"I wonder where they're going," said Yianni. "The way into the village is through a culvert, on the other side of the road."

The two men stopped, pulled open a narrow gate made of the same fencing, and stepped onto a set of stone steps mounted nearly invisibly up against a retaining wall made of the same stone.

"Son of a bitch," said Yianni. "When I asked the father if there was another way back onto the road he didn't tell me about the steps."

"You're such a trusting soul," said Tassos, making for the steps.

Yianni called out for the two farmers to wait for them. By the time they'd caught up, the grandfather had started working his hoe on a patch of unplanted soil.

"Didn't expect to see you again, Detective," said the father.

"I missed exploring culverts, Junior."

Junior grinned.

"This is my boss, Chief Inspector Andreas Kaldis, head of GADA's Special Crimes Unit and Chief Homicide Investigator for the Cyclades Tassos Stamatos."

Junior's grin abruptly faded.

"We're here because we don't think you told me the whole truth."

Junior clenched the shovel tightly in his hands. "Are you calling me a liar?"

"Don't bother to run that routine past me again. And in case you're wondering about these bandages I'm wearing, right after the last time we spoke, somebody tried to kill me and your hunting buddy's wife, Popi." Yianni pointed to the shovel. "Nothing would give me greater joy than for you to try using that on me. It would answer a lot of questions, plus give me the opportunity to vent a whole lot of pent-up rage."

"I had nothing to do with what happened to you or Popi."

"Just drop the fucking shovel."

Junior froze for an instant, then dropped the shovel.

"A wise decision," said Andreas. "No one is accusing you or anyone in your family of having anything to do with what happened the other day, but we do have some questions for your father."

"My father knows nothing about any of this. As I told him," pointing at Yianni, "he's not all there."

"Well, we still have questions for him," said Andreas.

"Klefteraki, how are you, my friend?" Tassos yelled out to the grandfather.

The father whirled to face Tassos. "Why did you call him that?"

"We all did back in the day. It was his nickname."

"I haven't heard him called that in forty years."

"Little Thief may not sound like a compliment, but that was his nickname when we first met. If we're trying to jog his memory, why not try a blast from the past?"

Junior shut his eyes, shook his head, and waved toward his father. "Okay, go ahead and try, but don't upset him."

Tassos walked over to the grandfather. "Klefteraki, it's Tassos. We worked together down by Alyko on that Junta hotel project. You did digging; I did guarding."

The grandfather looked up and studied Tassos's face. "I don't remember you."

"I was the one you always told, 'Keep your nose out of other people's business.'"

The grandfather kept staring at Tassos's face, then suddenly smiled. "I remember you. But you were so thin and good-looking then."

Andreas suppressed a laugh. Yianni wasn't as successful, and the grandfather shot him a stern look. "You need to show more respect to your elders, young man."

"Don't mind him," said Tassos.

"I apologize, sir."

"That's better." The grandfather turned back to Tassos. "So what can I do for you...uh..."

"Tassos."

"Sorry, I have such trouble with names these days."

"I do too. But that's sort of what I'm hoping you can help me with."

"Names?"

"Yes."

"From back then?"

"Yes."

"That's a long time ago."

"I know, but I think these names were important to you then."

He leaned against his hoe. "What are the names?"

"That's what I need from *you*. All *I* have are initials."

"Oh, my, I don't know how I'll possibly remember names from initials."

"Well, let's try. They're JSS, GTS, AKS, KSM, RIM, and BZ."

The grandfather's eyes appeared to glaze over. He closed and opened them three times. "Please, say them to me again."

He squinted and began nodding in concentration as Tassos repeated the initials.

He shook his head. "I'm sorry. I recognize nothing."

"Excuse me," interrupted Yianni. "Perhaps I can help, sir." He pulled his notebook out from his pocket and showed a page to the grandfather. "Can you tell me who wrote this?"

The grandfather leaned in close to the paper and carefully mouthed the words. His face lit up. "Yes, it was Giannis Nikiforou Konstantakis, a grocer up in Koronos."

He paused to swallow. "His mother, Sofia, was from here, and she twice saved him from the devil. He erected the plaque to honor her deep faith in God…"

He paused, shut his eyes, and gently rocked from side to side. "And her answered prayers to Saint Cyprian that he use his magic powers to save her son from the devil and bring joy back to his life."

"I thought the plaque had to do with the reason everyone left the village," said Junior.

"Yeah, like ghosts or disease," said Yianni.

"Ridiculous," said the grandfather. "People abandoned our village for the same reason as people abandoned other villages."

He spoke with a touch of newfound, flinty-eyed determination. "The same work that earned them five drachmas in our village would earn them fifty drachmas in Chora or Athens. And after the war, people wanted education for their children, but we had no school here. That meant a life of hard labor for the sons, and if our daughters were lucky, landing a job as a housekeeper in Athens. They all wanted better lives and more modern things. Education was the only way, so they moved. Even my grandson is looking for better opportunities."

Junior smiled. "He's off this morning on a college interview."

Yianni smiled and slapped him on the back. "Congratulations, you must be very proud."

Junior kept smiling. "We are, thank you."

"Who broke the plaque?" said Andreas.

"I can answer that," said Junior. "Some idiot in a rental car backed into it."

"So," said Yianni, "now that we've resolved that mystery, perhaps you can help us with this one." Yianni showed him a page from his notebook listing the six sets of initials.

The grandfather stared at the page for a moment, then waggled a finger in the air. "I've seen these initials before, but I can't quite place where."

Yianni gave him a bit more time to study the page. "Perhaps they relate to your work with antiquities?"

The grandfather moved his stare to the ground. "Yes, that could be it." He shut his eyes and again began to gently rock from side to side. "When I worked at that hotel site, I remember a very large woman in her sixties. I met with her many times. She always wanted to know what new things we'd found. We'd describe them, and then they'd disappear."

"Did she take them?"

"I don't know, but no one ever questioned where they'd gone."

"I can't recall ever seeing someone like that on the site," said Tassos.

"She only met with us who dug and her project manager who'd hired us. And we always met with her away from where we worked."

"What was her name?" said Tassos.

"I never heard it."

"What about the initials?" said Andreas.

"She had six children but never spoke of them by name, only initials."

"What would she say about them?" asked Yianni.

The grandfather opened his eyes. "Something like, 'These are right for BZ' or 'This should go to AS.'"

Tassos stared at Andreas. "Sounds like we've come across a dynasty of antiquities plunderers."

Yianni leaned into the old man. "Sir, can you think of anything at all that might help us identify the woman?"

"No, but her project manager would know all about her." The grandfather paused.

The cops perked up.

"But he's dead. Died in a car accident here on Naxos twenty-five years ago."

Tassos looked at Andreas. "At about the same time as Honeyman went into the antiquities storage business."

———

"Where to now, Chief?" said Yianni as Andreas made a U-turn, headed south, toward the village of Moni.

"I want to stop at the police station in Filoti. There must be someone around who can identify that woman. From the way the grandfather spoke of her, she spent a lot of time on the island and likely came from money. A big woman with six children? She shouldn't be that difficult to identify."

"Then what?" said Tassos.

"Not sure yet, but at least we'll know we're barking up the right family tree."

Yianni grimaced. "That was really bad."

Andreas smiled. "I happened to like it. And speaking of liking,

I really liked the way you handled the grandfather. Where did you learn to do that?"

"Too much personal family experience." Yianni paused. "The key to dealing with folks with teetering memories is to keep yourself calm, not to push them, and to do what you can to make them feel comfortable. Start with what they know or once knew well, and only when you sense they've regained some confidence in their memories do you risk probing gently."

"I'll try to remember that," said Andreas.

"On the subject of remaining calm," Tassos said to Yianni, "I'm all for the good cop, bad cop routine, but when you, with your two broken ribs and bandages, launched in on Junior over that long, hard shovel in his hands, I wondered if you'd taken into account the size of the man you were trying to stand down."

"Yes, I had."

"And what was your plan if he'd swung?"

"To keep ducking until one of you shot him."

"Great plan."

Ring, ring.

"Now what?" said Andreas, grappling for his phone with one hand and driving with the other. He looked at the screen. "It's the minister. Here, Yianni, answer and put us on speakerphone."

"Hello, Andreas?"

"Yes, Minister. Hello."

"Where are you?"

"Naxos, on our way to the police station in Filoti."

"How goes the investigation into the missing reporter?" The minister spoke in a measured tone, unusual for him.

"We've got some good leads on some bad folks, and once we locate them, we should be in a better position to find her."

"In other words, you have no fucking idea where she is."

So much for measured tones. "I guess some cynics might describe it that way."

"This is not a joke, Kaldis."

"Let's cut to the chase, Minister. Who's beating down your door on this?"

"I just received a letter delivered by hand from the reporter's publisher, charging you with gross dereliction of duty in your handling of her disappearance and threatening to wipe you and me off the face of the earth if I don't immediately fire you. He also accused you of making 'extortionate threats' if he sought the help of the public to find her."

Andreas answered calmly. "And what reason did he offer for my conduct?"

"To quote him, 'Kaldis's megalomaniacal ego and psychotic obsession for control endangers the very citizens he's sworn to protect.'"

"So, what's his bottom line?"

"If you're not fired by the end of today, he's going public with his charges."

"Good."

"*Good?* What the hell does *that* mean?"

"I told him to give me until midnight to find the reporter. He's obviously agreed."

"Maybe you are insane."

"I'll take that to mean I still have my job. At least until midnight."

"I'll fax a copy of the letter to you at the Filoti station. Once you've read it, tell me how you want to handle it. This man wants your head. Decide whether you want to resign or be dismissed."

"Is there another choice?"

"Yes, find his reporter before midnight."

The line went dead.

"Didn't we discuss this possibility when you decided to

threaten the head of the most powerful publishing family in Greece?" said Tassos.

"Is this an I-told-you-so moment?" said Andreas.

"No, more of a looks-like-now-you'll-have-more-time-to-spend-with-the-family moment."

Andreas glanced at Yianni, "Thank you for your help on that call."

"What are you talking about? All I did was hold the phone."

"No, for your advice on how to deal with the senile. It also seems to apply to bureaucrats. Stay calm, make them feel comfortable, and then pounce."

"Gentlemen, we only have until midnight," said Yianni. "What do you suggest we do?"

"I want to call Dimitri and see who he thinks can help us identify that woman and her children. No reason to waste time in Filoti if he can give us leads himself."

"But what about the letter?"

"Screw it. I know what it says. I don't have to see it in print. All it will do is cause me to lose my newfound *fucking calm* at that asshole publisher." He banged away on the steering wheel.

———

Lila, Maggie, and Toni left the house by nine, but appealing distractions along the way led them first to the Temple of Demeter and then on to a slew of historical sites, churches, and monasteries before they made it to Halki. They found the artist's gallery tucked away on a lane off the main road, but by then it was early afternoon and the gallery was closed. They stood staring in through display windows, wondering where to go next, when a woman's voice yelled out to them from a *kafenio* across the lane. "Sisters, I'm over here."

Artist sat at a café table, waving for the others to join her. "I never thought you meant it when you said you'd visit my gallery. I thought you were just being courteous."

"If you knew us better, you wouldn't say that," said Toni.

"I'll keep that in mind." Artist exchanged cheek kisses with her visitors and waved to a woman standing in the doorway. "Three more wineglasses and another carafe of white, please. And don't forget the meze."

Once they'd been seated, Artist whispered, "I ordered some things to nibble on, but if you're looking to have lunch, this isn't the place."

"The whole town has such a wonderful neoclassical atmosphere. I love it," said Lila.

"Thanks. I prefer calling it neohippie classical. At one time Halki was the capital of Naxos, and a few of us have done our best to revitalize the village. The trouble is, as soon as a new shop opens with a unique concept or product, others spring up copying the original idea and charging half the price for one quarter the quality."

"Welcome to today's universal business model," said Lila.

Artist glanced inside the *kafenio*. "Oh, no, she's on her phone. Probably with her boyfriend. Who knows when she'll bring our order. Come, I'll show you my gallery while we wait."

As soon as she stepped inside the gallery and saw the artist's work, Lila asked Artist to allow her to make an introduction to one of Athens's leading gallery owners. "I know her personally, and I can assure you she would love to represent you. That is, if you're interested."

"I thought you were some kind of psychologist?"

Lila nodded. "Believe me, I am, but art is my passion and I know what's good. If you're interested, let me know."

"Your drinks are on the table" came trilling across the road from the *kafenio*'s doorway.

"If you're serious, of course I'm interested. Thank you."

"As I said before we don't say things just out of courtesy, especially not this one," said Toni, pointing at Lila.

"I said the drinks are on the table."

"She must have had a fight with her boyfriend. Let's get back to the table before she explodes. Her voice could shatter my windows."

Over the ensuing hour, they finished off the carafe of wine; nibbled away at the bits of cucumber, cheese, and sausage offered as meze; discovered common interests; and elicited Artist's promise to hook Lila and Toni up with her friend on Naxos, who, like them, worked with abused and trafficked young girls.

"Usually, I don't have to say this," said Maggie, "because Tassos does it for me, but where do you suggest we have lunch?"

"Where are you headed?"

"No plans. We thought we'd stop by Eggares to see your friend," said Lila.

"She's not there today. Maybe tomorrow."

"Then we're wide open to suggestions."

Artist paused. "If you're up for it, a wondrous ten-kilometer drive from here gets you to a mountain village with a great taverna. A girl who used to work here now works there. She moved to Halki to be closer to her boyfriend, but when that fell through she went back home to work in her family's taverna. It sits on the edge of a mountainside."

"Sound's great. What's the village?"

"Apeiranthos."

"What's it like?" asked Toni.

"It's built between two valleys on the slopes of a mountain range. Some call it the *marble village* because marble's used everywhere, from the squares used to pave its streets to the construction of its houses. The village is dominated by two seventeenth-century Venetian stone towers, and for more than half a millennium, its people have mined emery, raised livestock, and grown wine grapes. Today, it's popular with tourists looking to explore the more remote parts of the island."

Maggie smiled. "That's a very good Chamber of Commerce presentation, but aren't you leaving out a few details?"

"Like what?" asked Toni.

"Shall I tell them, or will you?" Maggie asked Artist.

"I assume you're referring to the village's tough mountainfolk reputation."

"In body as well as mind," added Maggie.

Artist nodded. "I'm not an anthropologist, but I'd venture to guess much of that comes from their Cretan roots. To this day they speak in a distinctly Cretan dialect and know how to make it through hard times by being quick-witted and doing whatever's necessary to survive."

Lila said, "I have friends with Apeiranthos roots. Those same qualities have served them well in fashioning highly successful and distinguished lives around the world."

"It's also a place where vendetta is still practiced," said Maggie.

"I'm not so sure about that," said Artist, "but just to be on the safe side, I'd say don't offend someone from Apeiranthos."

They all laughed.

Lila called for the check, but Artist insisted that in *her* village, she paid.

Before saying goodbye, they exchanged phone numbers, and Artist promised she'd call her friend at the mountainside taverna to tell her to expect them.

As they walked back to the SUV, Artist yelled out to the three from her doorway, "Safe travels."

Toni looked at Lila. "Should we take that as a warning?"

Lila smiled. "Unlike us, I think she's just being courteous."

———

Dimitri told Andreas he had no idea who the large woman with six children might have been. He said, assuming she was an off-islander keeping a low-key presence in what back then was the isolated, undeveloped southern end of the island, she might have remained virtually anonymous to all but her neighbors. Then, too, she might have stayed on a boat, making her even less likely to mingle with locals. Still, he would reach out to old-timers from the area who might recall her or know of someone who would, but from how carefully she avoided being seen on the hotel site—and the suspicious death of the project manager who could identify her—he did not hold out much hope at getting an ID on her or her children.

On his own, Andreas reached out to the five locals he'd met with the day before on the off chance one of them, or their friends or relatives, might have known of the woman.

Chef said he'd check, but as she'd be well over a hundred by now, he doubted any local contemporary of hers would still be alive, although perhaps one of their children might know of her.

Shepherd said he knew little about that part of the island and nothing about the woman, but he'd ask around.

Andreas received similar responses from Farmer, Bookseller, and Artist, except Artist asked that he please tell Lila to let her know how she liked her restaurant recommendation. Andreas promised he would.

Finished with his calls, Andreas sat quietly staring out the cruiser's front window at the line of mountains rolling north, one off into the next. Yianni and Tassos stood a few meters to the left of the front of the car, likely talking football. He'd pulled over to make his calls, and they'd gotten out to stretch their legs.

Andreas liked being a cop. Make that, *loved* being a cop. Mostly the camaraderie. He hoped his bravado performance with the minister wouldn't prove to be his swan song on the force. But from the way things were shaping up, the odds weren't in his favor.

Worse, how am I going to tell Lila that, come midnight, I'll likely be hers, 24/7?

Chapter Seventeen

Artist's directions had them following a twisting mountain road into the heart of Apeiranthos, where they found parking across from the Panagia Aperathitissa, one of the oldest and most impressive churches on the island. Artist had recommended they visit the church as well as a small gem of an archaeological museum, one of several such museums in the village. But at this moment their minds were on lunch.

They strolled west toward a broad, marble-paved lane running south through the heart of the village at the eastern border with one of its two embracing valleys. *Kafenia*, tavernas, and tourist shops lined the lane's uphill side. Across the lane, tables offered parklike views out across a schoolyard and down into the valley, while farther on, tavernas and a few private homes claimed the more spectacular views.

Groups of three and four hard-looking men of broadly ranging ages sat scattered at well-worn tables on both sides of the lane, sipping *tsipouro* or beer, smoking one cigarette after another, and commenting among themselves on all who passed by. The men's eyes locked on to the women as they approached and did not shift away as they passed, but they said not a word to the women.

"Anyone care to guess what's on their minds?" said Lila.

"Bet it's not hard," said Toni.

"That's not what I asked." Lila winked.

"Hey, you made a joke," said Toni. "But whatever they're thinking, at least they're keeping it to themselves. On Mykonos, by now I'd have heard a dozen not so interesting proposals yelled out in a remarkable variety of languages."

"Amazing isn't it, how men have the same thing on their minds no matter where they come from?" said Lila. "Though I must say, these men have been respectful, aside from where they fixed their eyes."

"I'm past the age where I need worry about that sort of thing," said Maggie. "But before you get too enamored of their gentlemanly behavior, allow me to remind you that vendetta is very much part of this village's heritage. We're strangers to these men, so until they're sure we're not somehow related to one of their neighbors, they wouldn't dare insult us."

"Oh well, I guess that's a good side to vendetta," said Lila.

"Until the shooting starts."

"Wow, look at that," said Toni, staring up at a looming fieldstone tower surrounded by matching stone terraces and verandas. It sat anchored above the west side of the lane on a base of solid rock, framed at the level of the lane in complementing stone arches and the limbs of a massive plane tree.

"It looks like a fortress," said Maggie.

"I think the taverna we're looking for is named after that tower."

"I wouldn't mind living up there," said Toni. "It's only two stories, but the view must be terrific."

"Yeah, but just think of the heating bills," quipped Maggie.

"I'd only use it in summer."

"I think we've found lunch." Lila stopped in front of a taverna bearing a sign with an image of the tower. "Yep, this is it."

The place wasn't crowded and Lila told the lone waitress they had a reservation. She showed them to a table at the edge of a long veranda spanning the rear of the taverna that overlooked a valley dappled gray-green from the shadows of passing clouds. "I'm the one who took your reservation. Welcome to my village."

Toni stared down into the valley. "It's beautiful. I can't get over how green this island is compared to Mykonos."

"I can't get over how hungry I am," said Maggie.

"Don't worry, ladies. When my friend called to make the reservation, she said to treat you like family. And my family likes to eat. So, unless you'd prefer to order from the menu, I can start the food coming and keep it coming until you say stop."

Three hungry women exchanged shrugs. Maggie said, "Go for it."

"What about wine? We have wonderful local wines."

"Why not?" said Maggie.

"But only two glasses," said Lila. "I'm driving, and these roads and wine don't mix."

The waitress nodded. "There are far too many memorials along these roads attesting to the wisdom of your thinking."

"I will take a ginger beer, though. Nonalcoholic, please."

"Done."

She left, headed to the kitchen, and returned with a liter carafe of wine, a bottle of ginger beer, a bottle of water, and glasses. "Enjoy."

"I like this place," said Toni, looking around. "Not old, not modern, just right."

"Let's face it, in places like this it's all about the view," said Maggie.

"And, we hope, the food," added Lila.

Five minutes later the waiter arrived with platters of *taramasalata*, tzatziki, *melitzanosalata*, Greek salad, grilled octopus, shrimp *saganaki*, zucchini fritters, and pita bread. "How's this for starters?"

"Starters?" said Lila. "This is enough for lunch, dinner, *and* tomorrow's breakfast."

"Well, save room. The goat and lamb are in the oven."

By the time the main courses arrived, they'd insisted the waitress join them at their table, and soon had her sharing tales about the village and the wild and crazy people who lived there.

"I've heard it said that living and working in the mountains is what makes us crazy," she said. "If you're a fisherman, you're surrounded by the sea, and that's calming. But the wildness of all this," she waved her hand at the vista, "takes hold of your spirit and makes you just as untamed."

"I don't know if I wholeheartedly agree," said Toni. "At least insofar as this village goes. Frankly, I'm picking up a distinctly melancholy vibe. From what I can see, many of its magnificent homes look neglected, and as lovely as this view is down into the valley, it's an eastern-facing village, meaning no sunsets. Over time, that must play on the villagers' minds as a disappointment, for there's no visible, sensual closure to the day."

The waitress stared at Toni. "Where'd you learn to think like that? I mean, reading people so well."

Toni shrugged. "I guess from playing piano for tips in a gay bar."

"Perhaps that melancholy is why so few people live here year-round," said Sofia. "Most come only for the summer, and once they're gone, there's very few of us left to deal with the winter."

"Which I assume puts more stress on you?"

"You learn to deal with it. Life is hard."

"Let's change the subject," said Lila. "What can you tell us about that fortress across the lane?"

"The Tower? It's been in the same family since our Greek Revolution in 1821, but a Venetian family built it in the seventeenth century and the symbol of Venice still stands above the entrance."

"What is it with coats of arms?" said Toni. "Europeans seemed obsessed with them."

"Coats of arms and all that heraldry stuff is beyond me," said Lila. "All I know about them is that long before any of that became fashionable, ancient Greek Hoplite soldiers individualized their shields. Perhaps that explains why some modern Greeks create their own coats of arms."

"To me, all that's nothing more than another ego trip, this time to create a corporate logo for a family." Maggie lifted her glass of wine. "To pretensions, long may they perish."

"More wine?" said the waiter.

"Thank you, but I think not," said Lila. "My friends must stay awake on our ride home in order to keep me awake."

"Nicely played, Lila," said Maggie, waving her glass in salute. "Instead of saying 'cut her off,' you said help her save a life."

Lila laughed.

"Does anyone live in that tower?" asked Toni.

"If you're seriously thinking of living there, you *definitely* had too much to drink," said Maggie.

"I'm just curious."

"Yes, the heirs of the family come for a month in the summer."

"And the rest of the time it's empty?" said Lila.

"Sort of."

"What's that mean?" asked Toni, sipping from her water glass.

"The man who looks after it makes special arrangements for villager friends, and friends of friends, who wish to stay there."

"For a price?" said Maggie.

"Of course," smiled the waitress. "Everything is for a price."

"Could we possibly get in to see it?" asked Toni.

"I'm afraid not. It's rented at the moment."

"Oh well, just a thought."

"What sort of services does it offer?" asked Lila.

"Don't tell me you're interested too," said Maggie.

"Just asking."

"Whatever the client wants. The one in there now orders every meal from us. Doesn't even squeeze her own orange juice."

"I'd like that kind of life," said Maggie.

"I wouldn't," said the waitress. "She never leaves the tower, and every time I suggest she walk across the road to our place for a meal, she gives me the same answer: 'Why should I? My view's better than yours.'"

"That sounds like behavior symptomatic of a melancholic mind," said Maggie.

"More like clinical depression," said Lila.

The waitress gestured no. "I don't think so. I think it's more a function of her work."

Toni put down her glass. "What kind of work?"

"Writing away on a computer."

"What is she writing?" said Lila.

"A biography."

"Who is she writing about?" said Toni.

"I don't know. She doesn't like to talk about it. The most she ever said to me was that her book is about someone she met here."

Maggie picked up her nearly empty wine glass. "Is she a famous writer?"

"She looks vaguely familiar, but unless she were a TV, movie, or music video star, I wouldn't have a clue to her name. I try not to pay attention to what else is happening in the world. It keeps me from getting aggravated."

"Not a bad plan," said Toni.

"What *do* you know?" said Lila.

"I saw the title once."

"What is it?"

"A crazy-sounding one."

"How crazy could a biography title be?" asked Maggie, finishing off her wine.

"You tell me. It's titled *The Life and Times of My Black Hat Protector.*"

———

When Andreas saw the caller was Lila, he almost didn't take it. He sensed she'd know something was bothering him, but by the fifth ring he answered.

"Hi, my love."

"Hey, where are you?"

"In Moni, sitting under a big pine tree, breathing in the sharp, fresh scents of wild mountain herbs as we wait for our lunch to come."

"You've got to get over to Apeiranthos immediately."

Andreas sat up. "What's wrong? Are you okay?"

Lila repeated what the waitress had told them about the mysterious female guest in the tower. "And she's been here since last Thursday."

"Tell me again the name."

"*The Life and Times of My Black Hat Protector.* Nikoletta's hacker calls himself a 'black hat.'"

"I know, but what I missed was the name of the taverna you're in." She told him.

"Don't move an inch. We'll be there in twenty minutes."

"Please drive safely; we don't need another accident."

Andreas smiled. "Yes, dear."

He pushed back from the table and stood. "Let's go. We've got a lot of ground to cover in the next twenty minutes."

Yianni raised his eyebrows.

"What are you talking about? We just ordered," said Tassos.

"Lila said they think they may have found Nikoletta holed up in Apeiranthos. I'll tell you all about it on the way, but it's on the other side of the mountains from where we are, so we've got to hustle." He canceled the order, left a twenty-euro tip on the table, and raced out the door, followed by Yianni and Tassos.

They drove south past Halki and through Filoti before turning north, lights flashing all the way until a kilometer before Apeiranthos. Andreas parked in the plaza next to Lila's SUV.

"The taverna's just past the tower. Let's try to look casual so as not to spook the townsfolk."

"Spook them over what?" asked Yianni.

"No idea," said Andreas, "but in this village I'm sure there are more than enough guilty consciences to get some folks thinking *raid* anytime they see a cop, let alone three."

The men sitting at the tables lining the cops' way to the taverna turned away as the trio passed by.

"What do you think?" said Andreas.

"I smell lookouts," said Tassos.

"For what?" asked Yianni.

"I guess we'll find out soon enough." Andreas pointed ahead to the left. "There's the taverna."

As they entered, Lila jumped up from her table and waved for them to come out onto the veranda. Maggie and Toni remained seated, talking to a young woman Andreas assumed was the waitress who'd set off their mad dash across the mountains.

Andreas smiled and extended his hand to the woman, "Hi, I'm Andreas, Lila's husband."

The woman stood and shook his hand. "A pleasure to meet you." She waved to Tassos and Yianni. "And you, too. Please, come sit, we'll pull together another table."

Andreas motioned for her to sit down. "No reason to bother. We won't be staying long."

She looked surprised. "I don't understand."

Andreas sat. "I'm a chief inspector with the Greek police, and these gentlemen are also with the police."

Her face blanched but she said nothing.

"Don't worry; you did nothing wrong, and we're not here to arrest anyone. We're here to find a missing woman."

"What missing woman?"

Andreas reached into his pocket, pulled out a photo of Nikoletta, and showed it to her. His eyes fixed on hers, searching for any sign of emotion.

She jerked back in her chair. "Oh, my. It's the woman in the tower."

Andreas didn't bother to wonder what emotion his face betrayed at hearing those words. His rapidly beating heart had answered that question.

"What is your name, Miss?"

"Sofia."

"Ah, a beautiful name, the same as our daughter's. There are a few things I need to know that perhaps you can help me with. First of all, is there anyone else in the tower besides the woman?"

"No, not that I've noticed. That is, aside from Christina, who's the housekeeper. But she's only there in the mornings."

"Have you seen anyone other than Christina in the tower since the woman arrived?"

"No."

"Have you noticed any strangers hanging around the tower?"

"No."

"Are you certain."

"Ye-es." She strung out the word oddly, or so it seemed to Andreas.

He glanced at Yianni, who nodded.

"When do you usually deliver dinner to the woman?"

"Before we get busy, which would be around now."

"Do you have a key or does she let you in?"

"I press a button at the terrace door, she asks who it is, I tell her, and usually she comes down to open the door for me. Sometimes she just buzzes me in."

"I need you to go with us to the tower. When she asks who it is, don't tell her we're with you. As soon as she opens the door, get out of the way. We'll take it from there."

She looked around the table. "Really? You're making me worry."

"There's no need, Sofia. We're being cautious for the sake of the woman, just in case there's someone with her you don't know about."

"Don't worry, I'll be with you," said Toni, patting Sofia's hand.

"The hell you will," said Yianni.

"Don't mind him. That's my overprotective boyfriend, worried that I'll somehow mess up this very simple food delivery. Isn't that right, Chief Inspector?"

Andreas spoke through a clenched jaw. "Does that work for you, Sofia?"

She nodded yes and squeezed Toni's hand.

Andreas sighed and looked to Yianni. "Then I guess that's how we'll do it."

"What about video surveillance?" said Tassos. "Security's a big concern among homeowners these days."

"It wasn't so different four hundred years ago," said Maggie. "Why do you think they built this tower like a fortress?"

"And pirates still found their way in," said Sofia.

Andreas nodded. "I'm sure we will too."

Chapter Eighteen

A group of three couples armed with maps and snapping photos with their phones wound their way up beside a tower along a twisting path of marble steps. The steps led to a pair of bronze-clad doors framed in marble and crowned by the emblem of Venice carved in stone. The women stopped a few paces before the doors to snap photographs of the valley below, while the men argued over where to visit next. The group seemed oblivious to the young woman carrying a tray of food up the steps behind them.

As the arguing intensified, the three women turned away and started back down the steps, yelling back at the men that they'd be waiting at the car for them to make up their minds. The men kept up with their argument but slowly followed the women, stopping every step or so to accentuate a point.

The young woman with the tray pressed a button next to the doors and stood watching the men argue.

One of the doors swung open wide and a smiling, dark-haired woman appeared. "Good evening, Sofia."

"Evening, *keria*." As Sofia stepped inside, the three arguing men sprinted for the doorway.

Panic spread across the woman's face, and she tried to slam the door shut, but Sofia and her tray blocked the woman just long enough for the men to grab the door and force their way inside.

The woman screamed for help.

"Relax, Nikoletta, we're the police," said Andreas, pulling his ID out from beneath his shirt.

Yianni and Tassos did the same.

"You scared the bloody hell out of me," said Nikoletta.

"Are you alone in here?"

"Yes."

He turned to Yianni and Tassos. "Make sure that she is."

Yianni and Tassos headed into the tower, guns drawn.

"Is everything okay in here?" said Toni, stepping through the doorway.

"Seems to be," said Andreas.

"Who is she?" asked Nikoletta.

"More like who are *they*?" said Lila coming up behind Toni with Maggie.

"Don't I know you?" asked Nikoletta.

"I'm Lila Vardi."

"The socialite," she turned to face Andreas, as Lila frowned at the description, "married to Andreas Kaldis, chief of Special Crimes."

Andreas bowed. "At your service."

"I'm flattered by all this attention."

"Your newspaper is very worried about you."

"I bet. I'm sure they can't wait to hear my story."

"Personally, I can't wait to hear it myself. Why don't we start with a basic question: Where is your kidnapper?"

"Kidnapper? I've not been kidnapped. I've been protected."

"By whom and from whom?"

"I truly wish I knew. Why don't we go inside where we can sit down? I can try to answer your questions, and perhaps you can answer some of mine?"

"Sounds good to me."

Nikoletta turned to Sofia. "Please bring the tray inside."

"I'm sorry, ma'am. I had no choice. They are the police."

"Don't worry. I know you were only trying to help me." Nikoletta paused and looked at Andreas. "Are you expecting any others to join us?"

Yianni came out of the tower, followed by Tassos, caught Andreas's eye, and flashed him a thumbs-up.

He turned back to Nikoletta. "None of the invited sort."

———

Nikoletta led them to a second-floor library that could have passed for a museum dedicated to seventeenth-century baroque furniture. A large rectangular table fitted with marble inserts and adorned in elaborately carved cupids and shells dominated the center of the room. Bold scrolls embellished the table's legs and the legs and arms of twelve matching chairs. A comparably carved gilded writing desk sat to the side between two windows. An open laptop computer atop the desk served as the room's only visible sign of the modern age.

Nikoletta sat in a chair on the side of the table closest to the desk. She pointed at the computer. "I assume you know I'm working on a book about this experience."

Andreas smiled as he sat directly across from her. "We'd prefer not having to wait until it's published to learn what happened."

Yianni and Tassos sat next to Andreas, while Lila, Toni, and Maggie sat at the end of the table farthest away from the others.

"I'm sure you have a lot of questions for me, but before we get to them, I have one that's been gnawing at me since the night I disappeared from the hotel."

"What is it?" asked Andreas.

"Why hasn't a single word appeared anywhere in the media about my disappearance? Not even in my own newspaper."

"If you're able to answer my questions as easily as I can answer yours, I'll be a very happy cop." Andreas told her that keeping a lid on her disappearance was all his doing, and he'd done so out of concern that if she had been kidnapped, the inevitable avalanche of publicity might cause her abductor to panic and harm her. He emphasized that her publisher did not agree with his strategy.

"Thank you. I feel better knowing there were people out there who cared." She took a sip of water from a plastic bottle. "Where do you want me to start?"

"How about with what happened the night you disappeared."

Nikoletta shut her eyes, took a deep breath, opened her eyes, and began. "My planned final evening on Naxos had me joining some new friends for dinner in Chora, which in the inevitable Greek way led to way too much drinking and a very late night. I literally staggered out of the taverna, and in my haste to get back to the hotel, I decided to take a shortcut that involved leaving paved roads to climb a very dark, rocky dirt path that ran alongside a steep cliff high above the sea."

She paused. "That's all I know firsthand, because I reached my hotel without incident. The rest of what happened I learned from Soter."

"Who's *Soter*?"

Nikoletta laughed. "Sorry, I've been so immersed in my writing that I only think of my interviewee-turned-protector by the name I created for him in the book. In Greek mythology, Soter represented the male personification of safety and deliverance from harm."

"Do you know his real name?"

"No. I wish I did."

"You're probably better off not knowing," said Tassos.

"What did he tell you?" asked Andreas.

"On the day after my article about him appeared in the paper, he received an offer over the Dark Web to kill me. Obviously, the person making the offer didn't realize he was the man I'd interviewed. Though he turned it down, he knew someone would take the contract because the fee was extremely high. That's when he started following me."

Nikoletta picked up the water bottle. "At the time, he thought I'd been targeted because of his interview. He felt responsible. That his bragging had put me in danger." She took another sip. "The night of my disappearance, he'd been watching me from outside the taverna, and after I left, he followed me on a motorbike. When he saw me stop to stare up the hillside path, he guessed I'd take it, so he parked and made it onto the path some distance ahead of me. As he hurried up the hill, he saw a man crouched in the shadows across and back from the path at its closest point to the cliff edge. He recognized the man as a professional assassin—*definitely not top-drawer*, was how he later described him to me. The man did not recognize Soter or realize he'd been seen and stayed focused on my struggle up the hill. Soter walked by the man as if he hadn't noticed him, then circled back down and around to come up behind him. He knew the man had to be planning to push me off the edge of the cliff to make it appear an 'accidental death.'" Nikoletta used finger quotes for emphasis.

"But, as we all know, it didn't end up that way."

Nikoletta cleared her throat. "I was oblivious to all of that. After I'd safely reached my hotel, Soter made his way down to the rocks and stripped the now-dead would-be assassin of his mobile phone and identification. Once he'd finished with him, he called me on the man's phone and told me to meet him outside my hotel. He'd long before then culled my number from my mobile provider."

"But how did he know the password to unlock the phone?" asked Yianni.

She smiled. "Funny you should ask. I had the same question. He told me he didn't, but he just ran through the five most common passwords and 111111 worked."

"Clever guy," said Toni.

Nikoletta nodded. "When we met, he told me someone was trying to kill me and I had to come with him immediately. I told him my mother hadn't raised a fool, and I wasn't about to go off in the middle of the night with a nearly total stranger, especially one who'd recently bragged to me about being a master criminal. He told me my mother was a wise woman, but she wasn't here to protect me, and in a few minutes he wouldn't either. He walked to the edge of the cliff and shone a light down onto the rocks.

"He told me, 'The body down there would have been you if I hadn't intervened.' I looked over the edge and saw the man on the rocks. I almost fainted. 'He was waiting for you on your walk home,' Soter told me. 'Someone tipped him off that you were on your way back to the hotel. You have two choices. Come with me to a safe house I know while I figure out who's after you, or stay here and be a target. You've thirty seconds to make up your mind.'"

She exhaled. "Longest thirty seconds of my life. Obviously, I went with him. We took his motorbike to a parking lot in the harbor, where we switched to a car and drove directly here. When we got to the village, it was still dark, and no one saw us walk from the car to this fortress."

"You must have been frightened," said Lila.

"I believe the technical term is *scared shitless*."

"What did you two talk about on the ride up from Chora?"

said Tassos. "That was a long trip, especially at night along strange roads."

"He knew the roads. He said he'd hidden out in the tower several times, and the local people knew him. He said this time he wouldn't stay in the village but had arranged for some locals to keep an eye on me. He didn't say, but I got the impression locals knew what he did and might even have used his services."

"Why do you think that?" said Tassos.

"Because when I asked if the locals who'd be keeping an eye on me could be trusted, he said, 'They know what would happen to all of them and their families should any one of them ever break his word to me.'"

"That's quite a reputation," said Andreas.

"You said something before that piqued my curiosity," said Maggie.

"What's that?"

"You said, '*At the time*' Soter thought you'd been targeted because of the story about him. Did his thinking change?"

"The second day I was here he called to say that he didn't think our interview was the cause."

"Why did he say that?" asked Andreas.

"He said there was still a contract out on me, but a new contract had just gone up, offering even more money for anyone who immediately took out another target on Naxos, this time an Athens cop. That contract was attracting a lot of attention from a low-end crowd of thugs, indicating a state of panic on the part of whoever had put out those contracts. Soter's clients would never use such unprofessional types, nor would they have hired the inept one who intended to kill me outside my hotel.

"Besides, it made no sense for someone afraid of what Soter might say to go after the person to whom he'd told his story. He could tell his story to any number of journalists. The only way to keep more stories like it out of the press was to kill Soter, not the writer. All of which led him to believe there must be another motive behind why someone was after me."

"Any idea what that motive might be?" said Andreas.

"That's the kind of 'step back and think out of the box' approach I'm never good at when it comes to looking at myself."

"As the cop whose contract kill price topped yours, permit me to offer a possible answer." Yianni leaned in across the table. "You kept a sixth notebook. I've seen five of them. What's in the sixth?"

She appeared surprised. "I had the idea for another article I wanted to write after finishing the tourism piece. It's based upon a strange local character I came across purely by chance, selling honey from the back of a pickup truck." She took a sip of water. "He was a true fast-talker, and in the traditional style of Greek men, tried to impress me by claiming his honey-selling operation was just a hobby to keep himself in touch with local common folk. His real money-generating operation was in artifacts. I tested him with my slight knowledge of the subject and must admit he impressed me with what he knew. But not enough to buy his honey.

"Later on, in my interviews with locals, I'd ask if they knew Honeyman, and everyone had a story about him. Usually it involved the term 'con man,' and some had very sharp words to say. Most suspected he was involved in the illicit antiquities trade. But what really got my attention was when some said he'd approached them as the representative of different companies seeking to assemble vast parcels of beachfront land. I smelled a great story in this but didn't want to get into any of that in my tourism piece. I wanted to save it for a special article. So I put anything relating to his story into notebook number six, and as far as I know, no one knows about my plans for that story, except my editor and publisher."

"Did Honeyman know?" asked Yianni.

"No."

"But you did ask a lot of people about Honeyman?"

She nodded. "True, but if he knew, I doubt he would have showed up at my farewell party the night that man tried to kill me."

"He was there?" said Andreas.

"Yes, I was surprised too. I'd invited everyone who'd helped me with the piece, including Honeyman. I couldn't risk slighting him and losing his cooperation on my story about him. Frankly, I didn't think he'd fit in with the crowd, but he stayed to the bitter end."

Andreas looked at Yianni. "Well, now we know who the *some-one* was who tipped off the killer that Nikoletta was on her way back to the hotel."

"And why the killer had a phone," said Yianni. "Honeyman must've called him when Nikoletta left the bar."

Andreas decided not to tell Nikoletta that Honeyman was dead. No reason to alarm her further.

"You said Soter calls you?" said Yianni.

"Yes."

"Do you ever call him?"

"Sometimes."

"Do you have his number?"

"It's on speed dial on the phone he gave me when he brought me here."

"May I see it, please?"

"Sure, but it's locked." She smiled, "and not with one of those top five passwords." She punched in a code and, as she was about to pass the phone to Yianni, said, "I've got a new message from him."

She read the message and shook her head with a grin. "Wait until you hear this. 'Hi, Nikoletta. Now that you're safely in the hands of the police I can rest easy and go back to simply being a fan of your columns who's heading off into blissful retirement. Stay safe. By the way, these phones will get the police nowhere, and I'm dumping mine now.'"

Andreas nodded. "I guess the locals watching out for you are doing a good job of keeping him informed. Well, let's pack up and get you back to Chora and on to Athens."

"I don't want to go."

"What do you mean? You could still be in danger."

"As you said, the locals are keeping a close watch on me, and how will I be any safer walking Athens's streets or in my apartment than I am here? Until you find whoever's behind this, I think this is the better place to be. Besides, I've been remarkably productive with my writing here."

Andreas looked her straight in the eye. "Honeyman and two others involved with him have been murdered. This is real, Nikoletta."

She blanched. "Wow." She shook her head. "Wow, wow, wow." She shook her head again. "Where do you plan on keeping me?"

"I don't know yet. For the time being, at police headquarters in Chora."

She gestured no. "Despite what happened to those men, with all due respect, I feel safer here than in 'don't know yet.'"

"I don't think your newspaper is going to be happy about this. Your publisher has convinced my minister to fire me if I don't find you by midnight."

"You never told me that," said Lila.

Nikoletta looked at her phone. "We've got time left before midnight, so why don't you come around to this side of the table?"

"What for?" asked Andreas.

"For a selfie we can send to my paper and your minister. Proof of life, as they say. Proof you found me."

"You do have style," said Andreas.

"And it beats a sketch," said Yianni.

"For sure."

"May I see your sketchbook?"

"It's next to the computer."

Yianni went to look for the sketchbook while Nikoletta and Andreas posed for their selfie.

"Why do I have the distinct feeling that I'm going to regret this?" said Andreas.

"Because having salt rubbed into your wounds is painful and inspires a desire for retribution," said Tassos.

Andreas settled on what he considered a non-gloating photo, and after adding all the necessary recipients' email addresses, watched Nikoletta hit send.

"Excuse me, Nikoletta," said Yianni, holding the open sketch-book. "Does Soter know about your sketchbook?"

"I don't think so."

"You're very good. I recognize many of the faces." Yianni put the book down in front of her and pointed to a face. "Who's this?"

She bit at her lip. "I don't know."

"I know him. In fact, I believe we both met him at the same place."

"I don't recognize him." Now she was chewing her lip.

"Well, what about this one?" He pointed to another sketch of the same face, "Or this one?" turning to another page. "How many more pages showing this face do you want me to turn to before you tell me what we both know?"

She lowered her head. "He saved my life. And I protect my sources. I promised myself I'd destroy those sketches, but they were my only companions here. They made me feel safe."

Andreas and Tassos came around the table and looked at the sketches.

"So this is Soter?" asked Andreas.

"Yes," Nikoletta murmured.

"Where did you meet him?" Andreas asked Yianni.

"At the bar where she first met him. That snug little place down from the Kastro, where this guy kindly made me a pizza my first night in town."

Andreas pressed his finger on the sketchbook. "You mean Soter's the owner of the bar?"

"That's what he told me."

"Is that true, Nikoletta?"

"He never said anything like that to me, and he didn't act like the owner when we were there."

Andreas turned to Lila. "Ladies, it looks as if our night is just beginning. I suggest the three of you head on home and not wait up for us."

"Why do you have to do that?" said Nikoletta. "It's very late, the roads are tricky, you've had too much to drink, and this place has a zillion bedrooms. Please, ladies, stay here, at least until it's light out."

"I don't like that idea," said Yianni.

"Don't bother to tell us why; we already know," said Toni. "You're afraid an assassin will show up tonight and do us all in."

"It's not a joke."

"I didn't mean it as one," Toni said.

Maggie jumped in. "Why don't you get Dimitri to send a couple of cops to watch over us until morning? He's going to owe you big-time for all the great publicity his department will get for finding Nikoletta. Besides, this is a fortress."

"I'm not going to get involved in a losing battle trying to convince you otherwise, my love," said Tassos, reaching into his waistband. "But here, keep this." He handed Maggie his pistol and kissed her on the cheek. "I know you know how to use it."

"Isn't that overkill?" said Nikoletta.

"Only until you need it," said Maggie. "Now get out of here, guys, so we can get some sleep."

"What do you think we should do?" said Yianni looking at his partners.

Tassos smiled. "My vote is for leaving, because from what I've heard so far, I'd say we've likely got a better chance of winning the lottery than convincing these ladies that they need us keen-minded men to protect them from the bad guys."

Yianni glared at Tassos, "Soter, where are you when I need you?"

"With any luck," said Andreas, "we just might get your question answered tonight."

Chapter Nineteen

Andreas, Yianni, and Tassos made it to the bar by one a.m. The place was packed, with most of its customers focused on a guitarist playing a mix of American folk songs and old French chansons.

As their eyes scanned the room, Tassos said, "I can see why Nikoletta called this place Bohemian."

"Do you see him?" said Andreas.

"No."

"Me neither," said Yianni. "Let me ask the bartender."

Yianni made his way through to the bar and waved for the bartender.

"Yes, sir."

"Is Stelios here tonight?"

"Stelios? Stelios who?"

"The owner."

"The owner's name is Aris. And he's standing over by the door."

Yianni turned to see a short, pudgy clean-shaven man with long white hair wearing an "I adore Edith" T-shirt, rocking side-to-side in time with the music.

"I was in here a few nights ago, just after the kitchen closed, you were working at the bar, and a guy named Stelios told me he'd make me a pizza. I thought he was the owner. Maybe he was the manager?"

The bartender frowned, then smiled. "Oh, that guy. Yeah, I remember him. He tipped me big-time to let him make the pizza. Also a salad and fruit, right? Nice guy, but he's not the owner. Or the manager."

"You're new here, aren't you?"

"If five years behind this bar six nights a week is new, then I'm new."

"I'm sorry, sir. I must be confused, but tell me, did you ever see the man who called himself Stelios here before the night he made that pizza?"

"Yeah, maybe a week before. He'd tipped a waiter to invite a woman passing by to come inside for a drink. He struck up a conversation with her, and they spent hours together talking at a table by a window. He tipped me big that night too."

Yianni exhaled, shook his head, and took out his phone. "By chance, is this the man who tipped you?" Yianni showed him a photo of one of Nikoletta's sketches.

"Yeah, that's him. Is he someone famous or something?"

"You could say that." Yianni skimmed through until he came to another photograph. "Have you ever seen this guy in here?"

The bartender stared at the photo. "No, can't say that I have."

"That night, Stelios, or whatever his name is, told me when he was at the table with the woman, this man sat at the bar practically the whole time, watching them in the mirror."

"No way he'd have been here that long and I wouldn't have noticed. That was a very slow night, not like tonight. I'd have noticed him for sure. Is he famous too?"

"In some circles, yes."

"Who is he?"

"Peter Zagori."

"Never heard of him."

Yianni nodded, took ten euros out of his pocket, and handed it to the bartender.

"What's this for?"

"I should have tipped you for dinner the night I was in here. I thought Stelios had taken care of me."

Come to think of it, he did, and quite effectively.

———

Yianni sat outside the bar, telling Tassos and Andreas of his conversation with the bartender.

"What a con artist that guy is," said Tassos.

"Smooth as they come," said Yianni. "He had me thinking I was suckering him into giving up information, when all the while he was picking my brain and doing what he could to throw me off the scent. Peter Zagori wasn't even in Greece the night Nikoletta first met Soter, and though he never directly said the guy at the bar was Zagori, he tossed out just enough cop catnip to get me thinking there might be a new angle to what went down. He made it all up about the man in the mirror just to slow us down."

"Well, I think it's safe to say we're no longer slowed down," said Tassos. "We're at what I'd call a dead stop."

"There's another way to look at why Soter mentioned Zagori," said Andreas. "He might have made all that up to steer us toward investigating Zagori. Soter knew that Zagori wasn't in Greece the night he met Nikoletta, but he also knew that sometime after her article about Soter was published Zagori was hired to kill her. Investigating Zagori might have led us to who wanted her dead."

"That Soter guy grows more impressive every moment," said Tassos.

"But how did he know I was a cop investigating Nikoletta's disappearance?"

"You didn't exactly arrive undercover," said Andreas. "The morning after her disappearance, you were met at the airport by the chief of police and driven by him straight to where a body had been found on the rocks below Nikoletta's hotel. You questioned the hotel's night manager about her disappearance and spent time searching her room. The island gossip mill wouldn't have had to churn too hard to figure out there's a new cop in town. He might have started tailing you at the hotel, or just waited around the bar until you showed up. After all, the logical thing for police to do in a kidnapping is retrace the victim's steps, and for sure you'd be expected to check out the bar where she first met Soter."

"Damn. Four dead, two kill contracts still out there, and us without a clue as to who's behind them," muttered Tassos, slapping the table.

"We do know who killed Zagori," said Yianni.

"Only because the killer admitted that to a reporter," said Andreas.

"But we did find the reporter," insisted Yianni.

"Correction. Maggie, Lila, and Toni found the reporter." Andreas shook his head. "All we've found are a bunch of phony beehives, broken pottery, and an alphabet soup of initials."

"There has to be an explanation, a key we're missing that ties everything together," said Tassos.

"And what is *everything*?" asked Yianni.

"I don't know if it's a network, a pyramid, a sewing circle, or a lone crazy, but something's triggered a rash of violence unlike anything this island's seen in modern times. And whatever that trigger is, Nikoletta pulled it."

"Agreed," said Andreas. "I also agree with Nikoletta's point that anyone afraid of what Soter might have told her had to know it would do no good to eliminate her while he remained alive to tell his tales to others. Bottom line, I don't see her story as the trigger."

"Then what is?"

"My money's on something connected to that sixth notebook and those damn initials."

———

Andreas's phone rang at nine a.m. He struggled to find it on the nightstand next to the bed. "Hello."

"Good morning, my love."

"Morning. How's it going up in the tower?"

"You make it sound like I'm a Greek version of Anne Boleyn. Actually, it's lovely. We had breakfast on the terrace. Sofia joined us. She brought a nice young policeman from Filoti to watch over us."

"Terrific. When are you coming back to the beach house?"

"I thought you were busy."

"That's a relative term."

"I assume that means no luck at finding Soter."

"Or figuring out anything, really. Plus, we didn't get to bed until after three."

"I'm just calling to make sure you saw my email."

"The only email I saw before going to sleep was a two-word response from the minister to my selfie with Nikoletta. 'Got it,' was all he wrote. I'm not sure if he was disappointed or elated."

"A true politician."

"At least he's not corrupt; otherwise he'd have gotten rid of me long ago. So, what's your email to me about?"

"The policeman brought a letter with him. The minister faxed it to his office in Filoti for delivery to you. It's from Nikoletta's publisher, addressed to the minister."

"What's the letter say?"

"I took a photo of it and emailed it to you. It's demanding that you be fired by midnight yesterday."

"Oh, I know what's in that letter. I never bothered to pick it up in Filoti, but it's what triggered my race to find Nikoletta by midnight. Thanks anyway. Let me know once you and your merry band decide what you're doing today."

"Will do. Kisses. Bye."

Andreas lay in bed staring up at the ceiling. He missed his wife. She somehow always knew when something was bothering him. Even when he didn't know it himself. That's a rare quality to have in a partner.

He listened for the sounds of children. Not a stir, not a murmur. Or a scream. Yes, he missed even that. But not as much as he did his wife.

I'm one lucky guy.

His mind was waking up. He didn't want it to, quite yet. He'd have preferred sleeping but knew his preference was losing the battle to duty. He rarely slept this late, and even though he had no idea what to do next, he was awake. He picked up his phone and skimmed through a string of utterly useless email offerings, until he came to the one from Lila. He opened it and clicked on the attachment.

Andreas looked at the letter without bothering to read it. He didn't want to read it, for it would only remind him of how his father had been blackballed from the police force by another powerful man. One who'd set Andreas's father up to suffer a public shaming for something he had not done, ending with eight-year-old Andreas losing his father to suicide.

The letter was typed single spaced on the publisher's personal stationery, with a blue-and-gold coat of arms emblazoned across the top of the page. Andreas rolled his eyes at the crest.

Of course he *has one.* He looked at the coat of arms more closely, trying to discern what the publisher's family had chosen to portray about its history to the world. On one side stood a ship honoring the fortune his family had made at sea. On the other side, a printing press paid homage to the family's current financial engine. And in the central place of honor, the goddess Athena stood upon the pedestal of an open book. He wondered what the book represented and tried to make out what was written on its pages.

He casually tinkered with enlarging the words the family had thought important enough for Athena to stand upon.

One page of the book read,

JSS

GTS

AKS

Its facing page read,

KSM

RIM

BZ

Andreas bolted out of bed, yelling, *"Yianni, Tassos, wake up. The world as we know it is over."*

———

"I can't believe this," said Yianni, staring at the coat of arms on Andreas's phone.

Tassos sighed. "We've either hit upon a one-in-a-zillion coincidence or an explanation that ties everything together."

"Not quite everything, but a hell of a lot," said Andreas. "I asked Lila if she knew whose initials they might be. She said she'd ask her mother, the source of all knowledge about old-line Greek society."

"If the publisher's tied into this, he's involved in at least three murders."

"Plus two attempted murders," added Yianni. "Make that three, if you count Zagori's terminally unsuccessful plans for Nikoletta."

"It also explains how Nikoletta and you became targets. The day after her editor forwarded Nikoletta's sixth notebook to the publisher, Zagori showed up on Naxos to kill her. When that failed and you began retracing her steps, someone panicked, likely over your potentially discovering what she'd learned, and put out a casting call for local bad guys to take you down immediately."

"In the notebook covering her meeting with the hacker, Nikoletta wrote down the names of some persons who'd used his services," said Yianni. "But I don't recall any name fitting those initials, and certainly not the publisher's name."

"So that notebook isn't likely what set this off."

"Something in the sixth notebook is what did it," said Tassos. "And if those initials represent the members of some sort of cabal, there are at least six involved in this."

"But none of those initials is the publisher's," said Yianni.

"Which means it could be more than six. I know it looks like a perfect match to us, but with all the powerful players potentially implicated, we can't afford the slightest misstep. That's another reason I asked Lila for help."

"I don't mean to rain on anyone's parade," said Tassos, "but as the resident cynic in this trio of cops, do you think it even matters what we prove? Whoever's behind this undoubtedly has both the money and the power to *literally* get away with murder."

"As I see it," said Andreas, looking at Tassos while motioning for Yianni to give him back his phone, "my job is to chase down bad guys. After that, it's up to prosecutors and courts to seek whatever justice is called for. If I started thinking about what actually happens to so many of the bad guys I bust my ass to catch, I'd go crazy."

"Thanks for the pep talk, Chief," said Yianni, handing Andreas the phone.

"Hmm," said Tassos. "It makes you wonder whether the corruption among our brethren on the force is the cause of this sort of thing or the consequence."

"A bit of both, I suspect," said Andreas. He felt the phone vibrate in his hand and put the incoming call on speakerphone. "Hi, darling. We're all gathered around the phone to hear the results of your research."

"You mean my *socialite* efforts?"

"I knew you didn't like it when Nikoletta called you that, but I very much admired your self-control."

"I've since explained my feelings on that subject to her, and all is now fine in the fortress. She's even offered to do a feature on our Fresh Start initiative."

"That's great." He paused. "But could you please explain to us what those initials represent?"

"My mother's a better search engine than Google."

"No argument here."

"Okay. Let's start with the matriarch of the family. Her name was Athena."

"Well, that explains her namesake's presence on the coat of arms," said Yianni.

"Her father was a very rich and powerful foreign shipowner with vast investments in land across Greece, and one of the first twentieth-century off-islanders to invest in Naxos. He married a Greek who passed away when Athena was born, and he never remarried. He raised Athena to share his penchant for acquiring land—and his passion for collecting antiquities. When he died between World Wars I and II, she was in her twenties and inherited everything he owned.

"She had six children by three different husbands, and the initials are those of her children. All are male, except for RIM and BZ."

"But how does the publisher tie into this?" said Yianni. "His last name begins with none of those initials."

"His mother was BZ, and she took her husband's last name when they married."

"So, what are the names of these folks?" asked Tassos.

Lila slowly recited the names, including those of their spouses and children.

"Oh. My. God," said Tassos.

"You can say that again," said Andreas. "That's a veritable Who's Who of Greek politics, real estate development, shipping, and society. Not to mention publishing."

"And just to spice up your lives a bit, Mother said that for as long as she can remember there've been rumors of the family illegally trading in antiquities to finance their projects. Part of that comes from the family's uncanny success at gaining permission to develop real estate in areas where others were forbidden to even sink a shovel. 'Mining antiquities to finance modern development' is what Mother said should be written across that family crest."

"Oh," said Andreas, a look of dejection spreading across his face.

"What's wrong?" said Tassos. "We've got the bad guys in our sights and a motive."

"But if all of Athens already knows about their operation, why would they panic if a reporter threatens to do a story on it? Surely it can't be the first time. They'll just have their lawyers and friends in Parliament deal with it and continue on with their lives as if nothing happened. To that extent I agree with our resident cynic."

"Are you saying the publisher wasn't involved in trying to kill me and Popi?"

"No. I'm saying there must be a different motive. Something that the publisher and his network saw as so potentially explosive in that sixth notebook that they had to resort to murder to keep it from going public."

"And what, pray tell, could that be?"

"If I knew, Yianni, you'd be the first I'd tell. All I can say is that I don't think it's anything linked to what we know so far."

Tassos shook his head. "You have a unique ability for plunging us from a state of utter euphoria into abject frustration in a heartbeat."

"Now, now, that's my husband you're talking about."

"Then you know that even better than we do," chirped Yianni.

"Enough, guys. The answer lies in Nikoletta's sixth notebook. Somehow we have to get a copy of it." Andreas heard a muffled conversation on Lila's side of the phone. "Is everything okay?"

"Yes. I was just asking Nikoletta again whether she might have a copy of the notebook, perhaps photos of the pages taken with her camera."

"And?"

"She said no. She was so pressed to get it to her editor in a hurry that she didn't think to make a copy."

"Put her on the phone, please." Andreas sat so that his right elbow was on the table, with his right thumb against his cheek and fingers against his forehead. He held the phone out in front of him in his left hand.

"Hello?"

"Hi, Nikoletta, it's Andreas."

"Tassos."

"And Yianni."

"You must be as stunned by the news as we are," said Andreas.

"*Stunned* is an understatement. My own publisher trying to kill me? Utterly unbelievable. Made even more so by the fact it has to be true. It explains why he's been so desperate to let the world know I disappeared. He needed to find me to kill me. And for the literal life of me, I can't figure out what could possibly have made me his target."

"That's precisely where I need your help. You're the only one besides your publisher who knows what's in your sixth notebook. I'm convinced the answer's in there. The fact that you can't put your finger on what that is means it's only obvious to someone who knows the risk it presents. I'd like you to concentrate on any possible reference or thought you put in that notebook that conceivably could have triggered such a violent reaction in a guilty mind."

"Honestly, I've been trying all morning, ever since Lila told me about the initials."

"Forget about the initials. Forget about the real estate projects, forget about the antiquities smuggling. What else did you mention in your notebook?"

For thirty seconds, only the sound of slow and deliberate breathing came through the phone.

"I can't think of a thing."

"Empty your mind and start again."

This time it was a sigh, followed by more calm breathing, but as the silence went on, the breathing intensified until a rushed voice said, "I thought of something."

"What is it?" Andreas's voice was now as intense as Nikoletta's, his right hand pressed hard against the tabletop.

"At some point I read in a guidebook or brochure that the extraordinary library, furnishings, and priceless archives once housed in the former School of Commerce that is now the Naxos Archaeological Museum were completely destroyed by occupying forces during World War II. That struck me as strange, because those forces were well known for pillaging, not destroying.

Indeed, in the case of Germany, occupying forces were often under orders to send such treasures back to the homeland. I made a note to myself in that notebook to look into how many other Greek libraries, museums, and similar repositories were *destroyed* as opposed to pillaged. And I put a star next to it along with the words, 'Could be great story.'"

Andreas looked at his buddies. "Start your engines, folks. We're back in the race."

Chapter Twenty

Andreas dispatched Maggie to reach out to her army of contacts developed through shared lifetimes of service in the trenches of Greek bureaucracy. Her network ran deep, into all ministries of government, fueled by a camaraderie and transcending loyalty to one another born of knowing that they, not those blown in and out by shifting political winds, kept their ministries running. He wanted any information on valuables destroyed by occupying forces during World War II and any mention of the publisher's family in connection with those valuables or their destruction.

Maggie suggested they also ask for similar reports involving the opposing sides in the Greek Civil War that had followed.

Andreas asked Lila to dig up whatever other information she or her mother could find on Athena, matriarch of the publisher's family.

He called Dimitri for the twenty-five-year-old police records of the car accident that took the life of the project manager.

Andreas sensed they'd discovered the skeletal frame of a time line tying everything together. Athena, assisted by her project manager, had shepherded the family's business dealings through

World War II (1940–45), Greece's Civil War (1946–49), and the Junta Years (1967–74). At some later time, she turned over control to her publisher grandson, and on the project manager's death in the mid-1990s, Honeyman replaced him. All Andreas had to do now was flesh out the frame. Whether the result would be an angel, a devil, or something in between remained to be seen.

Andreas looked at Yianni and Tassos. "Anything else you can think of?"

"Yeah," said Tassos. "Start carrying a bigger gun. Like a howitzer. You do realize that by putting all this out there, word will undoubtedly get back to the publisher, and in his state of advanced paranoia, I don't see him missing where you're headed with this."

Andreas nodded.

"Seriously. The guy could be unstable enough to come after you."

"He could be."

"Or your family," said Yianni.

Andreas nodded again. "I'm sure he can justify that to himself, what with me going after his family." Andreas leaned back and stretched. "Years ago, I decided that anyone who threatens my family gets no quarter. Should he decide to take that route, he damn well better not miss."

"You're starting to sound like those vendetta guys up in Apeiranthos," Tassos said with a smile.

"They're not always wrong."

"Chief, your phone's vibrating."

"My mind's elsewhere. I still haven't switched it to ring." He picked it up off the table. "Hello."

"Hi, it's Dimitri. I found that file and took a look through it."

"Anything interesting?"

"Not *in* the file."

"What's that mean?" said Andreas, picking up a pencil.

"It's a routine report, describing the cause as excessive speed into a sharp turn on a treacherous mountain road and a subsequent loss of control sending car and driver on a terminal roll down the mountain."

"What about *outside* the file?"

"The person making the report was a detective at the time, and that wasn't the sort of thing detectives generally did. More significantly, he left the force under a cloud."

"What kind of cloud?"

"He was notoriously corrupt."

Andreas began tapping his pencil on the tabletop. "When did he leave the force?"

"Fifteen years ago."

"Where's he now?"

"He lives over by where you're staying. In a house almost as nice as yours."

"I guess police pensions are better on Naxos."

"For him, at least."

"Do you have an address? I'd like to pay him a visit." Andreas gestured to Yianni for a piece of paper.

"Would you like me to come along?"

"If you think it would help."

"He hates me."

"Perfect. That way you get to play bad cop. Can you pick me up?"

"I'll be there in twenty minutes. Bye."

Andreas hung up. "What do you think?"

"At the pace you're going," said Tassos, "I'm changing my firepower recommendation to a howitzer and a Sherman tank."

———

The ex-cop lived in a neatly maintained beach house on a wide and deep, bamboo-ringed parcel of land about a kilometer due

north of where Andreas was staying. A white late-model BMW
SUV sat on the gravel driveway connecting the house to a public
dirt road running alongside the property.

Dimitri parked beside the BMW. "I think we should sit in
the car for a few minutes, so Bear has time to notice we're here."

"Bear?"

"That's his nickname."

"And just what do you think he'll do if we show up at his front
door unannounced?"

"With this guy, there's no telling."

"Well, in that case…" Andreas leaned over and pounded on
the horn.

Ten seconds later, a gray-haired bear of a man, wearing nothing
but khaki shorts draped beneath a huge belly, came charging out
the front door headed directly for the marked police car.

"I see why they call him Bear." Andreas got out of the car and
walked toward the man.

Bear stopped a pace in front of Andreas, stuck his finger in
Andreas's face, and shouted, "Who the fuck do you think you
are, asshole?"

Andreas fixed his eyes on Bear's and grinned. "Dimitri, why
don't you make the introductions?"

Dimitri came around to the front of the car. "Permit me to
introduce you to Chief Inspector Andreas Kaldis, head of GADA's
Special Crimes Unit."

"I don't care if you're the damn archbishop; neither of you are
welcome on my property. So get the hell out of here."

"Would you care to get dressed?" asked Andreas calmly.

Bear hesitated. "I said get off my property."

"Then I assume you're willing to come with us dressed as
you are."

"I'm not going anywhere."

Andreas shook his head. "You're an ex-cop. Do I have to tell you the potential consequences of resisting arrest?"

"*Arrest?*"

"Why do you think we're here? I'm sure you're a fun guy to hang out with, but we're not here on a social call. So play nice, turn around, and put your hands behind your back." Andreas stepped back a pace, uncrossed his arms, and reached behind his back for handcuffs.

Veins popped on the man's forehead and he lunged for Andreas. Andreas sidestepped the charge, dropped his left shoulder, and thrust the heel of his left hand hard up against the side of the man's head. Bear stumbled for an instant, then spun around, looking for Andreas. But Andreas found him first, or rather the hard heel of Andreas's shoe found the exposed top of the man's bare foot.

A roar of pain, followed by a fall to the ground, had the man cursing but no longer fighting. "You miserable bastard, you broke my foot."

"We'll take you to the hospital for an X-ray on the way to booking you."

"For what?"

"For starters, how about assaulting a police officer?"

"That's a Mickey Mouse charge."

Andreas crouched down by the man's head. "You know what amazes me about so many ex-cops, especially dirty ex-cops? It's how they think that once they hit their pension years, they're home free and nothing from their past will ever come back to haunt them." Andreas fixed his eyes on Bear's. "Well, guess what? After that little macho performance of yours, permit me to introduce myself differently. I'm the man who's going to haunt your past, present, and future days for the rest of your life." Andreas stood up. "Get the fuck up and turn around. *Now.*"

"Chief, we came here hoping not to arrest him," said Dimitri.

"I've changed my mind." Andreas's eyes never left Bear. "I said *get up.*"

Bear got to his feet. "You guys are wasting your time with this good cop, bad cop routine. I practically invented it."

"You don't understand," said Andreas. "I'm the good cop in all this. You two don't get along at all, so I came here hoping to find a way to avoid charging you as an accessory to murder, but from the way you're behaving I think you've just become my primary suspect."

"What murder?"

"Turn around."

Bear hesitated but turned. Andreas cuffed him and spun him so they were face-to-face.

"What murder, you say? Have you been involved in so many you can't remember?"

"Stop the bullshit."

"Sure." Andreas said Project Manager's name. "And if that name doesn't jog your memory, how about this one?" He recited Athena's full name, including her maiden name and the last names of her three husbands.

Bear's eyes began to blink and he bit at his lip. "I don't know any of those names or anything about any murder."

"Of course you do. You conducted the investigation into Project Manager's death." Andreas paused, wondering whether to trust his gut and take a wild-ass leap into the unknown. "And for your efforts in that regard, you've been handsomely compensated ever since." Andreas pointed to the car and the house.

"I don't know what you're talking about."

"Permit me to describe your current situation more clearly. At present, you've got two things going for you. One, you're not who I'm after, and I don't even need your testimony. All I need is for you to tell me who was involved in that bogus report and why."

"I've nothing to say."

"Slow down. You haven't heard the second thing, which is: no one besides the three of us knows we're having this conversation. Once we take you in, the whole island will know. And when word gets back to you-know-who, how long do you think it will be before you end up wearing a marble necktie like your buddy Honeyman?" Andreas patted Bear on the shoulder. "You may be gone from the force, but you're certainly not forgotten by those who fear what you know. Talk to us so that we can get to them before they get to you. It's your choice."

A moment passed before Bear spoke. "Can we go inside? I have neighbors, and I don't want them to see me like this."

Andreas looked at Dimitri, who nodded, and the two followed Bear as he limped into his house. It was much bigger inside than it looked from the outside. Bear led them down to a room dominated by a wide-screen TV.

"Is this okay?"

"Yes," said Andreas.

"Could you take off the cuffs?"

"Not yet, talk first."

Bear dropped onto a sofa with fitted pillows. Andreas stepped forward and pulled Bear to his feet.

"What are you doing?" said Bear.

"Sit over there on that chair."

"But it's uncomfortable."

"Sit."

Bear sat on the chair, and Andreas took Bear's former place on the sofa.

"Now talk."

Bear exhaled. "You got it all wrong. Sure I've been getting paid by some folks for things I did for them, but nothing like murder. I wrote that report like I saw it, a simple accident. I only got paid to do what had to be done to keep certain people's names out of the report."

"Which people?"

"The old lady's family."

"Athena?"

"Yes."

"But she was dead by then," said Andreas.

"Yes, but the family was worried something might come out about her history with the man."

"What history?"

"He did things for her."

Dimitri jumped in. "Bear, I know when you're stalling. So get to the point or, so help me, on top of whatever other grief you're heading for, I'll have the buildings department all over your ass for all the illegal things you did building this house."

Bear shut his eyes. "He coordinated her antiquities smuggling. Had been doing it for years."

"How many years?" said Andreas.

"Since before the war."

"How old was he?" Andreas put his hands behind him and fidgeted on the sofa.

"In his seventies when he died in the mid-1990s."

"Did he have a pension like yours?"

"I never got a thing directly from the family. I got a percentage of what Honeyman made off of them."

"How'd Honeyman figure in this?"

"He's the one who had me keep their name out of the accident report. The project manager was driving a car registered to one of the family's companies when it happened."

"And Honeyman has been paying you ever since?" Andreas shifted again on the sofa.

"I was a cop then. He needed me, for a lot of things, and after I retired I agreed to take less."

"How noble of you," said Dimitri.

"No need to be a pig. I didn't want to risk ending up like the manager."

"Whoa," said Andreas, leaning forward, his hands still behind his back. "I thought you said you saw it as a simple accident?"

"I never found any evidence to the contrary, but over the years Honeyman told me things that made me wonder."

"What sort of things?"

"Honeyman had worked as a laborer for him for a couple of years before the accident, and he'd told Honeyman that Athena was a tough and controlling woman who thought her children weak and arrogant. Her grandchildren even more so. She worried how they'd behave after she was gone, so she made a contract with the manager, employing him for life to manage all the nasty projects that could come back to harm the family name."

"I assume that detail didn't make it into your accident report?"

Bear cleared his throat. "I didn't know about it back then."

"So, looking back, what do you think happened?"

Bear coughed. "No idea."

"What were the chances Honeyman arranged for the accident so that he could step into the project manager's shoes?" asked Dimitri.

Bear gestured no. "No way Honeyman could do what that guy did. Honeyman was a fast-talking laborer, and he knew his limitations. He was happy just making what he did off the deal. Besides, he liked the guy and complained that the person he had to deal with after the manager's death was an arrogant, privileged prick who ordered Honeyman around like he owned him."

Andreas nodded. "Perhaps he thought he did. What was this new guy's name?"

"I don't know; he just told me he was one of the old lady's grandsons. I never met him."

Andreas and Dimitri spent another half hour interrogating

Bear but came up with nothing new. Andreas led Bear back up the stairs and undid the handcuffs at the front door.

"No hard feelings, Chief," said Bear.

"No, none at all," said Andreas.

The men did not shake hands.

"Until the next time then," said Bear.

"For sure."

Andreas and Dimitri walked to the car, and once inside, Andreas said, "Hurry up and get us out of here."

Dimitri started the car and put it in gear. "Why the rush?"

Andreas reached behind his back. "Because, when he realizes why I kept squirming on that sofa, who knows what he'll come hauling through that doorway?"

He brought his hand out from behind his back. "This is what I found between the cushions where he wanted to sit." Andreas dropped a nine-millimeter semiautomatic on the console between them.

Spinning, smoking tires followed immediately.

———

By the time Dimitri dropped Andreas off at his borrowed home, Lila's SUV was parked near the front door.

"The women are back. Come on inside and say hello."

Once inside, they followed the sounds of voices out onto the terrace overlooking the sea.

"Look who's back from playing internal affairs," said Yianni.

"And look who's back from playing Rapunzel," said Dimitri.

"Nikoletta, what a surprise," said Andreas. "I'm so happy you decided to leave the tower."

"Only temporarily. My new girlfriends convinced me to spend the day with them, and I said why not?"

"Why not, indeed," said Lila. "Would you boys like to hang out with us today?"

"We'd love to, but things have just gone from hectic to horrific, so I'm afraid we'll have to pass on the invitation."

Toni waved her hand. "Excuse me, but after that bombshell, do you really expect us to simply say *toodle-oo* and be on our sweet way? Uh-uh. Give us the news, Chief."

Andreas turned to Yianni. "She's tougher to deal with than you are."

"Tell me about it."

"Just tell *us* about it," said Lila.

"Enough," said Andreas, raising his hands in a calming gesture. "Here's what happened."

After he and Dimitri finished describing their encounter with Bear, the first person to speak was Lila. "What do you think he planned on doing with that gun hidden in the sofa?"

"Nothing good."

"And you let him go?" said Toni.

"What could I charge him with? He's authorized to possess a pistol."

"And he *was* handcuffed," said Lila.

"Uh, that I didn't find comforting. With a round racked and ready to go, if he got his handcuffed hands around it, he could have spun around and started firing."

Lila shook her head. "I could have done without knowing that last part."

"Bad guys are always looking for a way to do their worst." He looked at Nikoletta. "And that's why I don't like the thought of you in that tower alone."

Nikoletta nodded. "So, what's your next move?"

Andreas looked at Maggie. "Any word yet from your friends?"

"Not yet, but I impressed upon them that this is a Code Red

Urgent matter, so I expect to start hearing back anytime now. If all my friends in high secretarial and clerical positions do what they've promised, our government ministries could come to a screeching halt over the next few hours."

"Not sure if that's a good or a bad thing," said Tassos.

Maggie shot him a glare. "I thought you were trying to stay in my good graces."

Dimitri grinned. "Remind me to change my vote in the next election."

"It won't matter," said Maggie. "We're everywhere."

Andreas stiffened suddenly and pointed at her. "You know what, Maggie, you're absolutely right. It doesn't matter. You *are* everywhere, and I bet *they're* everywhere."

"What are you talking about?" said Yianni. "Who's they?"

Andreas ignored the question. "Dimitri, I want you to set up a meeting with the mayor and the head of the Hoteliers' Association for later this afternoon. Tell them it's about important information relating to Nikoletta and that she'll be there with us." Andreas looked at Nikoletta. "Assuming that's okay with you."

"Not a chance in the world I'd miss that meeting." She paused. "But what do you plan on us saying?"

Andreas looked out toward the sea. "Good question. I'll let you know as soon as I know."

Chapter Twenty-One

The mayor bitched and moaned, threatened and cajoled, all in an effort to learn the agenda of the meeting in advance, but the presence of the once-missing reporter and attendant possibility of nationwide press coverage ultimately convinced him to attend—provided the meeting be held in his office and photographs be allowed showing him with the reporter.

Marco Sanudos, head of the Naxos Hoteliers' Association, said he was honored by the invitation and would gladly attend.

It remained to be seen which of the two turned out to be the better politician.

Andreas, Yianni, Tassos, and Nikoletta arrived at town hall in the SUV. Dimitri and two of his officers were waiting for them outside the side entrance. Andreas huddled with the two officers and Dimitri for several minutes, the officers nodding as he spoke. When he finished, the two officers left, and Andreas's group of five went inside.

They'd made it as far as the atrium when the mayor came rushing over to Nikoletta.

"Ms. Elia, I'm so happy you're safe. We've been working night and day to find you. All of Naxos rejoices and thanks God for your safe return." He crossed himself three times.

No one missed the film crew and photographer capturing the moment. Nikoletta allowed the mayor his moment of glory by standing next to him, smiling, and nodding.

Through a forced smile, she murmured, "Mr. Mayor, could we please go to your office now? I'm afraid my smile's about to crack into a million pieces."

"Why certainly, my dear. Just a few more photos, please."

Ten minutes later, they made it to the mayor's office. Marco was already there, sitting on the far side of the conference table. He immediately stood to shake hands with Nikoletta and Dimitri and nodded to Yianni, who introduced him to Andreas and Tassos.

"Please sit," said the mayor, taking his seat at the head of the table. "So, to what do I owe the honor of this meeting, aside of course from the rescue of Ms. Elia?"

"We've never met before, Mr. Mayor," said Andreas, "but I've heard wonderful things about you."

The mayor's chest seemed to puff out from beneath his snug suit jacket. "Why, thank you, Chief. As I'm sure you know, it's always rewarding to hear that the sacrifices we make to serve our constituents are appreciated."

Andreas nodded. "That's why I've come to you for your counsel and assistance on a matter of the utmost delicacy."

The mayor's brow furrowed and he leaned in toward Andreas. "Please tell me how I can help."

"Thank you. I knew I could rely on you." Andreas shook his head. "As you know, over the last week, four people have died, three clearly murdered, the fourth most likely as well. In addition, two police officers were the subject of another murder attempt."

"Horrible, horrible. All so unlike anything that's ever happened on our island."

"Yes, I know," said Andreas. "I've come to warn you of a

pernicious evil that's lain dormant on your beloved island for decades but has now come into bloom with a vengeance."

The mayor's furrows grew deeper. "I don't follow."

"Let me be blunt. All those murders and attempted murders are connected. They're tied into one family's efforts at keeping secret something I'm hard-pressed to believe many here on Naxos haven't suspected for years."

"What family?"

"And what secret?" asked Marco.

Andreas spoke Athena's full name.

The mayor leaned back, looking relieved. "That's old news. For a moment I thought you had something. Are you talking about their antiquities dealings?"

"In part, but I think illegal antiquities trafficking is a more accurate description."

The mayor waved his hand dismissively. "If we went after everyone who found and didn't turn in antiquities, we'd lose half our population."

"Even if your numbers were close to accurate, which I doubt, that's an interesting perspective on enforcing the law. It's the sort of attitude that can justify a lot of bad behavior."

The mayor's tone turned aggressive. "Like what?"

"Oh, I don't know; let's start with something simple, like murder."

"Are you accusing me of murder?"

"I didn't realize we were talking about you."

The mayor bit at his lip. "I'm very close to that family. They are big supporters of mine, and I take personal offense at any suggestion that they would be involved in anything like murder."

"I can understand your concern. Since you know the family so well, I assume you also knew the man who used to be their project manager." Andreas spoke his name.

The mayor smirked. "That piece of shit." He turned to Nikoletta. "Excuse me."

She said nothing.

"Why do you call him that?" asked Andreas.

"He was blackmailing Athena for years; everybody knew it."

"Who's everybody?"

"Everybody in the family. When he died, it was good riddance to bad rubbish."

"Wow, I'm impressed at how much you know about the family and its history. We should have come to you first. It would have simplified a lot of things."

"And saved you from wasting a lot of my time," the mayor added.

"The only question I have is, based upon all this knowledge you possess about the family, what secret are they so afraid of that they're prepared to commit murder to conceal?"

"That's just the point. There is nothing to hide. Everything's already out there."

"You know, I thought the same thing. But then I spoke to Nikoletta. And you'll never guess what she's learned through her investigative reporting."

"You mean she's a better investigator than our distinguished Chief of Special Crimes," said the mayor with a slight chuckle.

"Simply amazing, isn't it? Why don't you tell the mayor what you learned from your sources?"

Nikoletta smiled. "As you're well aware, Mr. Mayor, during World War II, Nazis plundered Greece. Much of our patrimony went straight to Germany, but some treasures were reported as destroyed. Take for example your island's School of Commerce, now the Naxos Archaeological Museum."

The mayor nodded.

"Over the years, our Ministry of Culture has documented

those destroyed treasures in connection with our nation's claim for war reparations from Germany."

Nikoletta paused to take a sip of water from a bottle in her bag. "In response, Germany submitted its own documentation contesting their alleged destruction and listing specific items claimed to have been destroyed that still existed."

"Are you going to believe the Germans?" snapped the mayor.

She smiled. "No, but the Germans weren't asking Greece to take their word for it. They provided auction-house records, gallery records, insurance records, private collection records, and other types of reputable third-party documents showing the items to still exist, decades after the war."

The mayor pulled a handkerchief out of his pocket.

"Many of those rebuttal records also reveal the provenance of the items and, lo and behold, guess whose family name, or companies recorded in other Greek ministries as being tied to that family, pop up? Athena's family appears in the provenance of a plethora of items allegedly destroyed in World War II as owning those items *before* the war. If true, that would convey legitimacy upon anyone subsequently acquiring an item through the family. But we know, don't we, Mr. Mayor, that before the war those items were the property of Greek institutions, *not* private individuals or companies?"

The mayor said nothing.

"In some instances, nonfamily members and unrelated companies are listed as participating with the family in ownership of the items." She paused. "Who those participants *are* is particularly interesting."

More silence.

"As I said, the German government went to great pains to demonstrate how claims by the Greek government were inaccurate. In its rebuttal documents, Germany listed military officers of the occupying forces, and persons and entities connected to those officers, found to have participated in transactions involving items previously reported by those same officers as destroyed. In many instances, those records show Athena or her children as participants in those transactions."

"This is insane! How could that be?" shouted the mayor, exploding out of his chair.

"If you're asking from a logistical perspective how such a distinguished Greek family could conspire with Nazi occupiers to steal Greece's national heritage, the answer's *very easily*. The family had both the means and experience necessary for smuggling and disposing of such treasures, and the officers had the incentive. If the Nazis didn't claim the items were destroyed, they'd be ordered to ship them back to Germany to enrich their superiors. Working with the family made sense for both sides." Nikoletta shook her head in disgust. "If you're looking for moral justification for robbing their fellow Greeks, may they find that answer rotting in hell."

Andreas cleared his throat. "Allow me to summarize. I think it's safe to say that this story shatters the image of the family as a stalwart supporter of Greece. After all, how is this going to play out against Nikoletta's publisher's crusade to have Britain return the Parthenon Marbles, when his own family pillaged Greece during its moment of greatest suffering?"

Andreas paused and motioned for the mayor to sit down. "That said, Mr. Mayor, which side of this story of Nazi collaboration and murder do you wish to end up on?"

He sat quietly.

A minute passed.

"Well, say something, already," said Marco. "This is outrageous. It's not even an issue open to discussion. We must cooperate immediately with the police."

Andreas wagged a finger in Marco's direction. "I'm so happy you said that. Because something has been percolating in the back of my mind that never quite sat right. I've heard that Spyros—you probably know him as Honeyman—was acting as the front man in efforts to acquire beachfront properties on behalf of Athena's family."

"Yes, I've heard that too," said Marco.

"But I've also heard that Honeyman knew his limitations, and negotiating those kinds of potentially sophisticated transactions doesn't seem to fit within his skillset. Nor do I think his boss— and I think by now we all know who that is—would trust him to be his man on this island in charge of supervising such significant ventures."

Marco nodded.

"I think the big boss would look for someone familiar with the terrain and the people, someone experienced in business who would know which buttons to push and people to reach out to, even if he didn't do it himself." Andreas stared at Marco. "Can you think of anyone who might fit that description?"

"No."

"Permit me to put it differently. We are investigating murders here. Anyone tied into doing that family's business on this island is a suspect. If you know anyone who might qualify for the role of Honeyman's boss and buffer between him and the big boss, you should encourage him to come forward *now*. The longer he waits, the closer he gets to a murder charge. And I can promise him that, in my experience, he can expect no assistance from the guy at the top of the pyramid. The only words that guy will say are, 'I knew nothing about what my subordinates might have done.'"

Andreas stared at Marco. "In other works, speak up now or be set up later."

Marco looked away. "I didn't do anything wrong. My only

dealings on behalf of the family were in connection with its efforts to acquire the properties. All told, this was a huge project. The biggest the family had ever attempted. Sovereign funds were banking on Naxos becoming bigger than Mykonos and were lined up to invest in the project once we acquired the land. It was my job to manage that, but I had to stay behind the scenes if we hoped to get all the necessary properties."

He paused to swallow. "If locals learned I was involved, they'd know something big was underway, and there'd be instant organized opposition."

Dimitri glared at his friend. "So, *that's* why you picked Honeyman to be the face of your project. Someone so ill-regarded by his neighbors that they wouldn't take him as a serious threat to succeed."

Marco looked down, avoiding Dimitri's eyes. "We needed a low-key, nonthreatening farmer type, but Honeyman was far from my first choice." He swallowed again, still looking down. "I had no say in hiring him. I was ordered to use him."

"Ordered by who?" said Andreas.

"By the head of the family, Nikoletta's publisher."

Andreas shifted his gaze. "Your turn, Mr. Mayor. Who's running the family's operations on the island?"

It was the politician's turn to lower his gaze. "The publisher runs all the family's businesses. The other family members have nothing to do with how he runs them. He treats them all like sheep, paying the six branches of Athena's family tree equal shares to distribute among themselves. They take what he gives them to maintain their lifestyles and ask no questions."

That's why there are no new initials, thought Andreas.

He looked at Marco. "If word got out that the publisher's family had been secretly collaborating with the Nazis against Greece, what effect do you think that would have on the development project?"

"It would kill it. Look, the publisher's potential investors aren't exactly upright citizens of the world, so I'd think the last thing they'd want to be is ensnared in that kind of emotion-charged public mess. They'd certainly still be interested in the project, but not if it involved the publisher's family."

"In other words, if the family's Nazi-collaboration past got out, the publisher would see his family's biggest deal ever disappear. Or, worse yet for a man with his ego, be snapped up by someone else."

Marco nodded. "Yes."

Andreas stood. "Thank you, gentlemen. I suggest you keep our discussion to yourselves. Not because I'm concerned about any of this getting back to the publisher, but because *you* might be concerned if that happens. Thanks for your time."

Andreas led his group from the mayor's office, down the stairs, and out of the building.

Once outside, Andreas turned to Nikoletta. "I'd say you have a pretty big story to write."

"Thanks to you."

"Just do our chief a favor," said Yianni, "and leave out the part where he talked about '*a pernicious evil* that's *come into bloom with a vengeance.*' He'll get razzed about that line for the rest of his life."

Andreas showed Yianni an open hand. "I was setting the mood for that pretentious putz of a mayor." He turned back to Nikoletta. "Do you remember our agreement?"

Nikoletta nodded. "I received all my information through my sources, and I will never reveal a source."

"Perfect. We don't want Maggie and her friends getting fired because of this."

"It shall remain our secret."

"By the way," said Andreas, "you might want to hold off for

a day or so on getting your story out there. I sense there are a couple more shoes to drop."

"No problem. I've got other things to do anyway."

"Like what?" said Yianni.

Nikoletta smiled. "Like finding someone to publish it."

———

"Gray puffy clouds drifting across the western sky transformed by hues of orange and gold into flowers, clowns, and big balloons as they pass across the setting sun." Lila smiled at Nikoletta sitting on a deck chair between Lila and a rattan outdoor couch. "There's nothing like an Aegean sunset, and sharing such a glorious one as this with my closest friends out here in the fresh air inspires me. Though, to be honest, I think I should leave the descriptive efforts to professionals like you."

"No, that was perfect. Besides, I write about crime, not sunsets."

"I never tire of sunsets," said Toni. "Even though they're really nothing more than nature's alarm clock, telling me it's time to get ready to head off to work."

"I wish we could share more sunsets," said Yianni, his head on Toni's lap and facing west, legs stretched out on the couch.

She stroked his hair. "Don't worry; you soon may have the opportunity. I was supposed to be back at my job yesterday."

"I'm sure he'll take you back," said Lila.

"He'd better," said Yianni.

"So you like the thought of me chained to my piano seven nights a week?"

"You got that right."

Toni smacked him lightly on the head.

"What's on the agenda next, Chief?" asked Maggie from a deck chair wedged between the couch and a recliner Tassos had angled toward the house while announcing he'd rather see his friends than another sunset.

"I head back to Athens first thing tomorrow. There's not much more I can do here."

"What about me?" asked Yianni, sitting up.

"Take the rest of the week off."

"I want to go back to Athens to see Popi and her husband. Thank God they won't have to remove her spleen, but I bet it'd make her feel a million times better to hear in person what we've learned so far."

"I can't argue with that," said Andreas.

"Nor can I. As much as I'd like to have you stay with me on Mykonos," said Toni.

SMASH.

"What the hell was that?" asked Tassos.

"Sounds like something broke one of the big windows by the front door," said Maggie.

Andreas stood up from his chair next to Lila and turned to go inside. He took one step toward the doorway and froze.

Bear stood in the doorway to the terrace, a shotgun aimed at Andreas's chest. "Like I said, *asshole*, until next time."

Yianni and Tassos jumped to their feet, and Tassos stepped toward the doorway.

"Don't try to be heroes. This is between me and him."

Andreas motioned with his hand for them to stay back. "Cool it, guys."

"You have something of mine."

"What would that be?"

"Don't play cute. You found it in the sofa. A cool but stupid move."

"Well, if we're speaking frankly, your move is definitely not cool and is seriously stupid."

"Just give me the fucking gun."

"Sorry, no can do."

"You're pretty cocky now, but what if I start shooting up these pretty ladies?"

"I still couldn't give you the gun. I don't have it."

"Who has it? That numbnuts, Dimitri?"

"Nope."

Bear pulled the butt of the shotgun tight against his right shoulder and clenched his teeth. "I'm done talking."

"Well, let's look at the situation. If I had the gun and gave it to you, your smart play would be to leave us alone and at worst face charges surrounding this little performance. So, if I had your gun, why would I risk you killing me and then everyone else in an effort to cover your tracks? Am I getting the general drift of your thinking so far?"

Bear snorted dismissively.

"Good, so let me give you another scenario. Walk away now and all you'll face are charges of owning the gun that killed Honeyman by that marble quarry and his two goons by the airport. With the right friends in high places, you'll likely get away with little if any time served. But if you go through with this, you just might singlehandedly get Greece to reinstate the death penalty."

"You're full of shit." He squeezed the gun tighter against his massive shoulder.

Andreas put up his hand. "Hear me out. There's no way the guy who ordered those three murders would ever risk doing the dirty work himself. What did he offer you? The chance to take over Honeyman's place in the food chain?"

"You've no proof of *any* of that," growled Bear.

"True, and even if the ballistics lab that currently has your gun comes back with a report tying your gun to the bullets dug out of those three dead guys, the *only* provable charge is that you owned the gun. So, do the smart thing and put down the shotgun."

Bear's nerves, plus whatever he'd taken to juice up for this confrontation, had elevated Andreas's own. He raised his hand to his head and begun running his fingers through his hair. "Put the gun down, Bear."

"*FUCK YOU.*"

"This is not going to end well for you."

"For me? I'm the one about to pull this trigger."

"Take a look at your chest."

A red dot twitted about the center of Bear's chest. His eyes jumped to find the source, the barrel of the shotgun drifting in sync with his gaze.

"Drop the gun."

"The hell I will." As he swung the gun back around toward Andreas, Andreas dropped his hand to his side.

Bear's chest imploded a microsecond before the *crack* of the sniper rifle reached the terrace.

Bear nearly toppled, and he struggled to turn his gun on Andreas, but Tassos leaped across the terrace and tore it out of the injured man's hands.

"Call an ambulance!" Andreas yelled to Yianni.

"This guy isn't going to need one," said Tassos. "That bullet took out his heart. He's been running for the last few seconds on pure venom."

"Shit."

"Why are you complaining? This dirtbag was about to kill you and all of us."

"He's the last witness we had who could tie the publisher to the murders."

"Shit."

Five other voices said the same.

———

It was dark by the time the ambulance drove off with Bear's body.

Lila stood with Andreas by the terrace doorway looking down at the bloodstains on the marble. The others sat on the terrace, waiting for local police to complete their investigation.

"How am I ever going to explain to my family's friend what happened in her lovely home?" asked Lila.

Andreas put his arm around her shoulders. "Don't worry; we'll get someone here first thing in the morning to take care of cleaning all this up and to fix the window he smashed to get in."

"How can you be so calm?" She rested her head on Andreas's chest. "I'm still shaking. He was going to *kill* you."

"But he didn't. So I put it all behind me. No reason to dwell on it. Just learn from it."

"And what did you learn?" said Dimitri, stepping out onto the terrace.

"That it pays to go with my instincts."

"What instincts?" asked Lila.

Dimitri answered for him. "He told me to arrange to have two men assigned to watch the house until you all left."

"That's what you were talking about with those two cops outside town hall?" asked Yianni.

"Yeah. Dimitri brought them there so we could meet. He introduced one as a former Greek Special Forces sniper, and I told him to bring along his rifle, just in case."

"Why didn't you tell us?" said Nikoletta.

"I get somewhat paranoid whenever my family is involved, and I didn't want to send everyone else off the deep end based on my hunch."

"How did the sniper know when to shoot?" asked Toni.

"We'd worked out three signals. If I brought one hand up to my head and began running my fingers through my hair, it meant dot him on the chest with his sight. If I brought my other hand up so that both my hands were running through my hair, it meant stand down. But if I had only one hand in my hair and dropped it to my side…well, you know what that meant."

"You do realize," said Dimitri, "that there's no way to keep this from the press. A total of five killings in one week in all of Greece would be front-page news. Five on one island…" He spun his hand in the air.

"Should do wonders for tourism," said Tassos.

"I can already hear the mayor's spin," said Dimitri. "'Through the keen investigative skills and bravery of our Naxos police, our nation has been cleansed of a murderous network responsible for the death of four men.' He'll play that tune long, loud, and often."

"At least you'll get some credit," said Andreas.

"Only because he has no choice."

"Excuse me, but I thought Bear only killed three," said Lila.

"Knowing our mayor," said Dimitri, "he'll add the death of Peter Zagori to his tally rather than leaving open the possibility of the public thinking another killer might still be at large on the island. Besides, it will give him a better excuse than the one he's been using for not keeping his promise to the press to turn over Zagori's name. He's been saying, 'We're waiting to hear back from the Americans.' Now he'll say he didn't want to jeopardize a far more significant investigation."

"Do these guys ever tell the truth?" said Toni.

"Actually, the mayor may be correct in saying Bear killed four," said Andreas. "If not more."

"Who's the fourth?" asked Dimitri.

"The project manager. Bear was Honeyman's natural go-to guy for that kind of thing. If the publisher told Honeyman to get rid of the manager, my money's on Honeyman hiring Bear to do the job. It would have made everyone happy because Bear could arrange to conduct the investigation of his own hit."

"But Bear said Honeyman liked the manager and disliked the publisher," said Dimitri.

"And the mayor said the project manager was a blackmailer," said Yianni.

"Putting aside that Bear was a pathological psychopath and the mayor is a pathological politician, all of that could be true," Andreas paused. "Or not. But my sense of Honeyman is that he was the sort of man who'd be loyal to whoever kept the easy money coming, and that meant the publisher. So, bye-bye, project manager, no matter what he thought of him personally."

"What goes around comes around," said Yianni. "Bear did away with his buddy Honeyman for the same reason."

"And on the orders of the same man," said Maggie.

"For twenty-five years, maybe more, Bear was on easy street, collecting money through Honeyman for doing nothing except possibly listening to Honeyman bitch about his boss."

"Something cops are used to hearing a lot of from their buddies," said Tassos with a smile.

"It wasn't until Honeyman's botched efforts at getting rid of Nikoletta, Popi, and me that the publisher panicked and reached out to Bear directly, offering him Honeyman's gig if he took out Honeyman and the two who'd run Popi and me off the road."

"The publisher must have known Bear killed the manager," said Dimitri.

Andreas nodded. "Bear was unstable. Knowing what Bear knew, I doubt the publisher would have allowed him to live much longer."

"This publisher guy must be a psycho himself," said Dimitri.

"Anything he considers potentially harmful to his family name, he eliminates."

"Precisely why I want Nikoletta to get her story out there ASAP. Once it's published, the harm will be done and he'll no longer have a reason to go after her."

"Except revenge," said Toni.

"I was thinking more about him going after you, Andreas," said Dimitri.

Lila's head jerked away from her husband's chest. Andreas kissed her forehead. "Let's see what happens after Nikoletta's article comes out." He pulled Lila snugly back against his chest. "Then I'll decide what has to be done to protect *my* family."

———

Later that night, before going to bed, Andreas took a walk around the house to make sure all the doors and windows were locked. As he pulled shut the sliding door to the terrace, he heard, "Whoa, there. Is this your way of telling me to go to bed?"

Andreas slid open the door and stepped outside. "Just taking precautions in an effort to limit my run-ins with two-legged madmen to one per day."

"At the risk of raising your count to two, come, sit beside me." Tassos patted the couch.

Andreas slid the door closed behind him, walked to the couch, and dropped next to his friend.

"Tough day, huh?" said Tassos.

"They all are, but when someone comes that close to taking you out…" Andreas shook his head. "Thanks, by the way, for taking the shotgun away from that nutjob."

"It was nothing."

"We both know that's not true. He had the barrel pointed

straight at you when you came at him, and he still had more than enough juice to pull the trigger." Andreas smacked Tassos on the thigh. "You can still move pretty quickly when you have to."

"For an old man."

"Nope, for any man."

Tassos sighed. "We do what we have to do to protect our friends."

"For sure."

"Now, it's my turn to thank you."

"Me?" said Andreas. "For what?"

"I don't know how many more years I have left, and—"

"Stop with that sort of—"

"Just let me finish." Tassos swallowed. "And that's had me wondering recently what really matters anymore. I can't contribute as I once did…so why bother to learn new things, visit new places, make new friends? What's the use? I'm just a relic."

"How much longer do I have to listen to this?"

"Shh, I'm coming to the good part. They say people suffering from deep depression—which I don't see myself as having—can benefit from shock therapy. It literally jolts them back to realizing how beautiful life can be. This afternoon on this terrace with that shotgun in my face, I experienced a sort of shock therapy. Not only did I realize in a matter of seconds that I could still contribute, but also how lost I'd be if I let anything bad happen to those I loved."

Andreas sat quietly for a moment, then thrust a fist into the air. *"Right on."*

Tassos laughed. "I'm serious. I feel…different now. Better, for sure. Like maybe I'm back on track, headed toward some purpose."

"What sort of purpose?"

"Not sure yet, but one will come to me. I'm certain of that."

Andreas smiled. "Look out, bad guys of the Greek Isles, Tassos is back."

Chapter Twenty-Two

Within a week of Andreas's return to Athens, Nikoletta's exposé appeared as a front-page story in the newspaper owned by her publisher's biggest rival.

The publisher countered with stories in his paper accusing Nikoletta of being, on the one hand, a deranged purveyor of libelous fake news and, on the other, a disgruntled employee under exclusive contract to his company, barred from publishing elsewhere. In bold letters across the front page of his paper, he threatened to sue her, the paper that had published her story, and anyone else who "dared to libel his family by repeating Nikoletta Elia's lies."

The trouble was, Nikoletta's story included copies of documents substantiating her claims, and news organizations throughout the EU found them quite convincing. With the Brits having been under siege by her former publisher's paper for years over Lord Elgin and the Parthenon Marbles, the bloodthirsty UK press had a field day, running story after story of how generations of the publisher's family had systematically plundered their own homeland while blaming others. The Germans seized on what they saw as an opportunity to undercut Greece's World

War II reparations claims by, "in the interest of full transparency," releasing a trove of previously unreleased documents listing the current owners and provenance of artifacts and other treasures claimed by Greece to have been destroyed in World War II. Many of those records related to transactions that in no way involved the publisher or his family, but they did name other prominent Greek families, now drawn into the spotlight.

As the publisher's defense of his family grew to ever more vituperative attacks on the European press, CNN got into the act with a special report titled "Has Greece Lost Its Marbles?" The premise of its piece questioned whether the broadening scandal might jeopardize even Greece's legitimate claims for return of its plundered treasures.

Despite all the heat, the publisher showed no sign of backing down. When members of Parliament and prominent citizens urged him to end the battle of words and address his concerns in court, he labeled them "useless, spineless embarrassments to those who know what it means to be Greek."

He used even harsher words to describe his longtime managing editor, Giorgos Pappas, who resigned in protest over his boss's treatment of Nikoletta. Never, though, did the publisher address his critics directly or, for that matter, the substance of Nikoletta's reporting.

Instead, he did what came naturally to him: he berated, bragged, and bullied.

———

Sunday mornings in the Kaldis household generally meant breakfast together, followed by church with the children's grandparents, coffee at a place of the grandparents' choosing, and in summer, a trip to the beach.

This Sunday morning, Andreas only made it to breakfast. Nikoletta's story had galvanized public opinion into demanding the prosecution of the publisher and his family for their crimes. State prosecutors, feeling the intense heat from this red-hot-potato of a case, ducked responsibility for deciding whether sufficient evidence existed to prosecute by kicking the decision back to Andreas and his unit.

Until now, the publisher's link to the murders had not been disclosed to the public. Nikoletta's story focused exclusively on the family's involvement in the illicit antiquities trade. Andreas had no doubt that, once the murders were added to the mix, an already bloody war would turn nuclear, unleashing fevered worldwide media attention upon this modern-day Greek family tragedy and triggering an unimaginable cornered-rat syndrome in the unhinged publisher.

Whether any of that happened would come down to the decision Andreas had to make by the next morning.

Once his family left for church, Andreas retreated to his wife's study to review the evidence, organize his thoughts, and formulate his recommendation.

Thirty minutes later, the building's intercom buzzed. It was a call from the doorman.

"Mr. Kaldis, you have a visitor." He said the name.

Andreas blinked. "Is he alone?"

"Yes. He'd like to see you."

Andreas hesitated. "Okay, send him up."

He put down the phone, left his wife's office, shut the door behind him, and went into their bedroom. Inside his nightstand's bottom drawer, he opened a small gun safe, removed a nine millimeter, racked the slide, and stuck it in the back of his jeans beneath his untucked shirt.

The doorbell rang as he walked through the rooms leading to

the entrance foyer, wondering what the hell this guy was doing here.

A man in his fifties, wearing an expensive blue suit, white shirt, and red tie, stood outside the apartment's front door. About Andreas's height and build, but decidedly pudgy, with a ruddy complexion and dyed jet-black hair, he reminded Andreas of a Greek version of a former Italian prime minister.

"Thank you for seeing me unannounced, Chief Inspector. May I come in?"

Andreas stepped back from the doorway and gestured for the publisher to enter. "But of course, sir."

He led the man to a sitting room offering a view of the Parthenon. "May I offer you a glass of water? The housekeeper and nanny are off to church, so I'm afraid I can't offer you much more than that."

"No need. I'm fine." Without asking, he sat in the most prominent chair. "You should exercise better control over your staff. No reason why you should be inconvenienced on their behalf."

Andreas forced a smile. "I'll keep that in mind." He dropped onto the sofa across from his visitor. "So, to what do I owe the honor of this visit?"

The man snorted. "No reason to play coy with me, Kaldis. We both know why I'm here."

Andreas raised and dropped his hands. "Sorry, but I can't say that I do."

The publisher leaned in toward Andreas. "It's about that recommendation you're due to submit tomorrow morning."

Andreas showed no reaction.

"And don't bother to ask how I know about it. I know everything."

"You must have friends in high places," said Andreas.

"The highest."

"And the lowest too, I suspect."

"They all have their usefulness."

Andreas wondered how often the man dyed his hair.

"I'm here to ask you what you plan to recommend."

Andreas nodded. "I admire your frankness."

"There's no reason to waste time."

"I agree."

"Well?"

"I haven't made up my mind yet."

The publisher first glared, then softened his look. "That's actually good news. It means perhaps I can convince you to make the right decision."

"I assume I know what you think that would be."

"May I continue to be frank?"

Andreas nodded. "Please."

"One thing you should know, if you don't already, is that in Greece I am all powerful. I know where *every* body is buried, where *every* scandal lies hidden, and where *every* prominent person has a pressure point. That means I can weather this round of unfounded accusations manufactured by my enemies and government peasants. And when all this is forgotten—and believe me, it all shall pass—I shall systematically destroy *anyone* who dared assault my family. Starting with that, that..." he stammered as if running possible adjectives through his mind, "slut Nikoletta Elia."

Andreas yawned.

"Am I boring you?"

"Not at all. Please, go on."

"I don't think you're taking me seriously."

"Oh, believe me when I say that I do. I was just up early with my children."

The publisher glowered at Andreas. "Children are important. I value mine. I'll do anything to protect them."

"I already got that point, sir, so how about getting back to the speaking frankly part?"

The publisher squeezed the arms of the chair, his face approaching beet-red. "If you make the wrong recommendation, I will destroy you and all you hold dear."

"That certainly is frank." Andreas leaned forward. "But what precisely do you think would be the *wrong* recommendation?"

"You have no proof supporting any charges implicating me or my family in any deaths." He smiled. "All potential witnesses to the contrary have sadly passed away."

Andreas smiled back. "If that's what you think, then why are you here?"

"I don't leave anything to chance. That's why."

"You mean you're willing to sit across from one of those government peasants, begging him for mercy."

The publisher yanked himself up to his feet. "I do not beg. I demand. And if you don't do as I say, I will destroy you and your family. And that includes your crooked-cop friend Tassos, who dealt in the same antiquities trading as you accuse my family. And that's just for starters."

Andreas struggled to keep his cool. He'd baited the publisher into revealing what he had in mind to do, and now that he'd heard, there was no reason to allow himself to be baited by his answers.

"Frankly, sir, you're wasting your time. Tassos has no fear of anything you might publish. I'd say you've got an empty quiver."

Spittle flew from the man's mouth as he responded. "And you've got a family to protect. Remember that accidents can happen to anyone, anywhere, anytime." He stabbed a finger at Andreas. "If you know what's good for you, Lila, Tassaki, and Sofia, you damn well know what you'd better do."

Andreas reached behind his back and squeezed the butt of

his gun. "As a matter of fact, I do." Andreas stood. "I think now would be a good time for you to leave."

———

Following his conversation with the publisher, Andreas arranged private security for his family and warned Nikoletta, Tassos, Maggie, Yianni, and Toni, of his threats. Yianni passed along the warning to Popi and her husband, now both back on Naxos.

The day after the publisher paid his visit to Andreas's home, prosecutors charged him and members of his family with crimes relating to their illegal antiquities activities, tax evasion, and fraud. They also announced a continuing investigation by Greece's Special Crimes Unit into five murders potentially linked to the publisher himself. As predicted, the charges set off a second worldwide media explosion and triggered verbal attacks by the publisher on Nikoletta, Tassos, Andreas, and everyone in Andreas's family.

In Nikoletta's new column, granted to her by her new publisher as thanks for his paper's booming boost in sales and growing international reputation as Greece's crusading publication of record, she gave no quarter to her ex-boss, starting with an online column titled, "I Defend My Friends."

When asked by the press for a comment on the war raging all around him, Andreas would only say, "This, too, shall pass."

"So, how do you feel this morning, Mr. Media Star?" said Yianni, sticking his head through the doorway of Andreas's office.

"I'd feel a lot better if we had even the scent of a lead on some way to pin the bastard to one of those murders. There's gotta be *something* out there."

"Hey, guys, turn on the television!" Maggie raced into the

office and straight for the TV remote. She tuned to a news channel, catching a reporter in midsentence. "No explanation yet for what went wrong, but the tragedy couldn't have come at a worse time for the family. Its patriarch has been engaged in a protracted battle to salvage the family's reputation, but now this."

"What the hell is *this*?" yelled Yianni at the TV.

Maggie pointed. "It's there on the chyron running across the bottom of the screen."

PUBLISHER OF LEADING ATHENS NEWSPAPER DIES IN HELICOPTER CRASH.

"Can't be," said Yianni.

Andreas stared at the screen. "I hope no one else died."

"I heard it was just him. He had a helicopter-pilot license."

"Where did it happen?" asked Yianni.

Maggie pointed at the TV as the reporter continued. "We're here with the Naxos chief of police, who's taken personal charge of the investigation. What can you tell us?"

"Hey, it's Dimitri!" said Yianni.

"We know," said Maggie, putting a finger to her lips.

Dimitri spoke directly into the camera. "The matter is currently under investigation by the U.S. military. What we know so far is that a United States drone based on Crete unexpectedly locked on to the victim's helicopter as it flew from Naxos to Crete and launched a missile that destroyed the helicopter in midair. As yet, the United States has offered no explanation for how such a tragic accident could have occurred."

"Seems poetic justice, doesn't it?" snipped Maggie. "Dimitri reporting on the investigation of the publisher's accidental death."

"Turn it off," said Andreas.

"Why? He's not done yet," said Yianni.

Andreas barked, "*I said turn it off.*"

Maggie turned it off. "What's bothering you, Chief? Were

you wishing he'd die, and now that it's happened, you feel guilty?"

"Maybe."

"Or maybe what else?" asked Yianni.

Andreas ran his hands through this hair and ended by rubbing the heels of his hands into his eyes. He looked at them and exhaled. "Maybe I could have prevented this."

"How?"

"I don't know, but with so many people angry at this guy, I should have done something to dampen down their rage."

"Bullshit," said Yianni. "You always took the high road."

"While letting everyone else take the low," mumbled Andreas.

"*STOP*. Enough already," said Maggie. "This guy had more people wanting to kill him than lined up to murder Samuel Ratchett on the *Orient Express*. No way you could have stopped them all."

"Not to mention that one of us would have had to do the job that drone did if that piece of shit had ever tried hurting your family."

Andreas rubbed at his eyes some more.

A message ping came through on Andreas's mobile. He looked at the screen. "It's from Nikoletta. Just after the publisher's death was announced on the news, she received an anonymous comment to one of her online columns. The one titled, 'I Defend My Friends.'" Andreas cleared his throat. "It reads, 'As you see, I also defend my friends. Your fan, Soter.'"

Read on for an excerpt from

Island
of Secrets

Book 10 in the Chief Inspector
Andreas Kaldis Mystery series.

Available now!

Chapter One

He never wondered about the purpose of life or how he turned out as he had. It all just sort of happened. He became a cop because he saw it as the surest way for a kid born into Greece's working class in the tumultuous early 1960s to make a living. He got lucky when, after the fall of the Military Junta in 1974, he joined the youth movement of a left-wing political party that came to power in 1981 and remembered to reward its loyal friends.

As he rose in rank, the more friends and money he made, the more power he amassed. He kept careful track of where the bodies were buried and possessed an uncanny instinct for digging up the ones he needed to achieve his purposes. An effort by the opposition party to paint him as corrupt failed when the prosecution's main witness died in a boating accident. An investigation into the witness's death faded away soon after he announced his decision to retire from the Hellenic Police force with the rank of colonel.

That's when he began to make truly big money, capitalizing on his contacts and former position as head of police for the South Aegean Region, home to Greece's most popular tourist islands for the rich and hard-partying globe-trotting crowd.

Tonight, the Colonel was far away from all that glitz and glamour. He sat in a restaurant in a nondescript, middle-class eastern suburb of Athens, virtually equidistant from downtown Athens, its port town of Rafina, and Venizelos International Airport.

"A convenient place for a meeting," said the one who'd arranged it.

The Colonel leaned back in his chair and yawned. The conversation had been as boring as the meal. Everything about the place was mediocre, from its tired, thirty-year-old decor to the hookers at the bar, and the ruddy-faced, pudgy man sitting across the table from him who had yet to say why their mutual business acquaintance thought they should meet.

"Am I keeping you awake, Colonel?"

"Barely."

Ruddy Face smiled. "How do you like my place?"

The Colonel leaned forward. It was long past time to get down to business. "If this is your joint, why don't you just tell me why you wanted to meet? You sure as hell don't need my services to run this operation."

"You're right, it's a dump." Ruddy Face paused. "But I have plans."

"What sort of plans?"

"I'm buying a club on the islands. It's going to be first-class in every way." He nodded toward the bar. "Including the girls."

"Which island?"

"One you control."

"Control is a mighty big word."

Ruddy Face smiled. "Let's just say, I don't like the idea of getting involved in a business where my investment isn't secure."

"That's prudent of you."

"Can you help me?"

"If you're asking for security, the answer is yes."

"I'm talking about *protection* for *all* aspects of my business."

The Colonel shrugged. "It's all a matter of price. You tell me what you want, and I'll tell you what it will cost you."

"I hear you're pricey."

"You heard right. But I make sure things run smoothly."

"How do you do that?"

"I don't have competitors stirring things up, jockeying for business. I maintain order among the chaos."

"They might see things differently."

"If by *they* you mean competitors, there are no *they* on my island. I'm the only game in town."

"I get your point," said the man. "I'm sure we'll come to terms."

"If you want to open a club where I'm in business, I'm sure we will."

The Colonel declined an offer of coffee, and the two men agreed to talk again once Ruddy Face had a better idea of what he might need from the Colonel.

He walked the Colonel to the front door, shook his hand, thanked him for coming, and wished him safe travels. "*Kalo taxidhi.*"

But the Colonel only made it as far as the front door of his Mercedes.

———

Greece's General Police Headquarters, better known as GADA, sat close by the heart of Athens's bustle, next door to a major hospital, down the block from Greece's Supreme Court, and across the street from the stadium of one of Greece's most popular soccer teams. GADA's Special Crimes Unit, charged with investigating potential corruption and other matters of national concern—at least those that piqued the interest of its Chief

Inspector Andreas Kaldis—occupied the eastern side of the fourth floor.

Andreas had been at his desk since shortly after sunrise. With two early-rising young children at home, it wasn't unusual for him to flee the morning domestic chaos for the relative calm of tracking down bad actors. His wife, Lila, never seemed to mind when he abandoned her to the ruckus, undoubtedly because she rightly considered him an active accessory to their children's early-morning mischief.

It wasn't as if he were leaving his wife alone to deal with their son and daughter; she did have a housekeeper and nanny to help, a decidedly suspicious luxury on an honest cop's salary. But all of that, and more, had come with his marriage to the daughter of one of Greece's most respected and wealthiest families. He appreciated his good fortune and considered himself a lucky man.

Too bad he couldn't say the same thing for the guy plastered all over the morning news headlines: RETIRED POLICE COLONEL STAVROS AKTIPIS ASSASSINATED. That summed up virtually everything the various news stations had to report on the shooting, though they tried their best to spice up their coverage with references to corruption allegations that had haunted the victim.

All the allegations preceded Andreas's time as chief of Special Crimes, but he'd heard the stories and much more about the Colonel. Instinctively, Andreas believed the victim had been corrupt, for the system far too often brought temptations to one in his position. Yet, if Andreas pursued every case of official corruption brought to his attention, he'd need all the offices in the building to house his staff—not to mention an unimaginable number of additional prosecutors.

Compounding all of that, innovative criminal types from around the world kept introducing new schemes and methods into Greece that added to his caseload. Overwhelmed as his unit was, and Greece a decade into a crippling economic crisis, he knew he'd be wasting his time asking for more support from the government. That left Andreas with little choice but to pursue the most egregious offenders, hoping to make an example of them in a manner that discouraged others from doing the same.

What happened last night to the Colonel, he knew, would be headed straight for his desk, in a file marked NASTY in all-red letters. The Colonel had been murdered for a reason, and it wasn't robbery. His wallet, filled with euros, and an expensive watch were untouched. Three quick bullets to the back of his head as he stood at his car door. No witnesses, and no terrorists claiming credit for the killing. At least none so far.

Andreas held a remote in his right hand, surfing through local news coverage on the wall-mounted TV screen to his right, while drumming the fingers of his left hand on his desktop. He looked at his watch. Detective Yianni Kouros should be at the scene by now. Andreas had called him at home as soon as he'd heard the early morning news. Yianni had been his right-hand man since their days together on Mykonos, back when Andreas was the island's police chief and Yianni a brash young bull of a rookie cop.

Andreas bit at his lip. Killing cops, retired or not, wasn't something even the most hardened criminals undertook lightly, especially when the victim was an ex-colonel. He'd been assassinated for a serious reason, most likely with the blessing of serious people. That's why he'd sent Yianni to the scene. He wanted his own people in on the investigation from the start. Screw-ups early on—unintentional or otherwise—haunted investigations, at times serving as a convenient pretext for bad guys getting away with murder. Not this time, though. Not if Andreas could help it.

Yes, this definitely would be a nasty one.

ACKNOWLEDGMENTS

Anastasia Antoniadou; Mihalis, Roz, and Spiros Apostolou; Marios Assimakopoulos; Vassilis Condilis; Diane DiBiase; Andreas, Aleca, Mihalis, and Anna Fiorentinos; Eleftherious Fiorentinos; Flora and Yanni Katsaounis; Panos Kelaidis; Giannis Nikiforou Konstantakis; Bogdan and Martina Kopec; Vicky Koromina; Marine Lascaris; Nikoletta Lianos and Dimitris Lianos; Linda Marshall; Tottie Mitchell; Terrence, Karen, and Rachel McLaughlin; Barbara G. Peters and Robert Rosenwald; Amargyros Protonotarios; Spyros Protonotarios; Dora Rallis; Alexander Reichardt and Katharina Bolesch; Grand Master Mark Shuey (founder of Cane Masters); Jonathan, Jennifer, Azriel, and Gavriella Siger; Ed Stackler; Yiannis Vassilas and Sophia Dimakopoulou; Barbara Zilly.

And, of course, Aikaterini Lalaouni.

ABOUT THE AUTHOR

Photo by Thanasis Krikis

Jeffrey Siger was born and raised in Pittsburgh, Pennsylvania, practiced law at a major Wall Street law firm, and later established his own New York City law firm, where he continued as one of its name partners until giving it all up to write full-time among the people, life, and politics of his beloved Mykonos. *A Deadly Twist* is the eleventh novel in his internationally bestselling and award-nominated Chief Inspector Andreas Kaldis series, following up on *Island of Secrets* (first published as *The Mykonos Mob*), *An Aegean April*, *Santorini Caesars*, *Devil of Delphi*, *Sons of Sparta*, *Mykonos After Midnight*, *Target: Tinos*, *Prey on Patmos*, *Assassins of Athens*, and *Murder in Mykonos*.

The *New York Times* described Jeffrey Siger's novels as "thoughtful police procedurals set in picturesque but not untroubled Greek locales," and named him as Greece's thriller writer of record. The *Greek Press* called his work "prophetic," Eurocrime described him as a "very gifted American author... on par with other American authors such as Joseph Wambaugh or Ed McBain," and the City of San Francisco awarded him its Certificate of Honor citing that his "acclaimed books have not only explored modern Greek society and its ancient roots but have inspired political change in Greece." He now lives in Greece.